Finding a Way Forward

by

Iona Morrison

A Blue Cove Mystery, Book 7

Finding a Way Forward

Cover Art by *Debbie Taylor*

The Wild Rose Press, Inc.
PO Box 708
Adams Basin, NY 14410-0708
Visit us at www.thewildrosepress.com

Publishing History
First Fantasy Rose Edition, 2019
Print ISBN 978-1-5092-2573-6
Digital ISBN 978-1-5092-2574-3

A Blue Cove Mystery, Book 7
Published in the United States of America

A flash of lightning lit up the living room with its brightness, followed by a clash of thunder that reverberated off the walls around her. The reflection danced eerily across the cove. She shielded her eyes, looking away for a few seconds. The air crackled with suspense. Jessie stared out the window, not wanting to miss…what? Motionless, she was spellbound, gazing into the heavens as the flashes of light and the darkness suddenly took on forms. With their swords drawn and gleaming shields in front of them, beings of bright light zipped in and out of the clouds. And then she saw him, a dark, terrifying dragon-like creature rising out of the dark waters and rushing toward the sky, warring with the creatures of light in the night sky. Suspended, he stood on his haunches, his sulfurous breath spewing fire, his red eyes glowing in the darkness. One large winged creature flew toward the dragon and thrust at him with his sword. The bright light streamed through the creature, pushing the dragon back into the darkness. Where did he go? She strained to see if she could find him. He retreated, circled around them, and streaked across the heavens from the other side, only to be pushed back again by another angel taking the first one's place. Back and forth they flew until all the light raced toward the dragon, driving him into the blackness.

Praise for Iona Morrison

"*THE HARVEST CLUB* by Iona Morrison is a well written, well executed murder mystery that takes place in a beautiful little New England town... I highly recommend this tight, fast paced romantic intrigue-paranormal-murder-mystery to anyone who loves a good book."

~Carol Kaufman

~*~

"I love reading Iona's books. Once I start reading one I can't put it down. Her books take me away and make me feel like I am right there in Blue Cove..."

~Carol Beier

~*~

"I just finished Iona Morrison's book *FLASHPOINT*, and I was drawn in from the first sentence to the last. She has not only created a world where we feel like part of the Blue Cove community and identify with the characters, but from her first book to this one has thoroughly engaged my emotions: joy, tears, fear, and hope."

~Rick Kess

Dedication

Dedicated to the memory of Mary Rosenblum,
my mentor and writing teacher.
Thanks for helping me to find my inner writing voice.
I miss your wit, critiques, and encouraging words.

Chapter 1

The pleasure of the moment, the clarity of the morning air, and the forest run filled Jessie Reynolds with exuberance. "Catch me if you can." She taunted the kids running with her. From the sound of her feet striking the ground in sync with her body's motion to the incredible sense of satisfaction that came with each mile she covered, Jessie enjoyed running. She was hooked instantly years before when she laced the new sneakers her mom had bought for her. And now here she was with a group of teens who felt the same way about it as she did. It was a win, win for her. The runner's high is how she often described it to her friend Katie, who didn't get it at all. Jessie smiled because this was perfect.

Suddenly the shrill screams of a woman sliced through the quiet afternoon air, bringing Jessie to a standstill, sending shivers racing down her spine. Chills mixed with the sweat of her heated body. "Did you hear that?" she asked to no one in particular.

Todd, the tall boy running up behind her, asked, "Hear what?" As he jogged past her, he glanced over his shoulder, giving her an odd look. "I didn't hear anything."

"Keep moving, Reynolds," one of the other kids called out after bumping into her and giving her a playful shove.

"Sorry." She started running again, this time dodging the runners who had tried to maneuver around her.

Who screamed? Jessie picked up her pace, wanting to stay close to the others.

Cries and screams no one else could hear meant she was about to meet another ghost. The routine was clear to her by now. In the beginning, until she understood what the spirit wanted, the experience had been a bit scary. For some reason, today, the experience had a whole different feel. She had no idea why.

Taking a quick look around, she saw there were no visible apparitions. Only trees and more trees as far as the eye could see. Rounding the curve, she pushed up the beginning of a steep incline. The sunlight filtered through the treetops, casting dancing shadows on the pavement in front of her. "Inhale, exhale, breathe," she muttered, repeating the cadence of the rhythm of her feet hitting the ground. Droplets of sweat dripped from her cheeks and neck, rolling down her chest and back. The locals claimed it was too early in the year for such oppressive heat and humidity, yet here it was. Thankfully, the current weather was forecasted to remain the same for only a few more days.

Several loose strands of hair escaped from her ponytail and plastered annoyingly against her wet cheeks. She wiped the hair away and, regaining her tempo, once again caught up to the main group. But another scary wail confirmed her suspicion. Ahead and off the path, a ghostly figure moved back and forth at the edge of a small clearing. The spirit screeched, shifting restlessly in front of a marker, drawing Jessie's attention until she changed direction and ran toward the spot.

Fresh, colorful flowers filled a vase at the base of a small monument across from a bench that appeared recently painted. The aroma of the sweet alyssum, lilacs, and gardenias filled the air with a fragrant scent. From the looks of it, someone cared enough to maintain the area on a regular basis.

A cold swish of air swirled around her as she jogged in place, a vivid reminder that she wasn't alone. The unnatural chill sent goosebumps creeping down her arms. This ghost wanted her attention. But why? Jessie stopped to read the words on the plaque:

In Memory of Elizabeth McKenzie. Our sweet daughter, and sister, Lizzy. May she rest in peace.

If her haunted eyes were any indication, Elizabeth wasn't at peace.

Jessie's hand clenched at her side, her heart racing in tandem with the images that flashed through her mind. There was more to the story of Elizabeth McKenzie than the simple marker inscribed.

"I don't know what you're trying to tell me, or why you wanted me to find you, but I'll try to figure it out," she whispered as she ran back to the path.

Catching up to the stragglers running ahead of her, Jessie made the push up the hill behind the final two girls. Discovering Elizabeth, finding out who she was and how she had died now topped her agenda. *What was this spirit's story?* Intrigued by another case, an unsolved murder from the past perhaps, had just thrust itself into her day. Call it fate, or kismet. It was meant to be.

The last-minute decision to run in a new area came

after Bob Harmon, the cross-country coach, asked her if she'd be willing to run with his running club to help keep them on pace. The club, a group of teens from the cross-country team, wanted to run all year to stay in shape. He promised her it was a beautiful spot to train. Bob had been right about the beauty, but it all seemed lost on her, now. Finally running past the slowest runners, she pushed hard up the last hill. At the top, Jessie ran full speed the last few miles, making her way to the high school parking lot, the team and pacing forgotten. Once in her car, ready to research the ghostly encounter, she headed directly for home.

Jessie opened the cottage door, discarding and kicking aside her sneakers. Half of her purse's contents scattered to the floor, rolling under the sofa when she tossed it over the back of the couch and headed straight to her desk. With the push of a button, the computer whirred to life. Her fingers drummed impatiently on the wooden surface of the desk waiting for the icons to appear on the screen. Why did it feel as if it took forever to open the program she wanted? *Finally!*

Jessie typed Elizabeth McKenzie's name into the Blue Cove Sentinel's archive site. Several articles popped up in the search. The first included a photo in the story. Elizabeth had been a beautiful, young girl with an enchanting smile. Reading one piece after another, Jessie held her breath as the story of Elizabeth's death took shape. And with it came a sense of despair. A gloomy cloud filled the room. At least one question was answered. Understanding dawned. Now she knew why this meeting was different. She reached for a tissue, debating what to do next.

Matt's unique ringtone sent her in search of her

phone. Where was it this time? The floor. Good grief! Nestled among several ink pens, a coin purse, and lip gloss, the phone continued to ring. Down on all fours, she mumbled under her breath, "Earth to Jessie." Reaching for the last lip gloss, she shoved the spilled contents back into her purse, placing it on the desk. "Hi, Matt. I was just about to call you."

"Are you up for company? I thought I'd stop by with dinner if you haven't eaten already."

"Sounds perfect. I'd love to see you. In fact, I need to talk to you anyway. Something happened earlier while I was running, and I hope you'll be able to shed some light on it."

"Sounds serious."

"Let's just say I need your input."

"Okay, be there in about twenty minutes."

"I'll be waiting." Jessie disconnected the call as she walked into her bedroom.

Setting her messy ponytail free, she ran a brush through her hair, letting the damp, loose curls fall against her shoulders and down her back. Grabbing her jeans from the drawer, she pulled them on, followed by a t-shirt. Reaching for a neutral lip gloss, she applied it mindlessly. Was this what her friend Reba had warned her about during the last case when she told her Matt had something he needed to deal with, or was this about her? There were too many instances and statements by Reba to keep them all straight.

Jessie paced from the kitchen to the living room and back again. "Blast it. Where is he?" Twenty minutes turned to thirty, and her level of tension rose with the ticking of the large clock above the mantel. She took a quick peek out the window, but Matt's car still wasn't there, and neither was he. "Well, this is a first. He's always punctual. Darn it. Why now?" she mused. Flipping the porch light on, she glanced at her watch for the umpteenth time. A few minutes later, the sound of him at the door sent her dashing to let him in.

"The restaurant was busy tonight. I hope you're up for Chinese. We haven't had it in a while." As he bent to kiss her, she turned her head, and he got her cheek. "Is everything all right?" He placed the bag on the table.

"I guess." She leaned against the counter.

He raised his brows. "You don't know. It's not a hard question, sweetheart. You're either all right or you're not."

"No, no, I mean I'm okay. We need to talk." She took a deep breath to calm herself and grabbed two plates out of the cabinet. She held them loosely between her fingers and thumb.

"What's up?" He stared at her with a perplexed look on his face. His hand reached for the plates. "Are you sure you're feeling okay? Let me take these before you drop them."

"What? Oh." She watched him take the plates from her limp hand. She nodded. "Here goes," she said under her breath. "I was running the path the cross-country running club runs each day near the school. Coach Harmon asked me to run with them and set the pace. I think I failed miserably today."

"Teen boys and a beautiful woman running with them is an idea probably doomed to failure from the start." Matt chuckled.

"I wasn't running only with the boys. There were girls, too." She scrunched her face as she blew out a loud breath, lost for a moment in her train of thought. "It doesn't matter anyway." She waved it off. "I forgot all about pacing after I heard the woman's screams, and no one else had heard her." She frowned. "Not screams exactly, more like screeches. Edgy, high, piercing, and having the same effect on me like fingernails on a chalkboard."

"Stop right there. What woman?" His motion halted with the plates in midair.

"I'm getting to that part of the story. Stop interrupting me," she snapped. Glancing away from him, Jessie slapped her hand to her forehead. "I'm sorry. I didn't mean to answer you that way. I'm still a little rattled by it all." She proceeded to tell him about what had happened with the ghost and the stories about Elizabeth that she'd read.

Setting the plates on the table, he sat on the edge of the chair. A sad look crossed his face. "I'm happy you know. Remember, I told you on your birthday I had a girlfriend murdered years ago. Now that the news is out, I want you to know you're the only person I've ever wanted to talk with about Lizzy."

"There's no time like the present." She rested her arms on the back of the chair, uneasiness settling over her. Lizzy's pretty face came to mind as she recalled the photo.

"I have no idea where to begin." He propped his arms on the table, resting his cheek against his fist. He started and then stopped to gather his thoughts. She could almost hear the words tumbling around in his mind.

"You can start wherever you want," she said, noting the weariness in his eyes. How had she missed it earlier?

"Lizzy was my girlfriend through most of high school. We thought we were in love but had no clue what our feelings meant besides our raging hormones. Mostly mine, I guess." He raked his hand through his hair. "After her body was discovered in the woods, it was one of the worst days of my life." He lowered his head, his voice flat. "I'm sure you saw I was the main suspect from the beginning. Handcuffed and put in the back of a police cruiser. The memory still disturbs me to this day."

"You must've been scared." She dropped in the chair across from him. This part of the story had shaken her to the core as she read it. But she knew him, and there was no way he could hurt anyone. She studied him. How many interviews had she done where she'd heard those exact words said by relatives of a convicted killer? She sighed inwardly.

"I couldn't believe people would think I could ever hurt her. I grew up in this town, and they knew me. Hell, I was the good kid. I played by all the rules." He leaned back in his chair. "There are plenty of killers who declare their innocence who are guilty, but I wasn't one of them. Getting mad is what saved me."

"What do you mean?"

"I was scared, and fear made me passive." He looked thoughtful. "While sitting in the interview room, I realized the police could quite possibly find me guilty of something I didn't do. The police pressed me for a confession. Wanted me to admit to a crime I didn't commit. You could say it was my wake-up call. My fear turned to anger, and I knew I had to convince them I was innocent."

She reached for his hand and covered it with hers. "That was a lot for you to deal with as a teenager. How'd you get through it?"

"My parents were my biggest supporters along with Coach Mac. Dad hired a private investigator who thought the authorities were trying to railroad me. He's the one who found out about someone else's DNA at the scene. Using their timeline, he also proved I had a solid alibi. I was practicing with the football team at the time Lizzy was murdered."

"The article I read said that the police exonerated you early on, but they never arrested anyone. Is that right?" She blinked, as her mind rushed ahead to more questions.

Matt nodded. "I was never charged. My file and record of arrest were expunged."

"Meaning what, exactly?"

"It's like the events on record never happened, and in my case, the file was destroyed. I never would've got into the academy if it hadn't been." He stretched his legs out in front of him. "The lead officer on the case apologized to the family, and I was sent home with my parents, but only after my father threatened them with a lawsuit for false arrest. Truthfully, I think that's why Chief Anderson trained me personally after I moved back to town. He was trying to make it up to me."

"Did the police ever suspect anyone else?"

"Not that I know of. I was the easy target, and after my guilt didn't pan out, it seemed like the police stopped searching. I'm sure that's not true, but at the time it seemed that way to me." He paused holding her gaze. "The people in town speculated for a while. Everyone became a potential suspect. In the end, the hottest theory was that a transient murdered her and moved on."

"What do you think?"

"The town's theory was too convenient. But it's equally hard for me to imagine anyone who knew her would have ever wanted to hurt Elizabeth. She was a sweet girl. Of course, I've wondered all these years who killed her, but no one ever came to mind. It made no sense then or now either." He shrugged his shoulders.

"No clue at all?" she asked. She tried to imagine a young Matt and his pretty girlfriend. Green with envy, not her, not ever. Green wasn't her color. Her pep talk wasn't working.

"Oh, I speculated like everyone else, but I was in high school, and my world had been turned upside down. Hell, before she was killed, my greatest worry was completing a pass for a touchdown and trying to survive my English class." He leaned his head back, closing his eyes. "I never stopped thinking about it, checking the evidence, but maybe I'm too close to the situation to see it clearly."

"What did you hear from her friends?" Her fingers drummed quietly on the tabletop.

"At first, most of them wouldn't talk to me, as you can imagine. Rumors were flying around. No one knew what was fact or fiction. After a while, the kids accepted me again, but not before it destroyed a few relationships." He moved his hand back and forth on the edge of the table. "All I can remember is that it was weird."

"People always suspect the worst. I guess, even our friends." Under the chair, her foot shook restlessly trying to keep up with the thoughts racing through her mind.

"Until I led the team to the state championships and, as teens' fickle natures would have it, I was a freaking hero again."

"Strange how that works. I think we have short memories while we're young." She paused. Jessie studied his body language. The pain was written on his face. How could she help him remember the details without them hurting him again? "Is Elizabeth's death one of the reasons you became a police officer?"

"In a way. I always wanted to solve her murder, and yet in many ways, I wanted to forget about it." He shook his head. "Try to make sense out of that if you can."

"I get it," she said, and he smiled. "Welcome to my world."

"I bet you do." His brows furrowed. "I often wondered what would have happened to me if I had been charged. Innocent people are sometimes found guilty."

"I know." Her voice softened. "I've done stories about a few."

"I was one of the lucky ones. People fought for me." Matt stroked her hand.

"Thankfully, you had them. Many don't." She laced her fingers through his.

"Can you see why after Lizzy's death, I found it hard to be serious about another girl? Don't get me wrong. I've had girlfriends and dated, but I could never let myself get serious."

"I understand." She leaned back in the chair, picturing Lizzy's captivating smile. "She was lovely."

"Why now after all these years?" He frowned, the lines on his forehead deepened. "It's been so many years. Why now?" He bowed his head.

"I suppose because I see and hear these folks. I might be the first person ever to have noticed or heard Lizzy's ghost." She waved away the idea. "It doesn't matter why. She wants her murder solved, and she's chosen this time because you're ready to face it."

The question was, was she? Jessie took the food out of the bag and placed the cartons on the table. Matt went to the cupboard and returned with two glasses filled with ice then handed them to her. Grabbing silverware and chopsticks from the drawer, he went back to his chair.

"You could be right."

"I know I am. Let's eat, then we need to put our heads together and figure out how to solve this cold case. It will mean closure for Elizabeth, the family, and for you. It's time." Jessie spooned some rice onto Matt's plate and then onto hers.

"Does it bother you that I was a suspect? Is that why you didn't want me to kiss you?" He added sesame chicken to the rice and mixed it.

"No, that was a knee-jerk reaction. Seeing her ghost, reading the articles, and waiting for you to get here stressed me out. Besides, you were only a suspect until your alibi panned out. If I had any doubts about you, it was when I first moved here, and they disappeared once I got to know you." She clasped his hand.

"What were your doubts, if you don't mind me asking?"

"I thought you were a tough guy. Not my type."

"And now?" His brows rose with the question.

"You're just about perfect in every way." She winked at him. "That's why I'm sure you didn't kill her." She rubbed her thumb across his. "But someone did. And whoever did...is free. Justice demands they pay for their crime. With the ten-year anniversary of her murder coming up, I think she's waited long enough for justice."

"You're right, and I've lived each of them, hoping some new piece of evidence would surface." He shook his head. "Another year and still no resolution."

She drizzled soy sauce on her rice. "This looks good." She picked up a fork.

"No chopsticks. What are you? Chicken?" He grinned at her, picking up his and changing the conversation.

"No, just hungry." She placed a napkin on her lap. "You must have a working theory of some kind."

"There was a strange janitor who disappeared after she died. Hell, it could have been a student or anyone, Jess. Lizzy was friendly and trusted everyone."

"An outsider is possible or, as is true in most cases, someone she knew and trusted. That's why you were their first suspect. I'm ready to discover new clues that will surface. All we need to do is stir people's memories." She took a bite of her rice. "Tell me what you remember."

His shoulders slumped. "The murder happened early in our senior year. Lizzy's smile could light up a room. What can I say? We did everything together and had been friends for years. We were excited about our senior prom, graduation, and college. Without her, it all became a fuzzy mess."

A twinge of jealousy seeped into Jessie's mind. How could she fight a ghost who could still own a piece of his heart? "How'd you face the pressure of your senior year?"

"My family and a few of my teachers helped a lot."

"Thank heaven for families. I had a close friend die, and my family helped me too." Jessie paused, remembering the moment as if it were yesterday. "It was a freak car accident right after she had dropped me and Katie off. A few blocks from her a house, a drunk driver crossed into her lane. She died instantly."

"It isn't easy losing someone at that age, or any age, to be exact." Matt shook his head. "It must have been strange for you, having been in the car with her right before it happened."

"I felt guilty. I was alive and my friend was dead."

"Strange, that's exactly how I felt at the time of Lizzy's death." His grip tightened around the chopstick, snapping it.

She handed him a fork. "Here, this might be safer."

"Sorry." He glanced at the broken pieces in his hand. "I should've been there to protect her."

"Most likely you would have been murdered too."

"I guess, but part of the male ego is to protect the people in our life, and I failed. It doesn't matter if it's realistic or rational."

"Stereotypes are hard." She shrugged her shoulders. "I hope one day we'll be free from them."

"I speak from experience. Some of those were my expectations and no one else's. Call me old-fashioned, but I kind of like the idea of protecting those I love." He smiled at her.

"I like being a strong woman, but it's nice to know

if I ever need you, you'll be there to watch over me."
She touched her hand to her forehead in a dramatic
fashion. "You already have."

He smiled. "You'd have a hard time getting rid of
me. It's a part of who I am."

"I've always envisioned myself as a sort of
warrior-princess standing up for women and girls
everywhere." She grinned at the vision in her mind.

"A warrior princess?" He shook his head.

"Yes, you know, strong enough to kick butt while
wearing my tiara."

"There's an image I won't soon forget." He
chuckled. "I've seen that side of you minus the tiara."

"We can stop if you want. But if you don't mind, I
have another question."

"Ask away."

"Do you remember hearing anything about another
missing girl at the time of her murder?"

"Yeah, Grace was her name. Her parents found a
note saying she was leaving. She was a missing person
for years. Eventually, her family gave up believing
they'd ever find her again." Matt frowned. "Why?"

"Something tells me the two girls are somehow
linked, and if we search, we'll find her body
somewhere in the woods near where they found
Elizabeth."

"What makes you think there's a body in the
woods?" Matt braced his hands against the table.

"Lizzy wanted me to read the plaque, she wanted
me to see her, and a picture in my mind showed me
another body. I'm sure the other girl is in the woods
somewhere."

"Damn, Jess, are you talking about a double

homicide?" He pushed his chair back from the table and jumped up. The chair crashed to the floor.

She stood with him. "That's what I'm saying."

"One murder is bad enough. To think of Grace's body lying there for all these years is terrible. What are we looking at?" He righted the chair.

She sat again after he did. "When we know the answer to your question, we'll be on our way to solving a murder." She took a bite of her chicken. "I need to do a little research on Grace too."

"I'll go through the old case files and see what I can find from the police interviews." He leaned closer to her. "You can see why I fought my feelings for you in the beginning. Still, you made me want to try." He stroked her cheek gently with the back of his hand.

"I'm happy you were willing to risk it." Jessie pushed the food on her plate around. She would not lose this man because of her stupid thoughts, or some ghost from the past.

"I am too. My life would be empty without you."

"Maybe now it's a little too full." She smiled at him. "With all my strange friends, it's bound to get crowded." She chuckled.

"What? I can almost hear the wheels turning in your head," he said.

"If both of the girls' families agree, I would like to write an article and stir the waters to see if we can get someone to nibble." She placed her napkin on the table. "Ten years is too long for a murderer to be free."

"I'm sure Lizzy's parents will help you any way they can. They're great people. I don't know if Grace's family is still in the area, but I'll check it out."

"Do you remember Grace's last name?" She

glanced at him through watery eyes. "Allergies are acting up," she responded to the puzzled look on his face.

"Oh, no fun." He handed her a tissue after she sneezed. "Walters. Grace Walters." He put down the fork in his hand and frowned. "If she's out there, then whoever murdered them took the lives of two gems. The police had to be inept to have missed all this. The head investigator failed at his job miserably."

She wrote Grace's name down so she could research information on her later. "Didn't you tell me once you lost your best friend Chad in your senior year too?"

"You have a good memory. It was a hard year. I'm still not sure what happened between us. All our fights centered on Lizzy during our senior year. The last time we talked, we both said some terrible things to each other. Chad left town after graduation. I've never heard from him again." He paused. "Back then, I was happy to leave Blue Cove for college and pick up the pieces of my life."

"I'm amazed you ever came back. Not sure I would've wanted to." She rose from her seat and walked to the fridge. "Do you want something to drink besides water?"

"Tea would be great, thanks."

"Tell me about her." Jessie placed the pitcher of iced tea in front of him.

"Are you sure you want to go there?" Matt asked.

"We have to talk about her life and death. There's no way around it now." She twisted the ring on her finger.

Matt spent the next several minutes telling her

about Lizzy. "She was fun, and for a while, we lived in the moment, the way one's apt to do during that phase of life."

"What?" She saw his expression change. "Do you remember something?"

"For a few weeks before she died, she'd become more secretive. She was always too busy to talk. I chalked it up to pressure from her parents because her grades were slipping. In truth, if I let myself think about our relationship, I'd say I had a strange feeling she wanted to break it off. Deep down, I didn't want to believe it. I kept myself busy and didn't examine my feelings too deeply."

"Maybe she was just troubled by something else. Do you remember anything more?" Hope rose in her heart. Perhaps she didn't need to worry about Lizzy.

"Chad was trying to convince me to break up with her. He thought she was cheating on me." Matt leaned back in his chair. "What can I say? If she was, I had no idea about it."

"Love is blind, as they say." Jessie thought of her crazy devotion to Katie's brother Liam.

"Lizzy had dimples and a smattering of freckles on her nose. I've always been a sucker for dimples." He ran his finger over Jessie's when she smiled.

"She sounds like someone I would have liked to know. A little like my friend Katie."

"In truth, Katie reminds me of her in some ways. For a guy like me who was socially awkward when I was young, Lizzy took me into the limelight and gave me confidence."

"I can't imagine you lacking confidence, ever." Jessie shook her head. "Nope, I can't see it."

"I was the middle of three boys. You'll have to trust me on this. Do you have memories of high school?" he asked. "The pressure to live up to my older brother was crazy. A close second to that was trying to make a man out of our younger brother through constant torment. Besides sports, at that age, my thoughts were about girls, sex, and maybe cars, if they were as hot as the girls." He grinned. "I wasn't what you'd call a deep thinker."

She laughed. "I doubt any of us are at that age. There were no sibling shadows for me to follow. Boys were the center of topic for me too, but having grown up around Liam, the difference between how guys and girls talked about sex was huge."

"It's strange how that works." He laughed. "It's a wonder any of us ever get together."

"May I ask you something personal?"

"You can ask me anything."

"How did you get over her death and move on?" Jessie shifted the food around on her plate.

"I pushed myself. I had to get good grades, play a great game, and do my best to please everyone. Lizzy's death was the end of my carefree life." He placed his napkin on his empty plate. "After college, I applied at the Bureau and was accepted into their program. It only took a couple of years for me to realize I was a small-town cop at heart and needed to come home."

"I know I'll have more questions about your days with the agency someday. I was shocked to discover you'd been an agent. Why did you leave? You never answered the question when Tom asked you."

"The job came with a lot of stress." He frowned. "As I learned in the last case, what you do can always come back to haunt you. At that point in life, I wasn't willing to risk having a family and go through the painful possibility of losing them." He shot her a grin and reached for her hand. "You changed that for me."

"How?"

"The fact you didn't want a relationship at all intrigued me and challenged me. It stirred my male ego, along with the fact you're smoking hot. I fell hard for you before I could guard my heart. Something I wasn't counting on, but I'm happy it happened."

"Thank you." A tear formed in the corner of her eye.

"I mean it." He squeezed her hand and then reached for the tear, catching it with his finger.

"What's our next plan of action?" Jessie pushed back her chair and reached for his empty plate. "She wants our help."

"What's strange is I talked to my therapist the other day about Lizzy. You're right. It's time for us to solve her murder."

"Do you want any more?" Jessie pointed to the cartons of food.

Matt shook his head. "You didn't eat much."

"There's too much on my mind to eat right now." She closed the cartons and took the leftovers to the refrigerator.

"I'll take you to meet her parents. They'll give you all you need for your human interest story on her. Knowing you, it'll shake things up. We'll see what happens and what the fallout is."

"I have an idea for a series of articles. I'll write the first one, but let you read it before I do anything with it. A story highlighting Lizzy's life and death seems like a perfect way to draw in any of the kids that were in the high school at the time."

"Sounds good." He put the plates in the sink and turned on the water.

"I'll do the dishes later. Bring your tea and let's watch TV." Jessie wasn't sure Matt would like her idea. She wanted to make a few calls before she told him her plan. He would see the rightness of it once it all came together. She grabbed her glass and walked into the living room. Sitting down on the couch, she patted the space beside her. "Hey, I'm your listening ear. Any time you want to talk, we'll talk, and when you don't, we won't. Right now, I want to be with you." She leaned into his side.

"Thank you, sweetheart." He wrapped his arm around her, hugging her tight. "You're the best."

"I feel the same way about you. We'll get through this, find their murderer, and Lizzy can rest in peace." At least that's what she hoped would happen.

Chapter 2

The days ahead wouldn't be easy for Matt or her. Besides closure for him, the girls' families needed answers too. Lizzy wanted her murder solved, and that's what they would do. The teakettle whistled, bringing her back to reality. Putting a slice of bread in the toaster, she went in search of her ringing phone. The darn thing was never nearby.

"Good morning, honey." Her mom's soft voice came over the line.

"Hi, Mom. Is everything okay?" She buttered her toast. A frown marred her cheerful countenance. Her mother rarely called this early.

"We're all fine. We had such a nice time at your birthday party. Matt is a fine man. Your father approves of him, and you know I can't say that often."

Her face relaxed into a smile. "Hey, I'm glad Dad likes him because I do, too."

"I know. I saw it in your eyes whenever you glanced at him."

"What's up?" Jessie asked.

"I don't call this early, as you know, but I have a surprise for you, and I couldn't wait to tell you."

"What kind of surprise?" Her thoughts immediately turned to guess what the surprise might be.

"One I think you'll love."

"Don't keep me in suspense. You know how I am." She sipped her tea taking a bite of her toast.

"I sure do. You're the girl who did everything but unwrap the gifts under the tree trying to figure out what was in them."

"The wait was too much." Jessie warmed at the image of her shaking her gifts every year. Even in high school, she was still doing it.

"I won't keep you waiting any longer." Her mother laughed. "During our visit to Blue Cove for your birthday, we drove around the area. We found a senior apartment complex near the ocean. Sadie fell in love with the place and convinced your dad that living by the ocean was on her bucket list. He has relented, and she'll be moving to Blue Cove in the next month."

"Are you kidding me?"

"No, honey, you know me. I'm always the serious one. Your cousin Peyton wants to come with us and help Sadie settle in, if she can get off work. Sally has graciously volunteered to help us too if she's needed. She's here visiting her parents and has been around to see us."

"Not to change the subject, but how's Sally doing?"

"She's healing, but her doctor and her therapist say it will take a while for her to fully recover. Who would've thought Bruce could shoot his wife?"

"I still find it hard to believe." Jessie wiped the breadcrumbs off the counter into her cupped hand and threw them in the sink. "The mental abuse over the years was equally bad, too."

"Probably, the hardest for her to overcome." Her mother sighed. "What do you think about having Sadie living in Blue Cove? It would mean us seeing you more often."

"Perfect." Jessie agreed it couldn't come at a better point. "Reba will be happy. They get along so well."

"Even your dad could see the added spark it gave his mother. Her apartment faces the cove, and she couldn't be happier."

"I can't wait, and it will be fun to see Peyton, too. I hope she can get away."

"I'll call you back when I have the exact date of our arrival. The apartment will be ready for your grandmother to move into at the beginning of the month."

"I'll call Grams later."

"Let her call you. She wants to surprise you. I know you have to get to work, but I couldn't wait to tell you. The plans all came together last night, and Sadie is excited. Don't tell her I called, and for heaven's sake, act surprised."

"I will. Love you, Mom. Oh, and before I forget to tell you, that red dress you talked me into buying was a big hit. Matt wants to thank you and Grams personally." Jessie chuckled. She could still see the look on his face.

"I told you. A little red dress works every time. I know. Just ask your dad." Her mom laughed. "Bye. Remember to act surprised when your grandmother tells you she's moving there."

"Okay." Jessie hung up. She couldn't wait to tell Reba the excellent news. Putting the last bite of her toast in her mouth, she placed her cup in the sink and grabbed her purse. The clock reminded her she needed to get to work.

****

"Gram's in Blue Cove." Jessie smiled as she unlocked the door to her shop. Reba would be happy, and she couldn't be more pleased. She flipped on the lights and the morning routine began. Reaching for the feather duster, she tackled a layer of dust she saw on the counter and took the window cleaner to the fingerprints on the doors. She stepped back for a better view. The glass looked much better.

Next, she got to work on the bookshelves and polishing the tables. "Umm," she inhaled the lovely lemony scent that filled the room. One more sweep of the duster and she was done. With the store tidied, what she wanted now was a cup of coffee. Unlocking the doors to Joe's, she waved at Molly as she walked in.

"Hey, Jessie. I was wondering if I'd see you this morning." Molly's cheerful voice greeted her. She placed a tray of fresh scones inside the glass display case.

"I saw the dust on my counter, and one thing led to another."

"I know the story. It's part of being a business owner. At least you left a few minutes for a coffee." She handed Jessie a cup. "May I tempt you with one of the newer items on our menu?" Molly pointed them out.

"I'll have a blueberry scone." Jessie reached in her wallet for cash. "After all, I need to do my part to support Blue Cove's local businesses."

"And may I say how much I appreciate your support." Molly laughed and handed her the bag. "You need to get over to your store. Reba's on her way across the street. I hope for your sake nothing is up and it's just a friendly visit."

"I have news for her. If you get a break, bring her a scone and tea. I'll pay for it. I can tell both of you the news together." Jessie scurried through the doors setting her stuff down on the counter. She grabbed her ringing phone on the way to unlock the front door for Reba.

"Hi, Matt, what's up?" She waved at Reba to let her know that she saw her.

"I talked to the McKenzies, and they would be happy for us to stop by after five if that works for you."

"Sounds good to me."

"I figured we might as well get started. I'll pick you up at your place."

"I'll be ready. I have some news to tell you when I see you. Reba is here. We'll talk soon."

"Okay, catch you later."

She held the door open for Reba. "I hope you can stay for a chat." Every hair on Reba's head was neat and in place. Jessie wondered how she did it. She couldn't imagine Reba any other way.

"Of course, dear, I planned on being here for a while this morning. Besides wanting to see you, I need to buy a few more books. I'm looking for a certain title for a friend's birthday gift. I also would like to check out your new card section. I'm happy you decided to include a selection of cards in your store. They'll give it a nice touch."

"I've added a few other nice book-related gift items, too." Jessie picked up a journal to show Reba. "Molly should be coming through the door in a moment with a cup of tea and scone for you. My treat."

"Sounds lovely." Reba went to the table in the middle of the room. She folded her jacket neatly over the back of the chair before she sat down. "I know you're dying to tell me about your latest adventure, and I'm all ears. Shall we begin?" She placed her hands on her lap, crossing her ankles.

Jessie told Reba about seeing Elizabeth McKenzie's ghost. "Do you remember her?"

A shadow crossed Reba's face, and sadness took its place. "Charlotte McKenzie is a dear friend. She was devastated by the death of her daughter. She's become a bit of a recluse the past few years. The anniversary of the murder is coming up it makes sense that Elizabeth would appear now." Reba opened her purse, taking out a pack of tissues, and dabbed at the tears forming in her eyes.

"I thought so too." Jessie patted Reba's hand. "Plus Matt is ready to tackle it."

"You understand what I tried to tell you about in the last case. Thankfully our Mr. Parker has faced most of the emotions already."

"Yes. Matt told me about their relationship last night at dinner."

"He isn't guilty of anything." Reba made eye contact with Jessie.

"In my heart, I know he isn't." Still, the doubts surfaced now and then.

"You have to believe in his innocence. Elizabeth was such a nice girl, but something was changing her. Her mother had voiced her concern to me several times. She had pulled away from the family, her grades were dropping, and she had become secretive about where she was going. It was completely unlike her. Charlotte was worried." Reba's voice trembled. "I'm afraid Lizzy's life had begun to unravel."

"The police had no suspect, which seems strange to me."

"Not really. There are many unsolved murders in this country. Something tells me this one will soon be solved, which makes me happy. At least my good friend will be able to put her daughter to rest once she knows what happened to her. It's the not knowing that makes it impossible to find peace." Reba dabbed at her eyes again. "Some thought the murderer was a transient, but I never did. Elizabeth knew her killer. I'm sure of it. He may still live close by. You're not telling me everything are you?"

Jessie shook her head. She described the scene that had played out in her mind. "Do you remember hearing about Grace Walters?"

"I remember she went missing while we were grieving for Elizabeth. The family found a note that led them to believe she was a runaway. Gracie's family was poor and lived in a small house on the outside of town." Reba got a faraway look on her face. "A remarkable family who did so much for the community. Grace was such a pretty little thing. A kind-hearted girl with startling blue eyes. To think of anyone murdering her is beyond awful. They would have to be the worst kind of person to have hurt such a sweet young girl." Tears sprang to Reba's eyes. "And yet, my goodness, that's exactly what happened. How could we have not known Gracie was dead all these years?"

Jessie leaned across the table closer to her. "Who knows? But this is the moment for the truth to come out." She patted Reba's hand. "Do you know if the Walter family is still in the area?"

"I'm not sure. After Grace was gone a few years

they were no longer involved in anything. They dropped out of the picture altogether."

"Hi, Reba." Molly came through the doors carrying her tea and scone.

"Such a nice surprise, thank you." Reba beamed at Molly.

"What's the news you have to share? You'd better be quick because a tour bus is dropping folks off as we speak."

"My grandmother is moving to Blue Cove." Jessie blurted out in her excitement.

"Sadie is moving here?" Reba clapped her hands.

"Yes, my mother called and told me this morning. I'm excited. It'll be great to have her in town. My parents and my cousin Peyton may come along to help her get settled in. My friend Sally has also offered to help."

"I hope they'll all come. The more, the merrier. This is good news indeed." Reba swallowed a sip of her tea.

"I need to get back. The line is forming as we speak." Molly jumped up.

"Scoot along, dear." She motioned to Jessie when the bell rang. "I'll be here a while, and we'll talk more before I leave. Take care of your customers."

When the last customer of the morning left, Reba brought her books and cards to the counter. Jessie rang them up. "I'm sorry I didn't get to talk to you as much as I hoped I would." She put Reba's items in a bag.

"A quiet moment alone to think can be good for a fresh perspective. I'm afraid my friend is going to learn some hard things about her family. Matt is going to feel betrayed and rightfully so, and the whole town will be surprised by the culprits involved and the one responsible for Elizabeth's murder. The possibility of a second murder is even worse. Several truths will surface, and some ugly secrets long hidden from view will come to light." Reba reached for the bag. "You, my sweet girl, are about to stir a hornet's nest, the sting of which will be felt far and wide. Be sure to protect yourself. There is more to this murder than meets the eye."

"Whew, that's a lot to digest."

"For you, my dear, it should be a piece of cake."

"From the sounds of it, you're talking about one huge piece of cake." Jessie rubbed her arms as the hair on her neck stood up.

"Jessie girl, be careful. It's your pen that will stir the hive."

Walking with Reba to the door, she waved goodbye as Reba's car pulled away from the curb. And she thought this would be an easy case. No murder was ever simple. What was she thinking?

Ugly secrets, intrigue, betrayal, weren't the words she wanted to hear. Simple would be nice. This sounded more like destroying a family, not bringing them closure.

As the day progressed, Jessie's curiosity got the best of her. The moment her last customer left, she closed her store fifteen minutes early and crossed the street to the cemetery beside the church. Jessie walked among the graves, searching until she found Lizzy's grave two rows from where Gina was buried. Fresh flowers were in the vase at the base of the headstone. Gone but not forgotten. Her hand moved across the top of the headstone as a gesture of comfort, but a gloomy foreboding settled over her. Something was amiss. Call it a premonition or intuition, but Jessie suspected Elizabeth had a dark secret she took to her grave.

Chapter 3

Matt pulled the car into the open space beside Jessie's red convertible. He liked Charlotte and Byron McKenzie, but it wasn't easy for any of them to see each other. Being near each other stirred up too many sad memories. He needed to work through the awkwardness. There was a crime to solve. No matter what, he owed it to Elizabeth and her family.

"Hi." Jessie opened the door and got in.

"Sorry, I should have opened the door for you. I wasn't paying attention." He reached for her hand. "Overthinking, I guess."

"In your place I would be, too. If you want, I can do most of the talking. I have a list of questions I'd like to ask the McKenzies." She fastened her seatbelt. If only she knew what he was thinking, maybe she could lighten the load.

"Your questions will stir some in me. It usually works that way with us." His voice was flat. He pulled out of the parking space. "What was the news you had to tell me?"

"Sadie is moving here next month. My cousin Peyton may come with my folks to help her get settled. We haven't seen each other in a few years. I feel a bout of matchmaking coming on. Peyton is a sweetheart, and she'd be a great catch for any man. Jeremy might be perfect or Gary."

"Whoa, slow down there. Let's get Sadie moved to town first. I like the idea of her being near you. We'll talk about Peyton after I meet her."

"Your brother might be nice too."

He slammed on the brakes. "We aren't going there yet."

Jessie grinned at him. "Lighten up. You're wound too tight. I can feel it sitting over here."

"It's true." He raked his hand through his hair. "I always get uptight before I see Lizzy's family. I never know what they think when it comes to me."

"From what Reba said to me today, they might feel the same way about seeing you. Reba told me, according to Charlotte, their daughter's life was unraveling before she died."

"I guess we rarely know what's happening in another person's life unless we choose to dig under the surface. I didn't think quite that deep in high school."

"Of course not, none of us did. We moved from one high to the next and from one crisis to the next. With all the emotions of growing up, it's a wonder any of us survived. For some, those years were great fun, and for others a nightmare. There seems to be little wiggle room in-between."

"In high school, I never thought much about the kids on the fringes. It's crazy how years can change perspective."

"You're not that old, Mr. Parker."

"No, but I'm far enough removed now that I can see how hard it was for the kids who didn't fit in. I would treat them differently now."

"A few years can give life a whole new

perspective. I mean—look at me."

"I'm looking." He grinned, winking at her.

"I used to drool over Liam. Crazy me." She glanced at him. "You can stop looking, you're making me nervous."

He leaned over and kissed her. "I'm sorry for being preoccupied earlier. Let's start over, shall we?"

"Sounds good to me." She reached for her phone and snapped a picture of him. "I had to capture the moment you relaxed."

"Thanks for lightening my mood." He turned onto the road to town. "By the way, I like when you wear blue, but my favorite is still the dress you wore on your birthday."

"Ah, the little red dress. I told my mom you were quite taken with it."

"That's one way to put it. I'm sure you don't want to know where my mind goes when I think of you in that dress."

"I might have to wear it again and make you tell me." Her eyes twinkled with merriment.

"You'll get no argument from me."

"On a more serious note, I went to Elizabeth's grave after work." She shrugged when he gave her a strange look. "Call me curious. I had the strangest feeling…" Her voice trailed off.

"What?" He glanced at her and then back on the road.

"Not sure how I'd describe it. I wanted to get away from the oppressive feeling. All was not well with Lizzy." The words hung thick in the air between them.

"What do you mean?"

She shook her head. "Forget it."

"Jess, I know you well enough to understand these feelings you get usually pan out right. You may as well tell me."

"It's probably nothing, but when I ran my hand over the headstone," she paused and went on to explain what she sensed.

"We'll know those secrets soon enough." He pulled in front of a pretty Tudor style home. "We're here." Matt turned off the engine. "I'll leave it to you how much you tell them. You seem to know what to say and what not to say better than I do."

She grabbed his hand. "It'll be okay. I'll be careful. They will dictate how much or little they want to talk about their daughter."

"You'll be fine. Let's do this." He opened the car door, and so did she. They paused at the porch then he rang the doorbell.

****

"Matt, it's good to see you," Charlotte McKenzie said as she opened the door and invited them in. She stopped his progress halfway in and gave him a big hug. "Please, sit." She motioned toward the living room. "Byron will be down in a minute. Matt told me you wanted to write a story about Elizabeth, Miss Reynolds. Do you mind telling me why?"

Jessie put her purse on the floor beside the chair. "Not at all. I was running with the high school running club yesterday when I noticed the memorial for your daughter. It is coming on ten years, and I would like to write a human-interest piece about her. I've found it can jog the memories of the public and a new detail might come to light." She smiled at Mr. McKenzie when he walked in the room.

"Matt, it's always nice to see you, son. We've been keeping up with your career in the paper. It seems our community has had more than its fair share of trouble lately."

"It sure has. Nice to see you too, sir. This is Jessica Reynolds."

"I've heard about you, also, young lady. I've read some of your stories in the paper. I loved the one about the kids saved from the human trafficking ring."

"Byron, why don't you show Matt your new workshop. I'll take Jessie up to Lizzy's room." Charlotte started up the stairs. "My husband can't stand to talk about her death, so he won't. Matt will keep him busy."

Charlotte opened the door to a typical teenage girl's bedroom, which had been frozen in time. Lizzy's favorite posters were on the wall, along with her cheerleader's photo. Several trophies were on the dresser. "I didn't have the heart to throw it away at first. After her murder, I would come to sit in here every day. Being in this room helped me to feel close to her and grieve." Charlotte's hand ran lovingly over the teddy bear on the bed. "This was one of her favorites as a little girl. She slept with it all through high school, too. She stood by the desk. "Look around, and I'll be happy to answer any questions."

"Thank you." The picture of Elizabeth hanging on the wall caught her attention first. "Her smile was beautiful."

"Yes, our Lizzy could light up a room." A shadow crossed over Charlotte's face. "I'm glad you came today because I have someone coming next week to pack her room and take it all away. It's time to let it go." She picked up the bear and clutched it to her chest. "I'll keep a few things, but only a few."

"I can't imagine how hard it must be to let it go." Jessie glanced around the room. It was as if Lizzy would be back at any moment.

"You never plan for your child to die before you do, Miss Reynolds. I mean you always know it's a possibility in the back of your mind, but who thinks about murder in their child's future? You have dreams of watching them grow up and find their place in life, but never of them dying before you. The best I can hope for now is maybe someday I will know why." Charlotte sat on the bed. She patted the spot beside her. She took an envelope out of the nightstand. "I want you to have this."

Jessie glanced at the envelope with Matt's name on it. "What is this?"

"I found this letter a few days before she was murdered. Lizzy had written it to Matt. I begged her to think long and hard before she sent it. Of course, she didn't live long enough to mail it. I probably should have given it to Matt years ago. He was too devastated by her death at first, and then later I didn't see any point in hurting him more."

"What do you want me to do with it?"

"Read it. You might find a clue to my daughter's state of mind and when you think you should, give it to Matt. It is rightfully his. I can't bring myself to do it." Charlotte stood and walked over to a box on the floor in the corner. She picked it up and handed it to Jessie. "Elizabeth loved to journal. These can tell you her story better than I can and in her own words. We never knew where they were because she hid them so her brothers couldn't find them."

"I'll return them as soon as I'm finished." Jessie took a peek inside the box.

"I came across them in a hiding place in the attic the other day. I've haven't read them. She wouldn't let any of us near them when she was alive. With the anniversary of her death coming, it is too painful to read them now. Maybe someday I'll be able to."

Charlotte showed her a photo album of Lizzy's high school years and answered several of her questions. She talked, cried, and told Jessie about the worries she had experienced in the months before the murder. "No one tells you when you're having a baby how much you'll love them. When you think it's not possible to love your child any more than you already do, your heart expands, and you find you are capable of loving them more." She dried her eyes. "We'll never forget our girl."

Jessie hugged Mrs. McKenzie. "How could you? Listening to you talk about her, I feel like I know her, and I'm saddened we'll never meet."

"Thank you. I needed to talk about my daughter. It's been stored up inside me for too long." Charlotte moved toward the door. "Let's join the men." She sounded exhausted.

"Before we do, can I ask you one more question?"

"Of course, go ahead."

"Did your daughter know Grace Walters?"

"Everyone in town knew Gracie. She was a sweetheart. What does she have to do with Lizzy? She was a runaway." Charlotte moved toward the door.

"It's not important. I was just curious is all. Both of the girls went missing around the same time, and it made me wonder." Jessie carried the box of journals down the stairs with her. "I appreciate you talking to me. I'll return these to you." She saw Charlotte nod. "I'll let you read my story before I send it to Max to see if it meets with your approval." Jessie handed the box to Matt to carry, gave Charlotte another hug, and grabbed her purse. They said their goodbyes and left.

"You two were gone for quite a while." Matt glanced at her when he got in the car shutting the door.

"Charlotte needed to talk, and I wanted to listen. I could use something to eat. How about you? You pick the place. I'll be happy with anything."

"Okay." Matt paused. "Are you going to tell me what's in the box or what you two talked about?" His deep voice cut through the silence.

"The box is filled with Elizabeth's journals. Charlotte wants me to read them. Of course, we'll talk. I have a lot to process." Jessie stared mindlessly out the window at the passing scenery. After listening to Mrs. McKenzie, the mystery had deepened for her.

Chapter 4

"Thanks for taking me to meet her parents. I have some heavy reading to do to get acquainted with Elizabeth. I want to do her story justice." Jessie latched her seat belt. "Dinner was nice."

"It was. You seemed distracted. Is everything, okay?" Matt started the car.

"Fine, I'm trying to process everything Charlotte told me. She did confirm what I told you earlier. Lizzy was going through a drastic change, and it wasn't good. She had no idea what was happening to her daughter."

"Did she ask her?"

"Of course, but Lizzy clammed up, and then they'd fight." She sighed. "I remember the drama and the war of words I had with my parents at that age. I was emotional."

"You? No way." He grinned at her. "I wonder where I was. I never saw a big change, or maybe I did, but it didn't compute with me. You know where my mind was. I was fairly shallow and uncomplicated. As I told you before, I was into girls, friends, and sports. Not much mystery. I was a typical guy." He shook his head. "Did I mention girls?"

"Yes, I think you covered the subject." She glanced at him with a grin. "Remember I grew up around Liam and Connor. Liam was attracted to anything that wore a skirt except for me, maybe."

"Boy, was he ever dumb. I know he must kick himself every now and again." Matt pulled in the spot next to her car. "I'll carry the box to your door and leave you to your work. I have some thinking to do myself." He opened her door and grabbed the box out of the backseat.

He placed the box on her desk and gave her a quick kiss on his way to the door. "I'll call you tomorrow."

Jessie followed him. "Come for dinner tomorrow night. It's warm enough to throw something on the grill, and we need to make plans on how we go about this case."

"Sounds good." He kissed her again and walked out the door.

* * * *

Jessie sat at her desk, shifting the envelope back and forth from hand to hand. Not sure if she wanted to read its contents, she placed it off to the side and picked up one of the journals. It was dated and labeled *My Junior Year*. Jessie scanned the first entries with a few smiles and laughter. Lizzy was a typical teen girl with all the drama and emotions that came along with growing up. Her description of Matt stirred memories of how she used to describe Liam. Lizzy had written four journals about her junior year alone. She seemed to be a happy, well-adjusted girl who loved her family and everything about Matt, of course. She wasn't as fond of Chad, who took too much of Matt's free time. Funny how small the world was, different girls, different towns, but the story sounded similar.

After reading for a while, she found nothing to indicate a dramatic change in Elizabeth's life. She decided to read ahead to her senior year. Picking up another journal entitled *My Senior Year*, Jessie began to read. The first pages began the same way as the others had until she got to the fifth entry.

I met someone. A dreamy man that makes Matt look like a child in comparison. My parents would flip out, but I'm going to meet him again tomorrow. I'll have to keep this a secret even from my BF Kendra who is sure to blab it anyway.

Jessie read on for a while. Lizzy's entries in the journal changed as did her language. Whomever this guy was he had made her a lot of promises. Easy money, a modeling career—a young girl's dream—and she wouldn't have to waste her life on more schooling.

Who was he and what was his angle? Did he have something to do with her death? Jessie was hooked reading on, hoping to find a name or description anything pointing to the man's identity.

Another thread throughout the pages mentioned a man she hated who wouldn't let her out, but she didn't say what from or who he was. Elizabeth's anger toward him came through every word she wrote about him. At midnight, she finished the last journal Charlotte had given her. Charlotte had been right. Elizabeth wasn't the same girl. They had to find her killer. Both the men in her journal had something to do with the change, if not her death. In her heart, Jessie knew they both were involved somehow.

The envelope off to the side of the desk caught her attention once again. Carefully opening it, she slipped the contents out, holding the letter written on pink paper in her hand. Another piece of paper with a hastily scribbled note also fell out. Jessie placed it in the last journal and began to read the long letter to Matt. In perfect legible penmanship, Jessie read one of the harshest and nastiest letters a girl could ever write to a guy. To put it bluntly, she not only wanted to break up, but she had met a real man. Whatever a real man meant to a seventeen-year-old. She punctuated the letter with some ugly colorful remarks about Matt being less than stellar and a child in comparison in every way. Maybe it was good Matt had never received it. It would have given the police motive for Lizzy's murder. Charlotte had kept him from a world of hurt.

Jessie placed the letter back in the envelope on the desk. How would she ever know if and when to give it to him? One more clue to add to the mystery of Elizabeth McKenzie. Reba was right. Matt would feel betrayed. Who was this man who outshone Matt and made Elizabeth feel like a desirable woman? Find him, and you might find the killer or someone close to him. Whoever he was he sounded like quite the salesman.

Jessie stretched out on her bed. The morning would be here before she knew it. Closing her eyes a vivid scene began to play in her mind.

Lizzy, young and full of life, stood at the edge of the woods. Pushing her hair from her face, she stared off into the distance. *Where is he?* She checked her watch. He promised he would come today. Hope was replaced with fear. *Grace, oh no, Grace.* Lizzy ran and realized too late that she was running into the woods. She was going the wrong way. He would catch her. Who told him? Betrayed. The dark shadow grabbed her, and they were hidden from view among the trees.—

Jessie pushed up, swinging her legs over the side of the bed. The shadowy figure was the one who had killed her. They had to go into those woods. No way would she go there alone. Matt would have to come with her, and maybe Radar too.

****

Matt had spent most of the night trying to figure out what was going on in Jessie's head and thinking about the strange conversation they had at dinner. It wasn't what she said, but rather what she didn't.

His mind moved into high gear as he stretched out on the bed, stacking his arms behind his head. Jessie had been quiet on the drive home, too quiet. The opposite was true at dinner. She talked about everything, but never mentioned Lizzy once. Maybe he was asking too much of her to be involved in this case. Okay, so he didn't ask her. Lizzy's ghost had. Still, it could mean trouble.

How would she handle the information she read in the journals? Better yet, what had Lizzy written in them? He raked his hand through his hair. He had no clue. What kind of junk did a girl write in a diary? Writing, if you weren't being forced, made no sense in his world during those years. The high school years were a blur and too many years had gone by. It was news to him that Lizzy had even written journals. He didn't read about them in the case file.

At the time, he'd believed he loved Elizabeth, but now he knew the difference. How Jessie would interpret it, though, was another question. The thought of losing her was something he didn't want to entertain. To think of her alive and not his girl made him shudder. Matt frowned. Life was too damn complicated. How could he expect Jessie to understand when he had no idea how to explain it to himself? He simply knew.

None of it mattered. The case was open, and he was in it to solve it. Jessie was right. The smallest detail could open a trail gone cold. Blue Cove needed her fresh eyes to look at the file. Maybe she would see a connection no one else could see. She was strong, but he had no idea what this case would dredge up. Hopefully, the details of the murder wouldn't drive her away from him, but it was a risk he had to take. He rolled over scrunched the pillow under his head and closed his eyes. It was going to be a long night.

Chapter 5

Sadie called first thing in the morning. Jessie could hear the excitement in her voice. "I've always wanted to live by the ocean and being near you will be delightful for me. I'm waiting to hear if Peyton will help me move. It would be nice for you girls to be together."

"I would love to see her, Grams. It'll be great to have you nearby. Reba will love having you around."

"I want to work at your store. It would be a good way for me to meet new people."

"I can always use another person to fill in once in a while at the store. Who's helping you pack?" Jessie asked.

"Your dad is having movers do all the work, which is fine by me."

"Sounds perfect. Keep me in the loop. I want to know the details when you have them."

"I'll call you as soon as I know. See you, sweet girl. Tell Matt I said hi." Sadie paused. "I hope you two get married soon. I want to be around to see the wedding."

"We'll see. You never know, Grams. I'll tell him you said hello. Talk to you later." Jessie disconnected. She would point to this moment as the time when the plan formulated in her mind.

Jessie grabbed her purse and headed out the door. A few years had passed since she last saw Peyton. She was a couple of years older than Jessie, about the same age as Liam. They wouldn't be a good match. Her cousin never liked Liam, and the feeling was mutual. Connor maybe, or Gary? Of course, the years could have changed everything. Still, Matt's oldest brother Evan seemed like the wisest choice. He was single and a year or two older than Liam. Mature enough, handsome, with a good business sense. He'd be perfect. Yes, now all she had to do was get Matt to invite Evan for a visit while Peyton was here. How would she pull that off? Matt wouldn't be easy to convince. He'd be on to her in a minute. Darn, she shouldn't have playfully mentioned his brother earlier. *Think.*

Jessie began her morning routine at the store. She pulled her ringing phone out of her purse. "Hi, Matt, I was just thinking about you."

"Oh yeah, in a good way I hope."

"What do you think?" It was now or never. Jessie pursed her lips. "All good. You know, it's been a while since your brothers have been here to see you, and I have yet to meet your parents, which makes me wonder if you don't want them to meet me." *Good one.* She grinned.

"What brought this on?" Matt sounded perplexed.

"What can I say it's how my mind works? I have all kinds of random thoughts. Why did you call? Did you want to tell me something?"

"I found Grace Walters' family. I wanted to make sure tonight works for you if they agree to meet with us."

"Don't you think we should wait until we see if

47

there's a body?"

"I thought maybe we should give them a heads-up that we're reopening the case."

"Of course you're right. They need to know, so it doesn't take them by surprise. I can go tonight if they agree."

"I'll pick you up at the store." The phone was silent for a moment, and then his deep voice came across the line. "I want you to meet my parents, Jess. In fact, you won't have to wait long. They'll be in town on the first of the month, my brothers included. It's as if you somehow know. I find it hard to get used to you always being one step ahead of me."

Jessie did a fist pump and was happy Matt couldn't see her. "I had no idea. I thought it would be nice to meet them, that's all, and to see your brothers again."

"The question is why would you be thinking about my brothers at all?"

"It's been a while since I last saw them. No great mystery. You've met my family, and I'd like to think you want me to know yours too."

"Okay, as long as you aren't planning to match one of them with your cousin."

She heard him chuckle. He knew her too well.

"What gave you that idea?" she asked.

"You did, if I remember correctly. Jess, you're an amazing woman, but you're not clever at scheming. You're too sweet and easy to read to be sneaky."

"Peyton can speak for herself. I'm glad your brothers will get a chance to meet her. I'm not sure yet if she'll be coming anyway. Sally might replace her if she can't get off work. Besides, Gary or Connor might be more to her liking. It's quite possible she already has a steady guy, so you won't have to worry at all."

"I'm not worried, sweetheart. I don't want you to be disappointed."

"I won't be. You and Evan are a lot alike. He's been dragging his feet longer, is all. I hope some girl comes along and knocks him off his feet."

"As long as it's the girl doing the knocking and not someone who will remain nameless for now, meddling. We'll see. I'll catch you later. I'm going to read the Walters file."

"If I remember, we had some folks pushing us together.

"Yeah, and neither one of us were happy about. Let things run their natural course."

"I wouldn't think of doing anything else." She crossed her fingers behind her back. "Let me know what you learn about Grace. We'll talk later." She would let him believe he had won for now. Opening the doors to the coffee shop, she waved at Molly. Her day was off to a good start.

****

Matt shook his head and smiled. Evan wouldn't know what hit him if Peyton was anything like Jess. He could only hope his brother landed softly. Placing the Walters file on his desk next to Lizzy's, he began to read. How were they connected, if at all? The McKenzie file had a detailed crime scene. It made him sick to read it. Lizzy's death was horrific. If what Jessie saw was true, then Grace had suffered in the same way. Damn, they needed to solve this one. Why hadn't they searched the woods for Grace at the same time? Had their suspect killed only two or were there more?

Matt picked up the phone and paged the front desk.

"Kenny, would you tell Kip and Dylan to come to my office."

"Sure thing, Chief."

"Kenny said you wanted to see me." Dylan stood in the doorway.

"I have an assignment for you and Kip." He motioned for Dylan to sit down while they waited. Kip knocked on his open door. "Come in." Matt motioned to the empty chair.

"What's up?" Kip sat, careful not to spill his hot coffee.

Matt brought them up to speed on the cold case and what Jessie had seen. "She seems to think that the two girls are connected. She feels Grace is buried somewhere in the woods. I have Frank from the Bloodhound Search and Rescue group coming in a few days to help us search for Grace."

"What do you want us to do?" Dylan asked.

"I want you to search through police records of missing and murdered girls in the area over the past ten years. Look for similarities between the McKenzie girl and other murder sites. I'm wondering if Lizzy and possibly Grace are the only victims or are there more."

"Where do you want us to begin?" Kip asked.

"You can start by making a copy of these files to study. If we find Grace's body, then her file will change."

"What are you thinking?" Dylan frowned.

"I know we'll be changing her file. Jessie is damn accurate." Matt pushed the files toward the edge of his desk.

Kip grabbed them. "I'll make copies and bring them back to you."

"Okay. Here's another one to copy." Matt handed him the paper.

"Can you handle this case, Matt?" Dylan stood. "I know it was a long ago, but it's sure to bring up some old wounds."

"I need to do this, Dylan. Ten years is too long for a case to go unsolved. We owe the girls' parents answers."

"You too, I think." Dylan walked out of his office.

Maybe he didn't want to know the answers. New memories were surfacing. Jessie was right. All was not well with Elizabeth. Her parents' hearts were about to be broken again. He didn't relish the idea.

Chapter 6

When Jessie worked for Neil in New York, he had drummed the literacy statistics into his reporters. Those numbers hadn't changed much in the last ten years. Fourteen percent of adults or approximately thirty-two million people can't read. Twenty-one percent read below a fifth-grade level. Add to those numbers the forty-one percent who said they hadn't read a fiction book in over a year and a mere one percent higher number for nonfiction. The picture was grim for book lovers. The key had to be getting people hooked on reading at an early age. She wanted to do her part to help and knew from the first day she opened the store she would have a story hour for kids. It would have to be fun and exciting to keep the kids coming back for more.

Working most of the afternoon on her ideas, Jessie put her plans together for a children's summer reading program. Typing one detail after another into her computer, she saved the information. With a bit of colorful clipart added, the announcements and fliers began to take shape. She and Sadie planned to split the program so the kids of Blue Cove would have two story hours a week at Idle Time Books.

Larissa's ghost had given Jessie the idea for the perfect spot to read to the children. She would sit in the leather chair near the front window, the same one Larissa had sat in when she took up residence in the store. If the crazy antics of Larissa's ghost didn't inspire great stories, nothing would. Jessie could still see the books lifting from the book table, spinning in the air like bees near their hive. Larissa's willingness to pitch a book at someone she didn't like made for a few interesting moments

As a child, Jessie had often gone to the local library for story hour. Every story she heard made her love books all the more. She thought about the stories long after she heard them read and often rewrote them in her head. From adventures to mysteries to be solved, she would play out those scenarios at night in her bed. The perfect story to her would always be Mary Poppins and the tea party on the ceiling. She never tired of hearing it. She laughed along with the Banks children, wishing she could be up there with them.

Blue Cove's local library had a program too, but as far as she was concerned, you couldn't have too many reading programs to get children involved in books. Jessie wanted the children to love reading as much as she did. She'd spent many enjoyable moments with a flashlight and a book.

A smile spread across her face. Molly promised to make special treats for the kids to eat for each story hour. The excitement was building, and she could hardly wait for the first day. All she had left to do was finish designing her fliers and get the word out. Jessie carried a stack of books to replace the ones on the table. She could almost picture the excited children filling her store.

Audrey, her employee and new friend, had given

her several great suggestions including a treasure chest that the children could pick a special gift from for every ten books they read. Ten books seemed like an easy enough number to reach over a three-month period to get a least one prize. Some kids would do more. Great prizes would be an excellent incentive to get them reading. Her hope was the stories would keep them coming back, or at least the parents who could use an hour coffee break would bring them.

"I'll close these doors for you." Molly's cheerful voice startled her.

"Thanks, I didn't realize it was so late." Jessie looked at the clock. Matt would be there in ten minutes. "My mind is deep in plans for my summer reading program, and I haven't even locked the front door yet." She walked over to the door, locked it, and turned the Open sign to Closed.

"I was wondering why these doors were still open. I thought maybe you were going to stay open later tonight."

"I'll stay open later during the summer hours, but not yet. I appreciate you checking on me. I'd still be daydreaming if you hadn't."

Jessie rushed through her closing routine and finished as Matt pulled in front of the store.

****

"Hi, how was your day?" Matt held the door open for her as she walked out. He closed it, checking to make sure it was locked.

"It went fast." She took her place in the front seat and fastened her seat belt. "I stayed up last night reading Elizabeth's journals. Her last entries changed dramatically from the earlier ones."

"In what way?" Matt glanced at her as he clicked his seat belt.

Jessie described a couple of the things she'd read. "Someone promised her a lot, and she fell for their spiel."

"I can't imagine who she'd been talking about." Matt pulled out onto Main Street. "Why would she believe that junk?"

"Easy. Our culture places a high price on beauty and youth. Girls feel the pressure early in life to have the perfect face and body. I know I did and often still do. To be told you're pretty enough to be a model plays right into a young girl's vulnerability. One of my first articles for Neil was about girls who were trapped in porn movies and magazines on the promise of a modeling career. These were all underage girls. Believe me, a lot of men will take advantage of pretty young girls with the promise of making them the next top model."

"Damn, I never thought of that angle. I've got Dylan and Kip looking into police reports to see if there are any other cases similar to this one. Maybe we should ask your friend Jeremy to work his magic on the computer and research this, too."

"It wouldn't hurt. Did you call Frank?"

"Sure did. Your friend will be in town for a couple of days." The sound of the signal beeped before Matt changed lanes and headed toward the highway.

"Don't forget to ask for a scent article," she reminded him.

"Frank told me a scent article wouldn't be necessary," Matt informed her. "He has a different technique he uses to work his dog when it comes to a cold case involving murder."

"I'll have to ask him to explain it to me. He's been involved in several cold case searches, lately. They've had some successes but not all were by any means. Still, if it's possible, I'm sure Radar can pull it off." She leaned closer to him and placed her hand on his arm.

He glanced at her with a smile. "The Walters have moved. It took me a while to find their new address and phone number. They're still in the area, but no longer live in Blue Cove."

"What did you find out about Grace?" she asked.

"The file had a few holes in it. It seemed from the beginning it was viewed as a missing person case and then a runaway." He scowled. "No one, not one single person, tried to connect Grace's disappearance with Elizabeth. We're talking basic investigation here." His voice grew angrier as he recalled the details. "When two girls go missing at the same time, and one is found dead, you always look for connections. After the letter to her parents had been entered into her file, the investigation was over."

Jessie let him rant for a moment until he finished.

When Matt turned onto the highway, his frown was even more pronounced.

"It's sad when you think about it." Her words came out thick and heavy with emotion. She fiddled with her purse strap and blinked a few times. The pesky tears were gathering in her eyes.

"I know." He handed her the tissue box. You wouldn't sleep at night if you knew how many people vanish in our country, much less globally, and no one ever sees them again." Matt glanced in the rearview mirror with a grim expression on his face. "As we learned from Abigail's story, some are taken and sold into slavery, and others are murdered. Some get lost to change their identities and start a new life. Children are often abducted by another parent, and some kids leave home and live on the streets. The numbers can be staggering, and there's never enough manpower to investigate each case the way they should be. Look how long this case has waited to be solved. To friends and family, ten years can feel like a lifetime. No one should ever have to wait that long."

"Especially, if you're the family waiting to hear about your child or, in Charlotte and Byron's case, who murdered your child and why." Jessie turned to look at him, the tears finally running unrestrained down her cheeks. "I feel sad and angry at the same time." She dabbed at her eyes with the tissue.

"Me, I get angry. It comes with the job, but I'm human, and I can't bury the emotions deep enough to forget them." He patted her hand, and she squeezed his arm. "I would never sleep nights if I didn't have my therapist to talk to."

"What did Grace's letter say?" Jessie changed the subject.

"The damn thing sounded a lot like what you told me you read in Lizzy's journal, but I don't think the letters were written by either of the girls. That's my opinion. Her file is in my case on the backseat. You're free to read the letter for yourself. Tell me what you think." Matt pulled over on the shoulder and reached in the back for the file and handed it to her.

Jessie read the letter. "I can't believe no one connected this before. This is almost word for word like Lizzy's letter. The handwriting is similar too, I'm sure of it. Did the police file mention anything about Lizzy's journals?" Jessie tugged on the seatbelt that rubbed against her neck.

"They were never mentioned in the evidence. I'd say probably not, and I wonder why." He maneuvered back onto the road. His jaw looked like granite.

"Maybe Charlotte never told the police Lizzy kept a journal. I don't think she knew where they were hidden until recently. Charlotte told me she found them in the attic last week when she was moving stuff around. Lizzy always hid her journals so her brothers wouldn't read them." The memories prompted images that made her smile. "I know from personal experience growing up with Katie that brothers can be pests. Liam was always searching for her diary. He loved to torment her with what he read."

"It seems to be the way of boys. Tormenting girls is in our genes until we grow up." He stroked his chin. "I guess we still torment and chase after them, but in a different way." Matt grinned at her. "If you get my drift." He waggled his brows at her.

"I get it," she chuckled, leaning her head back against the seat. "You have a good way of changing the subject at just the right moment."

"It comes from growing up with brothers. We joked around all the time, unless of course, we were fighting." He smiled at the memory. "My parents were saints."

"I guess most parents are." She chuckled. "All though it takes a while to recognize the fact. Did I mention that Charlotte told me she hasn't read any of the journals yet, but wanted to someday?"

"Why, I wonder." Matt glanced in the rearview

mirror. "Any ideas, or feedback."

"With the anniversary coming up, her emotions are raw and the memories are too painful right now. My takeaway from all of this is the police probably didn't know about the journals, and her family had forgotten about them until Charlotte stumbled across them. With hindsight it's easy to second-guess their investigation, but who knows what evidence they sifted through during their investigation." Jessie glanced at him. "What's amazing is we went to the McKenzies' in the nick of time. Charlotte is having Lizzy's room packed up and removed next week."

"From what I've read in the files so far. They skipped a lot of clues staring them in the face." He paused looking off into the distance "All I know is the answers are out there. You heard Lizzy's ghost, and now you have her journals. It's our moment to solve this one. I hope we can provide the McKenzies with a few answers and closure. We need to bring Grace back home to her family." Matt pulled into the right lane and turned.

"Where are we headed?" she asked.

"The small town of Hanover. The Walters have been living there for about five years now." He slowed down as he drove through the quaint little town.

"What a pretty place to live." Jessie noticed the freshly painted store fronts as they drove down Main Street. "Look at that awesome ice cream parlor." She pointed at the cotton-candy pink building. "You'll have to take me there someday. This is a great little town." Her enthusiasm made him smile.

"It's a popular stop for the fall tours because of all the color." He pointed to the enormous trees that lined both sides of the street and nearly touched the trees in the grassy median. The effect formed a canopy all the way down Hanover's town center.

"I bet." Jessie closed her eyes, picturing how beautiful the street would be.

"You're not moving." He chuckled. "I wouldn't want to drive here every day."

"Nope, no ocean view. Blue Cove is picturesque, too, but it also has the cove." She reached over and squeezed his arm, marveling at the feel of his bulging biceps. "I'm not going anywhere."

Matt turned left onto a side street. Half way down the block, he stopped in front of a lovely Cape Cod style home. The white trim and picket fence were freshly painted, as was the gray siding on the home. The black shutters added to its charm and the bright red door was the final touch. The house had a beautiful curb appeal. "Nice house, not my style, but nice."

"You have to admit that this house fits perfectly in this town and on this street. Is this their home?"

"Yes, this is the address they gave me." Matt got out of the car and opened the door for her. "I wonder what we'll find out and how it'll change the investigation."

"I think we're in for a few surprises."

****

Jessie was silent when they walked out the door a while later. She had spent an hour alone with Mrs. Walters, who had needed to talk. The picture that emerged about Grace broke Jessie's heart. Gracie, as her family lovingly called her, was one terrific kid. She had never given them any trouble, and they still hadn't wrapped their minds around her being a runaway. A tenderhearted soul who wrote beautiful poetry, played the piano, and loved her family did not seem a likely candidate to leave home because she was angry.

Matt closed the car door. "What's your take on Grace?"

"She doesn't fit the profile of a runaway, that's for sure. A gifted student, musician, and aspiring poet." Jessie reached for the seatbelt.

"I hear you. Grace's father still thinks she will walk through the door any day now. It's been ten years."

"I have two things troubling me. I think Grace was lured into something. She had no idea what she was getting into. She trusted the person. The handwriting on this letter isn't similar to samples of her other writing. I have a copy of a poem she wrote, so you can have it checked by an expert. The letter is word for word like the one Lizzy left her mom. Did either of the girls write it or did someone else write it?" She scrunched her face in thought.

"What's the second thing?" He twisted the key and started the car.

"Her mother mentioned that several months after Gracie's disappearance, they received a large amount of cash. They had no idea who it was from. It simply said 'We are sorry for the loss of your daughter.' No name, no return address, and it was left inside their screen door. Mrs. Walter's mentioned it was more money than they had ever seen. The money paid for a trip with the whole family, a substantial down payment on their new home, and some they tucked away for a rainy day." Jessie frowned and toyed with her purse strap. "It makes you wonder if someone was feeling guilty enough to give money because he or she knew what happened to Grace. At that point, Gracie was considered a runaway, not an abductee and not dead."

"I wonder if the police knew anything about it?" Matt glanced at her.

"I doubt it. The case had already been closed as a missing person. I imagine they kept the money to themselves. Mrs. Walters said she felt it was a gift. Someone who cared about what they were going through and wished to remain anonymous. She even thought it could be a church member. Reba told me the family was active in the community and did a lot for others."

"Sounds more like a bribe to me. It's too damn bad the police weren't notified, though. It might have changed the nature of the case back then." He raked his free hand through his hair. "It gives us another angle to consider." Matt drove through the center of town and back to the highway before he added. "Frank will be here in a couple of days, and we should know more soon. In the meantime, I want to have the writing samples checked for both Grace and Lizzy's letters."

"Sounds like a plan. I have enough material on both girls to write my first article. I hope some of their friends will come forward and want to talk."

"The waiting begins." He glanced over at her, and then back at the road.

"I hope we don't have to wait too long. All I know is Grace loved life. Her optimism filled her writing, her music, and art. She was a sweet, generous young woman and someone robbed her of life. We have to find her and the person who murdered her."

Chapter 7

Jessie had two restless nights filled with bizarre dreams. Senseless dreams, strange, and nonsensical. She had no idea what they meant. Matt had been busy in court, and she was writing her first article, but it lacked something. Talking at night with Matt helped, but she missed seeing him. Inspiration is what she needed. There was plenty of material, but she had to make the girls' lives mean something in her words, and right now the whole article seemed flat.

She answered her ringing phone. "Hi, sweetheart, checking to see if you want to go to dinner tonight. I should be there at five-thirty. The jury has the case now."

"Of course, I'll be ready. Are we still on for the track tomorrow?"

"Yes, do you want to go?" he asked. She could hear the laughter in his voice.

"I wouldn't miss it. If I remember I was the one who suggested it." She heard him chuckle. "It was my idea, and I invited you to come along." She emphasized the I, holding the word out.

"You make it too easy, Jess. See you later."

"Sounds good." She hung up as Audrey came in the store.

"I'm glad you're here already. I can always count

on you if I need you to work an extra shift. Thank you." Jessie eyed her store critically. It looked good. "I told Pastor Kevin I'd be a little late," she said, putting on her jacket. "I have something I need to do this morning." She grabbed her purse, stuffing her phone in it.

"I'll be early tomorrow too. Reba will answer the phone at the church until I get there." Audrey took off her sweater, hanging it up in the back room.

"I appreciate you both more than you'll ever know. I need to be a part of the track tomorrow. I can't explain why right now, but it's important to a story I'm working on." Jessie opened the back door, waving as she left for the small memorial. She needed answers and maybe she could find some there.

She drove to the school and parked in the upper lot near the top of the path. Walking a short distance, she made her way to the bench at the entrance to the woods, the place where she had first seen Lizzy's ghost. Elizabeth wasn't there. Had she expected the ghost to be waiting for her? Seeing no sign of Lizzy disappointed her. Lizzy's ghost was the one who knew what had happened that day, and clarity would be nice at this point. Peace from the crazy dreams. Whenever she thought about Lizzy, a dark, gloomy feeling descended over her like a thick cloud. Elizabeth had tumbled into a terrible trap from which she couldn't free herself, and the same trap may have ensnared others.

Jessie was positive Grace was buried in the woods. Did Lizzy have something to do with her death?

She hoped not. The trees moved with the breeze, sending strands of hair fluttering around her face. For all the sorrow that transpired in this place, it was still peaceful.

"Grace, we are searching for you. We want to bring you home to your family," Jessie whispered beneath her breath, her words muffled by the wind.

The longer she sat there, the stronger the sense became someone was watching her. Not a ghost, but a living, breathing person, and it agitated her. A group of students talked nearby, and she casually walked toward the path where they stood. She stayed close behind them, taking a quick peek back to where she had been. It hadn't been her imagination. She rubbed her arms against the chill. Someone was observing her.

****

He watched her from his favorite perch high in the tree. It was his favorite spot ever since he could remember. The tree didn't matter. All he cared about was being up high. The higher the better. People paid him no never mind. Thought he was dumb. This was his secret spot. He could see everything from here, and he had seen plenty. He knew these woods like the back of his hand. Even in the dark, he could find his way.

"Never seen her before," he muttered to himself. "Shut up, Billy, don't you be talking to yourself like some old fool" He lifted his pa's fancy glasses to get a better look.

He stared at the girl sitting on the bench, her golden hair swaying in the breeze. He adjusted his looking glasses.

"She wouldn't listen to him, either." He clamped his hand over his mouth.

The only person who had ever talked to him was in the woods where he'd buried her after he found her.

She belonged to him, and no one else knew where she was now. He swatted at the tears running unhindered down his cheeks. The back of his dirty hand wiped his running nose. He sniffed. "Old Billy wouldn't leave you out there all alone."

Her hair had been the same color as the wheat growing in his papa's field. Every day, he'd waited for her to pass by on her way to school, and she always waved. Her smile made his heart beat faster.

A tear rolled down his grubby cheek. She hadn't thought he was dumb. He shoved his stringy brown hair out of his eyes, rubbing his wet hands on his dirty jeans.

That day, he had tried to tell the men what happened.

"Get on home to your papa, Billy. This here is a crime scene."

He whispered their words over again, hitting his hand against the tree trunk. "Billy knew, he knew." He shimmied down the tree to get a better look at the girl as she walked away.

"Be careful, Billy, don't get caught." He ducked behind a tree when she turned around. Maybe she was a nice one too. She sure enough looked nice.

****

"Good morning, Jessie." Pastor John greeted her at the door before she walked in the church office.

"Do you have a moment to talk?" Jessie placed her purse on her desk.

"I do." He sat in the chair in front of the desk.

"Were you pastoring here when Elizabeth McKenzie was murdered and Grace Walters went missing?" She pulled out a piece of paper and a pen.

"I was and knew both families from the

community. The Walters were a charitable family, and Grace was as sweet as they come. Besides being a great student she was gifted. I always thought of her as a gentle soul. I can still hear the way she played 'Moonlight Sonata' in the community talent show. It was hauntingly beautiful and moving." John closed his eyes for a moment. "When she ran away, it was if the light went out in the family." Pastor John shook his head. "A sad state of affairs."

"What if I told you I don't think she ran away, but her disappearance is linked with Elizabeth's in some way?"

"Grace didn't move in the same circles as the McKenzie girl, but anything is possible, I guess. It never made sense to me that she would run away. She loved her family too much."

"Exactly. What about Elizabeth? Did you know her?"

"I did. Her family used to attend church here. Lizzy, as they liked to call her was a sweet girl, but something was going on with her in the weeks before she was murdered. Her death was an awful shock to this town." John frowned. "Hard memories. What brought this up?"

Jessie explained how she came upon Elizabeth's memorial by the school. "It will be the tenth anniversary of her death, and I think it's past time for her murder to be solved."

"What makes you think Grace's disappearance is linked to Elizabeth's murder?" John asked.

"It's a hunch, is all." Jessie moved to the edge of her chair.

"Your hunches," John said, smiling at her.

"They're almost always one hundred percent accurate." He reached across the desk and patted her hand. "It's okay to be who you are. You're a blooming miracle if you ask me."

"Thank you. You don't know the half of it. During our last case, I saw something different." Jessie closed her eyes remembering the images in her mind. Three ghosts and angels interacting with them was over the top even for her. Everyone involved in the case knew things had happened to save Matt that were beyond normal.

"Different in what way? Most of what you've seen is highly unusual."

"I saw a being of light, an angel, on more than one occasion. It happened at Ryan's memorial service. He was the murdered college student whose body was found on the beach." Jessie described what happened at the service and again in the woods.

"Was this the first angel you've seen?" the Pastor asked.

"Yes, and I'm still a little in awe of seeing what I see, to be truthful."

"I can imagine. As Melinda, the church lady who knows it all, has told me more than once, you live a charmed life, young lady. I'm glad you still work a few hours a week for us so I can catch up on what's happening in your life."

Their conversation took a whole new turn to upcoming events at the church and before she knew it her shift at the church was over and she could leave for the day.

"Jessie, if you find out more about Grace, please let me know. I've often thought of her over the years."

"I will." Jessie slipped on her jacket. "Thanks for talking to me. It helped a lot. Sometimes I wonder why me?"

"What's to wonder? Everything you have seen or heard has been for a good reason. It's not for profit, or even for ego, but only to help others. Relax. The gift will be with you for as long as the circumstances call for it."

Jessie would always be grateful to First Community Church. She closed the doors as she left. It was her first job when she moved to town and where she met Reba and the place where she saw her first ghost.

Walking back to her store, her arms swinging at her sides, a smile lit her face. She took a deep breath, a measure of contentment soared in her heart. Pastor John didn't think she was crazy. He had called her a miracle.

Chapter 8

The morning air was crisp and brisk. In a few weeks, she would long to feel this cool breeze again. Jessie zipped her sweatshirt and shoved her hands in her pockets to warm them, jogging in place for a few minutes before she stretched. Strange thoughts raced through her mind, bringing up scenes from her dreams. None of them made any sense. Maybe they were symbolic. Who knew? Lizzy had come here the day of her murder to meet someone, but who? Matt? Annoyed with where her thoughts were taking her, making sure she had her keys in her pocket, she started to run. Her feet pounded the ground in a steady rhythm. The trek would take her from the school parking lot to the small memorial across from the entrance to the woods. A good five miles there and another five back is what Bob Harmon had told her. Up the first small incline and around the curve, she ran. Her body warming with each quarter mile.

First, to arrive, she saw there were fresh flowers again. Someone tended the site regularly. She made a mental note to mention it to Charlotte to see if it was a family member. If not one of them, then maybe a person feeling the guilt of their crime kept their eye on the area. Was it possible they were watching her now? Not a pleasant thought while waiting alone. She sat on the bench to wait for the others. The tree branches swayed in the cool morning breeze. The murder had happened in this place, or at least the body was found not too far from here. Yet the location remained beautiful and peaceful. How could that be? Grace was hidden somewhere in these woods, she was sure of it. Someone had killed her, but another had buried her there with love. At this moment, she had no evidence of her theory. Maybe they would find some proof today. Call it premonition or a feeling. She'd bet on it.

Who was it? He might have seen it all, or maybe he had accidentally killed her.

The first indication she wasn't alone was a wet tongue licking her hands. "Hey, big fella." She patted Radar's head and ran her hand down his smooth coat. "Hi, Frank." She looked from his sturdy walking boots up to the broad smile on his aging face. She smiled back at him. It was always good to see her kind-hearted friend.

"Where were you? You were so lost in your thoughts, you didn't even hear us approach." He sat on the bench beside her. "We weren't quiet, either." He glanced around. "This is a beautiful spot. It's hard to believe anything awful happened here, much less a murder."

"I was thinking the same thing. Look." Jessie pointed to a majestic hawk soaring overhead. His sharp extended cry continued as he flew in a circle above their heads.

"A red-tailed hawk," Frank said. "You can tell by his dark brown mantle and red colored tail." He shielded his eyes from the sun as he watched the soaring bird. "We are going to have a successful track today."

She tilted her head, shielded her eyes, and continued to watch the hawk soaring high above them. "No doubt about it. Radar is always successful."

"He does well when he's on, but not all tracks are successful. Today will go well. I know because of the hawk."

Puzzled, she asked, "What do you mean?"

"Do you want to hear an interesting story while we wait for the others?" Frank patted Radar's head as he plopped down beside him.

"Of, course, I'd love to." She turned to see him better.

"A few weeks back, I traveled to Montana to be a judge for K-9 nose work. It was a long drive. By the time I arrived in town, I wasn't feeling well. I was hungry and basically wanted to go to my hotel and sleep. The Little Big Horn site was nearby, and I wanted to see it." He stared off into the distance.

"Oh, I've always wanted to go there," Jessie said, paused, then continued, "I've read it's a haunted area. I guess most battlefields are. People don't get a chance to say their goodbyes. Gettysburg is said to be one of the most haunted places in our country."

"I've read some of the stories about the Last Stand Monument area, and I wanted to see it, too." Frank glanced at the hawk, now sitting on a branch. "Knowing I might not make it to Montana again, I decided to go and see the monument before the park closed. If I had stopped to eat or done anything differently, I would have missed it."

"Missed what?" Jessie asked.

"Here's where it gets interesting. Standing near the

Last Stand Monument an older Native American man approached me. 'I like your hat,' he said. I thanked him. I was wearing this one with the dog prints on it."

"I think you always wear the same hat."

"You're right, I do. Anyway, he shook my hand and told me he had a message for me. 'You've seen many bad things and so has your dog. The cries of all the lost and hurting people keep you awake at night. Your dog hears them, too.' I was dumbfounded. How did he know? All I could do is nod my head."

"What happened next?" Jessie was fascinated by Frank's story.

"A hawk appeared over our heads as we talked. The man told me to look up. He said I was being given a spirit guide to protect my dog and me while we were tracking. Whenever I saw the hawk, we would have success and be protected. He told me there were still many people for us to find and bring home to their families." The hawk circled and squawked as he soared above them as if on cue. "I've seen a hawk on several of my tracks since his words to me. I had never seen one before he told me."

"Wow, that gave me goosebumps." Jessie folded her arms around her middle. "If you had stopped or not gone, you would have missed his message."

"I know. I've always been a skeptic of this kind of stuff until you came along."

"You and me both." She pursed her lips.

"Still, this is me and not you we're talking about. It's hard for me to wrap my head around it. Yet, I have to say it's comforting to see the hawk before I begin a track." Frank petted Radar's head as he stirred.

"I can imagine."

"The idea of protection appeals to me. Radar and I have been in some sticky situations with some bad dudes waiting on the other end. Haven't we, fella?" The dog leaned into his hand.

"I'd say you were supposed to meet the man. It's another one of those mysteries we don't understand. The world is filled with mystics and truly spiritual people who see and hear what we don't. Just because someone doesn't understand things the exact same way we do doesn't mean they're wrong." She looked up at the hawk circling above them. "I will take comfort in this beautiful bird's presence and never look at one the same way again."

Radar stood when he heard the voices of the group approach. The hawk flew into the woods and out of sight. Jessie was more optimistic than ever that they would find Grace today and take her home to her family. She briefly closed her eyes and smiled, thankful that she wasn't the only unconventional person on the planet.

****

Matt stood beside Jessie. "I saw your car in the school parking lot. I suppose you ran here." He saw her nod. "How long has Frank been here? I hope you didn't have to wait too long."

"Not at all." Her hand brushed his. "We had an interesting talk and a visit from a beautiful red-tailed hawk. Someday you'll have to ask Frank to tell you his story about the hawk. It was fascinating."

"Are you ready for this?" Matt's arm rubbed against hers, nudging her.

"Yes, I think we're going to find Grace. She is hidden somewhere in there." Jessie pointed to the woods. "By someone who thought they were taking care of her."

"What makes you think that?" he asked.

"Call it a gut feeling, but I could see and sense it inside of me. You know what I mean."

"Is it the same person who murdered her?"

"I don't think so, but it could be. We can't rule it out." She stepped back as more of the team got on site.

"Let's get started." Matt walked over to Frank.

Frank put a second collar on Radar. This one had a skull and crossbones on it. "He's trained to know with the second collar and leash, we're not looking for a living person." Frank pulled out a small bag. "I use the HRD for scent."

"HRD?" Jessie looked at him.

"Human remains detection or decomp to me. I use a small amount of human decomposition as a scent. It can be as small as a drop of blood or even a tooth. Along with a new command, and he knows he's in search of a body."

"Wow, it amazes me that he can track off something so small." She patted the dog's head.

"I work with him on a daily basis. I know what my dog is capable of, and he still amazes me." Frank bent down holding the decomp at Radar's nose. "Find the grim reaper. Let's get to work."

As soon as they entered the woods, the hawk circled overhead. "Would you look at that, Frank?" She pointed to the sky.

Frank's face lit with a smile. "I'm happy to see him."

"Me too." Jessie watched the majestic bird circle the air above them.

Radar began tracking, pulling Frank with force. They walked for about a mile when an old cabin came into view. He circled the old building, pawing the ground. After circling several times, he sat down. "It's hard to know, but I wonder if she was in this place at some point."

"She probably was. The kids in the area all know about this place." Matt walked beside them.

His words made her uncomfortable. She shook her head, frustrated with where her thoughts were going. This was Matt. She knew him. He was not involved. "Should we go inside?"

"Not yet, let's see if he takes us anywhere else, first." After Frank's command, Radar took off into the wooded area, circled back around, and ended up sitting outside the door of the cabin again.

"What should we do?" Matt asked.

"Now, we go inside. She must be here, or something dead is." Frank stood aside allowing Matt and his team to go in first.

At first glance, the place was clean; or at least as clean as an old cabin in the woods could be. The bed had a handmade quilt on it and was tidy. Fresh flowers, like the ones Jessie had seen earlier at Lizzy's small memorial, were in a vase on the table. Was it possible the person placing the flowers knew about this place also? *Who?*

"Does someone live here?" she asked. That's when she noticed the light shining around the room. No one else reacted to the magnificent creature, standing by Grace. The angel was shielding her under its wings.

"Not that I know of. It was abandoned when the kids stumbled onto years ago. It sure has the appearance of being cared for though, doesn't it?" He glanced around the cabin. "Someone had a fire recently." He bent down and stirred the ashes with a stick until he noticed a strange look on Jessie's face. Radar rushed past him, pawed at the floorboards in the small space, and whined into the corner.

"Are you trying to tell me something, fella?" Frank bent down. "I think you need to look under these boards. There has to be decomp he's smelling."

Dylan pried up one of the boards. "Well, I'll be. There's a body buried here, Chief. Damn, I was hoping we wouldn't find anyone."

"I knew we'd find her. It's Grace." It has to be. She pushed her hair behind her ears and moved out of the team's way.

"We don't know that for sure, Jessie," Kip said.

"I know. I'm sure." She walked outside and leaned against the huge pine tree. The cool breeze rushed over her face, cooling and calming her. She would never get used to what was happening to her. At peace with it, yes. Used to it, never.

Matt approached her. "Jess, what did you see?" He placed his hand on her shoulder. "I know you well enough to know something was going on in there."

She explained what she had seen. "I know it's Grace. There isn't a single doubt in my mind." She hesitated to tell him about the angel. Ghosts were enough. "I saw her standing there watching Dylan pull up the floorboards."

"I guess we'll be expecting a confirmation from Lewis then." He raked his hands through his hair. He started to leave but turned to look at her with a perplexed expression on his face. "You're not telling me everything. Why?"

"I guess I'm not sure how to tell you. Since the last case, my world has kicked it up a notch."

"What do you mean?"

"I don't only see spirits, but I see other manifestations."

"What is stranger than seeing a dead person walking around?" His brows raised.

"Try a being of light or an angel..." Her voice trailed off. "Interacting with a dead person."

"Okay, you finally managed to surprise me. I don't know what to say."

"Imagine being me for a day." She wrapped her arms around her middle.

"Not on your life, sweetheart." Matt walked into the cabin.

Great, she shouldn't have told him. She had given him enough to think about without adding anything else to the equation.

"Jessie, my girl, you should buy a cat. I think you're destined to live a strange and lonely life," she whispered to herself and swiped at the tears forming in her eyes.

She pushed away from the tree and walked with no destination in mind. What she needed was to clear her head. Walking in a circle, she kept the cabin and a few landmarks in sight.

No, feeling sorry for yourself. You have been privileged to see what you've seen. Any man would be lucky to have you. She stopped and grinned. "Especially, Matt. He'll come around," she spoke the words aloud.

The sudden squawk of the hawk soaring overhead,

the snap of a branch, and the rustling movement in the tree in front of her heightened her senses. Jessie glanced up at the tall tree. An odd-looking man, sitting high up on one of the branches, stared down at her.

She smiled and waved. At first, he glared back at her, but then he waved timidly. He wasn't dangerous, but she had wandered too far. As she turned to head back to the cabin, she sensed someone else watching her, too. She picked up her tempo. Even without seeing the second person, she knew he wasn't harmless. She ran.

Chapter 9

"Where have you been?" Matt asked as he walked to where she was bent over with her hands on her side. "Are you all right?"

"Yes. I needed to be alone to think." Her words sounded breathy after her fast sprint.

"From your breathing, it sounds like more a run than a walk. I wished you would have told me you were leaving. I was worried about you." Matt grabbed hold of her hand. "We are about to wrap things up here. When I came out and saw you were gone, I thought maybe I'd upset you."

"No, you didn't. I'm still unsure of why I see what I do. I thought maybe I had managed to run you off with all my talk of spirits and angels." She shifted from foot to foot. "Please keep the angel to yourself. I haven't told anyone, but Reba and Pastor John about seeing them."

"I'm sure it's stressful for you." His thumb stroked the palm of her hand. "You aren't going to get rid of me that easy. I'm made of sterner stuff. Though I'm never sure what's going to happen with you next, it's rather exciting in a strange way. As long as it doesn't happen to me," he spoke quietly leaning close to her. "Then I might hide and cry like a baby. You're the strongest woman I know."

"The fact you can say that with all the tears I've shed in front of you makes me wonder about your judgment." The smile formed slowly on her lips as she gauged his reponse. "We might need to talk about these oddities in my life seriously. They don't seem to be going away. Actually, they seem to be intensifying. Would you want to wake up next to me one morning to find a ghost perched on the edge of the bed or have an angel bar you from entering the room?"

"Damn, sweetheart, I'd love to wake up next to you under any circumstances."

She nudged him playfully. "I'm serious. It could happen to you, and you might not like it. I'm getting stranger by the day."

"Jess, have you ever met anyone who was perfect? We all have some odd quirks. I guess that's what makes us who we are and separates us from the crowd." He grinned at her. "Take me, for example. I'm in love with a woman who sees and hears what others don't. The whole package entices me."

"You're incorrigible." She pulled her hand away from him. "Promise to think about what I've told you, at least."

"I'll think about it, but it won't change anything for me."

"Before I forget to tell you. There was a strange looking man with binoculars up in the tree. I waved at him, and eventually, he waved back at me."

He studied her face. "That's why you were running. Angels and ghosts don't scare you, but a strange man sends you fleeing back into my arms."

"Excuse me, I'm not in your arms."

"I was speaking symbolically." He put his arm

around her and leaned close to her face. "Where did you see him?"

"I saw him on one of my circles around the area. I'm not sure I could find him now if I tried."

"Friend or foe?" Matt asked, pushing a curl out of her eye.

"I'm not sure. It was the man I couldn't see that spooked me. He's the reason I might have run all the way back here. I was stunned to see the man in the tree, but I wasn't afraid of him exactly, even though he seemed a tad unfriendly at first."

"Was he kind of a straggly looking fella?"

"Yes. Do you know who I'm talking about?"

"I know him, and I've heard of him. People rarely see him. These woods have been his playground since he was a kid. Billy is slow, but he hasn't harmed anyone that I know of. He's scared a few folks who wandered into his woods. As for the man you couldn't see, I have no idea what to say about him, but stay close and don't wander off." He pulled her to his side.

"Hmmm." Jessie lifted her hair off her neck and let it fall down over her shoulders.

"What?" He turned her face toward him.

"It gives me something to think about. I wonder if the man in the tree knew Grace or saw something."

"He could've been here, only he would've been much younger then. As we all were. Let me know when you have a theory."

"I will. Let's say he fits in the story somehow, and let's include the unseen observer. I'm not sure of how, yet."

"I was about to send Radar out to find you," Frank told her as he came out of the cabin. "You were gone for over an hour, which isn't like you."

"She was thinking, and if I know my girl, she forgot all about how long she was gone."

"She did," Jessie chuckled.

****

From his vantage point high in the tree, Billy could watch the other man. "Billy doesn't like you." He frowned, looking through the glasses his pa had given him. "These are Billy's woods." He rubbed his hand on his pants. Agitation swirled through him, squeezing his chest, making him gasp for air. "Billy won't let you hurt this one. She waved at me. She's nice."

He scampered down the tree and followed her from a distance. Picking up several rocks off the ground, Billy hid in the bushes. He took the sling from his pocket and placed one stone in it. Pulling it back, he let it rip. End over end it sailed through the air toward the man hiding behind the tree. It missed him by mere inches, taking the bark off the tree near his face. The man jumped.

"Billy just about got ya." He grinned and loaded the sling again. The second rock came closer, still just missing the man's arm, leaning against the trunk. The third stone was on the mark, hitting the man hard on the shoulder before he had finished looking to see who his attacker was. The man took off running, rubbing his shoulder.

Billy shoved his slingshot in his back pocket and climbed up the tree to keep an eye on the people in the cabin. "Ah, Billy likes a dog." He liked the nice lady too. He didn't leave the tree to go home until the people left the cabin, his woods, and took his special friend with them.

****

"Jess, do you want a lift back to your car?" Matt asked her as the approached the parking area in the upper lot.

"Sure, I don't feel like running now, and I'd rather not walk all the way back by myself."

"Hop in." Matt opened the back door for her.

Frank put Radar in his crate and got in the front to drive. "What's next on the agenda?"

"Right now, I'd say something to eat." Matt latched his seat belt.

"Sounds good to me." Frank pulled out of the space.

"We can take Radar to the house so he can move around. How about if we meet up at Mindy's about five-thirty? Will that work for you?"

"That works. I'll close up the store and meet you at Mindy's."

Chapter 10

Reba rushed in the door the first thing Monday morning. She pulled Jessie aside. "I'll get some tea and scones. We need to talk."

"Okay." Jessie shook her head. Reba wasn't herself this morning. Her usually neat hair was half up, and well she wasn't quite sure how to describe the hairdo actually. Without makeup, her face was pale and tired looking. *Maybe she was sick. No, she can't be.* Her mind raced off from there. Jessie needed Reba. She was the one person who understood what was happening to her.

"Sorry for my appearance. I knew I needed to get here early this morning. I'll be right back. Molly will be over in a minute."

Jessie stared at her as she walked in the back room. When Reba came out a few minutes later, everything was as it should be. Her hair was neat, her lipstick on, and a tinge of color had magically appeared on her cheeks with the help of blush. What woman didn't need its magic from once in a while?

"Let's sit, shall we, dear?" Reba sat in one of the winged back chairs. Crossing her legs at the ankle, she straightened her dress.

"Are you okay?" Jessie studied Reba's face.

"Perfectly, and soon to be even better. Here comes

our tea." Reba patted the small table. "You can place it right here and thank you, Molly dear." She handed Molly a large tip for the jar. "Tea makes everything better, I always say."

"You're welcome. You look different now. Not so, ah…frazzled." Molly smiled at her

"I admit, I did look a bit off earlier. But as you can see, everything is in place now."

"I noticed," Molly said. "Enjoy your tea, ladies."

"We will, dear." Reba looked around the store. Her voice quiet. "I have so much to say to you, and I have no idea where to begin. It's not like me to be this unsure of what I should say." Reba pursed her lips and frowned.

"Start wherever you want. I'll listen." The foot under her chair began to shake from side to side. What could possibly make Reba this nervous? Jessie wasn't sure she wanted to know.

"Jessie girl, I love you as if you were my own daughter. You're a generous, warm-hearted girl with lots of love to give to everyone."

"Thank you. I think I hear a but in there somewhere."

"Maybe one or two." Reba patted her hair. "Matt had nothing to do with Lizzy's death. Don't let your mind go there. He is a free man, and he loves you with all your idiosyncrasies, but I'm afraid…" Reba's voice trailed off.

"Afraid of what?"

"Well you see, you need to deal with your own issues."

"I don't know what you mean."

"Of course you don't. I come in here and throw

stuff at you and have little other information to give you." Reba gave her a puzzled look. "All I can give you is what I get."

"I understand."

"Jessie," Reba grabbed her hand. "You nearly lost Matt in the mill explosion a few months ago. We all did. I know you are warming up to him. You love him, yet something keeps you from moving forward with the relationship. Are you afraid to be hurt? Why? Nothing is safe."

"I've only known him about a year, I'm a cautious person, and I've had a lot of crazy stuff to deal with since moving here. I think I'm handling things pretty well." She moved to the edge of her seat.

"You are, dear. Blue Cove has been a dramatic change for you. Yet, I know what I sense. You need to find out the real reason you're dragging your feet. You might find yourself being challenged to face it."

"In what way? Why? Haven't I been challenged enough? I've faced bullets, ghosts, and a serial killer to name a few. Isn't that enough?"

"I don't know. But I am sure you will discover the real reason. Jessie girl, you weren't made for a tepid romance or a safe harbor. You were meant to challenge life passionately, stand your ground, and love with all your heart. You're about to face yourself and grow into the woman you're meant to be." Reba took a sip of her tea and bite of scone. "Our lives are a tapestry of all the events that shape us. Yours needs a little work, dear. I hope I haven't made you mad or destroyed our friendship."

"Of course, not. I have no idea what you mean, but I'm sure I'll find out soon enough, like everything else you've ever said to me."

"This gift we've been given is strange. You only see what you can see. To add anything else would be making it up. Still, I know you'll do fine, dear. I'll be the one cheering you on." Reba patted her hand. "Now, with that off my chest, how's your handsome fella doing? Is he handling this whole Lizzy thing well?"

They chatted until a customer came in and then Jessie got to work.

****

"Matt, Lewis is on the phone," Kenny told him when he answered.

"Thanks, I'll take it." He pushed line two. "What do you have for me, Dave?"

"I have the ID of your victim. It's Grace Walters. From the condition of her skeleton, it's safe to say she was beaten with a blunt instrument. The weapon of choice made a distinct pattern on her body where it broke the bones and the base of her skull. I wonder why no one thought to look at the idea of a possible homicide with regards to her."

"Good question. Compare your report with the one on the McKenzie girl and see if there are any comparisons then get back to me."

"Will do."

After Dave hung up, Matt added the new information to Grace's missing person's file. He had the unpleasant task of informing her parents. At least they wouldn't be wondering anymore if she was out there and why she wasn't coming home.

Chapter 11

"Idle Time Bookstore. May I help you?" Jessie answered the phone.

"Do you have a few minutes to talk?" Matt's deep husky voice came over the line.

"I have a few customers. What's up?" She glanced at the woman who walked in the store. Her pixie haircut framed a pretty face, enhanced by gorgeous big brown eyes.

"How about I come to the store at lunch? We can talk then."

"Sounds good. I'll see you later." She hung up the phone and approached the young woman. "Can I help you find something?" Jessie towered over the woman's petite figure.

"I'm just looking." She smiled at her. "Are you the owner?"

"Yes," Jessie answered.

"You have a nice store." She glanced around the store. "Charlotte McKenzie told me you're writing a story about Lizzy." The woman paused. "Is that true?"

"Yes, it is. Did you know Elizabeth?"

"We were best friends." She swiped at the tears starting to run down her cheeks. "My name is Kendra Jones. Simpson was my maiden name. In high school, Lizzy and I were inseparable."

"Would you consider telling me about her? I am looking for ways to bring her to life in my article." Was this the break she needed? Kendra's memories could add a special touch to the article.

"I need to talk to someone. So many years have passed, and yet, for me, it seems like yesterday. We were friends since our first day of kindergarten."

"You must have some happy memories of her. Let's sit and you can tell me about them." Jessie motioned to the chairs in the corner.

"Many happy ones and some sad ones, too." Kendra placed her purse on the small table beside the chair. "I was shy and she was outgoing. She grabbed my hand on the first day of school and told me she was going to be my friend." Her lips turned up at the corners and her eyes sparkled. "I never questioned the wisdom of her words. Lizzy never asked. She told me and that was that. She was the perfect person to be my friend. There was no way she'd let me be shy around her."

"My friend sounds exactly like her. Life was never the same after we met," Jessie recalled with a smile. "Katie never asked, either. She told me what we were going to do, and her escapades usually got us both in trouble."

"Lizzy was fun and I was level-headed. We were good for each other. Until our senior year. I'm not sure what happened." Tears filled Kendra's eyes. "She began to change. At first, I thought she was struggling with the stress of school until she told me she was going to dump Matt. Her reasons made no sense, and I couldn't believe what she was telling me. Needless to say, we fought. I saw her every day after that, but she wouldn't talk to me. Whenever I approached, Lizzy turned and walked away from me. She was murdered before we had a chance to make up." Kendra wiped her dripping nose with the tissue Jessie handed her. "We had been friends for so long. I felt guilty and even more once I found out she was dead."

"Do you have any idea what was going on in her life?"

"No, we'd always shared our deepest secrets, but she wasn't telling me anything. The thing is, Lizzy was crazy about Matt. I had no idea why she'd want to break up with him. He was a great guy. Of course, being loyal to my friend, I blamed him at first, but he was such a mess after her death. He was lost. I never believed he'd hurt her. Something strange was going on with her. I wish I'd known. Maybe I could've helped her."

"Maybe, but probably not." Jessie paused. "If she'd wanted your help, she would've told you. The fact she was keeping the secret from you, her best friend, meant she didn't want to get caught or be found out." She reached for Kendra's hand. "There's nothing you could've done to save her if she didn't want to be helped. It's hard to watch a friend's life unravel. It's hard to stand by and watch them self-destruct. I bet you took several opportunities to talk to her."

"I did, but she wouldn't listen to me."

"You tried, and that's what's important." Jessie reached over and squeezed her hand.

"I'm sure you're right, but there're days I wonder if I could've done more."

Kendra told her several stories. Each one added another dimension to Elizabeth's life. How sad that no one saw what was happening before it was too late.

She stood when Kendra did. "Before you leave, may I ask you a question?"

"Sure." Kendra turned to look directly at her.

"Did you know Grace Walters?"

"Yes, everyone knew her. She was popular and super nice. I still don't believe she ran away. It was out of character for her."

"Did Grace ever hang out with Elizabeth?"

"Lizzy liked her. Everyone did. She was one of the super smart girls and involved in the student body. She didn't hang with our crowd. At least not while Lizzy was still talking to me."

"What do you mean?"

"The last few weeks when Lizzy was ignoring me, she seemed to be real chummy with Grace, and then just like that," Kendra's voice trailed off. She snapped her fingers. "They were both gone."

"Did anyone ever wonder what happened to Grace?"

"Of course, there was talk. No one believed Grace had run away, but there was never a body found. It seemed strange that they both went missing at the same time and no one ever heard from Grace again." Kendra fidgeted with her purse, pushing the strap on her shoulder. "I need to go. I've already stayed too long." She glanced quickly around the store, her eyes lighting on something in the coffee shop. "Goodbye." Kendra raced toward the door, her face suddenly pale.

Jessie sensed a change in the atmosphere. She wanted to ask more questions, but they would have to wait for another day. "Please, stop by any time. I'd be happy for the visit. You've given me a lovely picture of your friend. If you have any old photos of the two of you together or remember anything at all, call me." Jessie followed behind her, she handed Kendra her business card. "My private number is on the back. I can be reached at either number." Giving her a hug, Kendra scurried out the door. What had changed? Jessie glanced in Joe's when she walked by the open doors but had no idea what she was looking for. Something or someone had bothered Kendra.

She got busy helping other customers and was more than ready for lunch when Matt arrived.

"How was your morning?" he asked when he walked in the door.

"I'd call it productive." She lifted her face for the kiss that was sure to come. He didn't disappoint her, and neither did the kiss.

"Sit tight, sweetheart. I'll be back with lunch." He smiled at her as he walked into the coffee shop.

"He seems nice," a customer said as she brought her books to the counter.

"He is," Jessie said, her voice taking on a dreamy quality. She rang up the books and placed them in a bag. "I noticed you like to read mysteries, if your book choice is any indication. We have a mystery book club that meets here every week." She handed her a flyer advertising the group. "You should check them out. They are open to new members and seem to enjoy being together."

"Sounds like something I should look into. We recently moved to the area. My husband was hired at the school. One of the teachers took early retirement due to health. I've been looking for a way to meet new folks."

"You'll like Blue Cove. I moved here last year, and

the people are friendly. When you get a chance, go to the coffee shop next door. Molly, the owner, is the first person I met when I moved to town, and she's been a friend ever since. She also makes and serves some of the best food around." Jessie placed her receipt in the bag. "My name is Jessie, and I hope to see you often."

"I'm Rachael Tanner, and I'm sure you'll be seeing me again. I'm an avid reader. I'll stop by the coffee shop and meet Molly now. Is it okay if I tell her you sent me? I promised my husband I'd try to get out and meet people today. There's no time like the present for getting out of my shell."

"Of course, you can tell her. You've got this." Jessie smiled at her when she left.

****

Matt walked in her store, carrying lunch. "I wanted to talk to you before you heard it somewhere else. Lewis identified the body, and you were right. It's Grace Walters. Do you want to go with me to tell the family?"

"I'll go with you, but I was hoping I was wrong." She leaned her head back against the chair, shutting her eyes. "Her family needs to know, but it's sad that it'll kill any hope they've had."

"Truthfully, sweetheart, I think it'll confirm what they've known in their hearts for a while." He reached for her hand and pressed it to his lips.

"You're right, but it doesn't make it any easier." She gazed in his eyes. "Why are people so cruel? I've never met Grace, but everyone I've talked to thought she was a special young lady. The question becomes did she stumble into something or was she targeted? I hope the details of her final days will tell us the story."

"The forensics should help lead us to the killer and hopefully to the whys we all seem to need."

"It didn't seem to help find Elizabeth's killer, but maybe with the advances in technology, and the clues from Grace's body their murderer will be found." She took a bite of the sandwich Matt brought her. "Speaking of people, Kendra Simpson was in earlier, and we had a nice talk."

"Kendra, wow, it's been a few years since I've seen her. Lizzy and Kendra were inseparable. I think I heard she got married a few years back."

"Yes, she did," Jessie told him the details of their conversation. "She was open and gave me a lot of information for the article until right at the end." Jessie frowned. "Something or someone in the coffee shop bothered her and then she couldn't get out of here fast enough."

"Did you see anyone?"

"I wish I had. All I know the atmosphere changed in an instant, and Kendra left quickly. When I looked in the coffee shop, I didn't see anyone. Of course, I had no idea who I was looking for." She picked up her glass of tea. "Kendra did tell me a few weeks before Lizzy died the two of them had a fight. Elizabeth wouldn't talk to her after that. Kendra said she tried, but Lizzy ignored her."

"I wonder what the fight was over. Did Kendra tell you?"

"Yes, but I'm hesitant to tell you." She pinched a piece of her sandwich off and nibbled on it.

"You can't withhold information. It could be crucial to the case." He leaned toward her in the chair.

"If you must know, they fought over you."

"Me? Why?"

"Lizzy told Kendra that she was going to break up with you. Kendra thought she was making a big mistake. She told me none of her reasons made any sense. She also confirmed that Elizabeth was changing and something wasn't quite right with her."

"I was clueless. I wonder why I couldn't see it then." Matt popped the last bite of his sandwich in his mouth.

"Maybe you did. Sometimes it's easier to see what we want to believe is true than what is right in front of us." That could be her problem. She couldn't see what others could when it came to herself. It was frustrating. *Darn Reba.*

"Chad tried to tell me the same thing. I refused to see it." Matt stood and extended his hand to her. He pulled her gently to her feet and placed a kiss on her cheek. "If you can find someone to watch the shop around three, I'll swing by to get you. The Walters need to know about their daughter as soon as possible."

"I'll find someone." She walked him to the door and waved as he left. "Why are you dragging your feet? He's everything you've ever wanted. You'd better work this out before he gives up and walks away." She stood at the window until his car was out of sight.

Chapter 12

Jessie sat on the window seat looking out into the night sky. A storm was brewing. Lightning lit up the dark clouds, flashing through the sky like a light turning on and off in a room. The occasional rumble of thunder grew louder as the storm approached. She could still see the devastated faces of Grace's parents. Matt had been right. In their heart of hearts, they knew their daughter was dead. Yet, they hoped and prayed their gut instinct was wrong.

The longer she stared out at the ominous night, the angry clouds took on the faces of Grace and Lizzy. Conflict ensued around them. Thunder and lightning, darkness and light were clashing in the sky as if to capture their essence. She shook her head at her fanciful thinking. Yet, it seemed to be true at this moment, and maybe it was true then. Light at war with darkness, love battling hate, kindness trying to overtake cruelty. She had seen enough ghosts to know there was a lot she didn't understand. An angel stood with Grace, and there was peace around her, and Lizzy seemed to be tormented. Maybe Elizabeth was trying to make it right. She had no idea if it was possible. All she could do was hope for Elizabeth's sake that it was.

A flash of lightning lit up the living room with its brightness, followed by a clash of thunder that reverberated off the walls around her. The reflection danced eerily across the cove. She shielded her eyes, looking away for a few seconds. The air crackled with suspense. Jessie stared out the window not wanting to miss…what? Motionless, she was spellbound, gazing into the heavens as the flashes of light and the darkness suddenly took on forms. With their swords drawn and gleaming shields in front of them, beings of bright light zipped in and out of the clouds. And then she saw him, a dark, terrifying dragon-like creature rising out of the dark waters and rushing toward the sky, warring with the creatures of light in the night sky. Suspended, he stood on his haunches his sulfurous breath spewing fire, his red eyes glowing in the darkness. One large winged creature flew toward the dragon and thrust at him with his sword. The bright light streamed through the creature, pushing the dragon back into the darkness. Where did he go? She strained to see if she could find him. He retreated, circled around them, and streaked across the heavens from the other side, only to be pushed back again by another angel taking the first one's place. Back and forth they flew until all the light raced toward the dragon, driving him into the blackness.

What had Elizabeth McKenzie gotten into? Jessie closed her eyes in vain, trying to shut out their images. Taking a deep breath, she opened her eyes. The storm raged on, but the creatures were gone. She grabbed the throw from the chair, cocooning herself in its warmth as chills raced down her back and up her arms. It was clear she had seen a glimpse into another world. As crazy as it seemed, what she witnessed was another piece of the puzzle. A new clue fit into this case, and all she had to do was figure out how.

****

Matt woke from a deep sleep and shot out of bed. The flash lit up his room, followed immediately by the crack of thunder. The sound of crashing thunder resounded still through the room. The lightning must have hit something. He heard the sizzle and smelled the sulfur.

Sitting on the edge of his bed, he rubbed the sleep from his eyes. He glanced at the clock. Three o'clock. What an ungodly hour for a noisy storm. Damn, it was loud. Walking down the hall on his way to the kitchen, he jumped when the living room lit up with the next flash of lightning. Night storms always seemed more ominous to him. They were sure to have some damage from this one. The howl of wind, the rain hitting the windows with force, and the constant rumble of thunder, all seem more intense in the dead of night. He reached for his phone then sent Jessie a quick text. *Call if you're awake.* In a matter of moments, his phone rang.

"You couldn't sleep either?" she asked.

"I was doing fine until a while ago. It got loud enough to wake the dead," he chuckled.

"Funny you should say that."

"Why?" His body tensed.

"I've had a most unusual night. I'm not sure you'd believe me if I told you." The line became quiet as she paused.

"Try me, Jess. I sense you're afraid to open up with me. Don't you trust me?" He raked his hand through his hair. "I've told you often enough I'm not going anywhere."

"No, I'm not afraid to tell you. Okay, maybe a little."

He could barely hear her last few words. "Well, now is the moment I need the assurance from you." He stretched his legs out in front of him.

"Why, I don't understand?"

"I don't know what you think when it comes to the McKenzie case. Can you handle the fact this is my past? I have no idea what is going on inside your head." He frowned. "I know how jealous I was of Liam, and I have no idea how you feel about any of this."

"I'm still here aren't I?"

"Yes, but you hold a part of you in reserve. Is it me or is there another reason?"

"I'm not sure what you want from me." She sighed.

"Yes, you do, Jess." He stood and paced. "At least tell me what you saw tonight. I don't always understand all the stuff that happens to you, but I've been damn accepting when it comes to this part of your life."

"I know you have." Her voice softened. "This is a lot even for me. I know there was a puzzle piece missing in this case. I think it's what I saw tonight." She explained the war she witnessed in the night sky earlier. "I'm not sure if it's a metaphor for what happened to the girls, or if it is happening in an unseen world, but for some reason, I got to see it."

"Whew, I wasn't expecting that. Damn, Jess."

"I know. Like I said, it's new ground for me. As for your other question, I'm careful. I want a relationship that will last a lifetime. I guess what I think of as *cautious* might seem distant to you or to others. At least, for now, I can say I find it strange that I'm jealous of a ghost from your past. I'm not sure what that says about me. I'm here and working through the emotions one by one as they come up."

"Thank you for being honest." Matt fought a smile. Jealous was a good sign. Right now he'd take it. It meant she was invested. "I know this can't be easy for you. It isn't for me either. Communicating will be important. Ask me anything and I'll try my best to answer you. When it comes to angels and dragon-like creatures, you might have to be the one answering the questions. What does it have to do with this case?"

"I'm still thinking about it. Maybe it's something to file away now that will make more sense later."

"You're probably right." Lightning lit up the room again, followed by a loud rumble. "This storm shows no sign of being over." Matt got a glass of water from the kitchen.

"The rain is coming down hard. I'm going to try to get a little sleep. I'll talk to you tomorrow. Sleep well."

"Back at you, Jess."

"And, Matt, I'm here for the long haul too."

"Good to know." He sat in his recliner, put his legs up, and watched the light show until his thoughts quieted and sleep overtook him.

****

He was sorry he got mad at his pa and ran into the woods. *Billy doesn't like the noise.* He covered his ears and put the pillow over his head. The walls of the old cabin shook with each rumble of the thunder. "She's not here no more," he whispered, swatting at the tears forming in his eyes. *No reason to come here no more.* He was alone, all alone, and plenty scared. Pa would tan his hide for sneaking off in the night. The damp cold wind whistled through the cracks in the wall. He couldn't stop the shivers. When he reached for the blanket at the foot of the cot a splat of rain landed on his hand. He wondered if the big fella watching her was gone, too. *Billy hates to be all alone.*

Chapter 13

With the morning's light, Matt got a clear picture of the severity and damage from the storm the night before. From the shredded new foliage on the trees to their downed limbs, it was visible all through the town as he drove to the station. He was sure there were plenty of messages waiting to tell him about the damage that he couldn't see.

He still struggled over processing what Jessie told him last night. His comfort zone had been blown to smithereens since he'd known her. Dragon-like creatures, beings of light, and dreams were only the tip of the iceberg. What more could possibly happen? Maybe he shouldn't ask. If he knew his girl though, something was bound to happen.

"Hey, Chief," Dylan's voice came over the radio.

"Go ahead," Matt answered.

"Are you on your way?"

"I'm about there. What's up?" He turned into the station parking lot.

"The calls are piling up, and you're going to need to assign the cases."

"Place them on my desk. I'll be right in."

"Okay, see you in a few. Over and out." Dylan laughed. "I always wanted to say that."

Matt made his way from the parking lot to the

station door. The park in the town square looked like someone tossed all the young trees around like cabers.

"Good morning, Chief." Kip poured coffee into a cup and handed it to Matt.

"Thanks, Kip." Matt added cream.

"Boy, that was some storm last night, wasn't it? Did you see all the young trees ripped up in the park?" They walked down the hall together toward the offices.

"It's that way all over town. I noticed quite a few branches down on my drive in. We'll be busy with calls all morning."

"The mountain on your desk is growing." Kip stopped at his cubicle.

"It's always the same. They call us, and we have to tell them to call their insurance companies." Matt continued on, walking toward his office. As soon as he sat behind his desk, he went through the list of calls to return and assigned officers to make them. He still had one call that he needed to make personally. He closed his office door.

"Hello, may I speak to Mrs. Tanner?"

"This is her." Her pleasant soft voice came over the line.

"I'm Chief Parker, and I had an urgent message to call you."

"Thank you for being so prompt. I'm calling for my husband, Gordon. He's a new teacher at the school. Today he discovered something in the art supply room that he thinks the police should see. It's important to be discreet about it because he doesn't want to tip anyone off."

"Did he mention what it was?"

"My husband didn't tell me much. He said he

didn't want to get me involved." She paused. "I know it can't be good because he wanted me to contact you as soon as possible."

Matt gave her his cell phone number. "When you talk to your husband have him call me at this number. I will meet him somewhere, and we can talk. I'm well known at the school, and there would be too many questions about why I'm there." He turned his chair around to watch the city crew begin the park clean up.

"Thank you. I'll tell him when he calls." She hung up.

Matt wondered what the new teacher had found. He couldn't imagine. It was a high school after all. He pulled out the McKenzie file and began to go over every entry from the beginning. There were too many unanswered questions. The lead investigator was inept, or there had to be some kind of cover-up going on. Why? Dammit, even the basic questions were never asked, which made no sense at all. There was no mention of the journals, a major piece of evidence to Lizzy's state of mind. How could they have missed them? Were they forgotten or hidden on purpose by someone other than Lizzy? Matt tapped his pencil against the notebook his eyes strayed to the clean-up work going on in the square. It didn't make sense. Anderson signed off on the case. What was he thinking? Matt shook his head in disbelief.

A knock on his door interrupted his thoughts. "Come in."

"I hope I'm not bothering you," Dylan said. "I have some new information I thought you might like to see. Kip and I have been researching like you asked us to and I thought you might find some of this interesting."

Dylan placed the papers on his desk, and the two of them began to go over the crimes in the area similar to their case.

****

Jessie's morning was off to a slow start. She had plenty of time to think, which might be good or maybe not. Her night had been a wild one. There had to be a clue there somewhere, or what was the purpose of seeing all that crazy stuff? One thing for sure, she would have to be careful who she told. Ghosts were bad enough, but creatures fighting in the sky on a stormy night might get her committed to an institution. It all seemed real, but how could it be? Jessie waved at Molly, who was waving at her.

"Are you okay in there?" Molly called out to her. "You looked lost in thought. I waved at you several times, and you never saw me."

"Oh, I'm sorry. I didn't see you."

"Are you sure you're all right?"

"I'm fine." She focused on Molly standing in the doorway. "Daydreaming is all. I have too much time on my hands this morning. I hope business picks up soon."

"It should if the group of tourists from the RVs in the church parking lot heads over here. Either way, I need to get to work." Molly pointed and pushed away from the open doors.''

Molly was right. There were several motor homes and trailers parked at the church. What were they doing there? Better yet, how did she miss seeing them earlier?

"I should at least appear to be busy," Jessie walked behind the counter and began to straighten the bookmarks. The longer she stood there, the more it made sense. All at once it hit her. She couldn't wait to talk it over with Matt. She scribbled down some notes. It would have to wait a little longer. A group of ladies walked in from Joe's, and her store was about to get busy.

****

Matt picked up his ringing mobile phone. "This is Matt."

"Sir, this is Gordon Tanner. My wife told me you said to call you at this number."

"I did, Gordon. When would you like to meet?"

"How about my lunch break at noon if that works for you? The sooner I can give this to you the better."

"That works for me. Where?"

"My wife told me about Java Joe's Coffee shop. Is that all right?"

"It's a great place to meet. I'll be there at noon." Matt hung up the phone. He opened the email from Jessie and began to read the first article about Lizzy. How did she do it? Her words made Lizzy come to life on the page. He could see her smiling face and hear her laughter all in Jessie's words. The more he read it dawned on him that the familiar ache, the one that had always been present when he thought of Lizzy, was gone. She was his past, but Jessie was his present, and future if he could only convince her. One of his current job descriptions was to help her see it. He had been sure the explosion that had nearly killed him when it took out the gristmill would have done the trick. He knew how he felt and was confident about their relationship, but once in a while, he wasn't sure how she felt. Hell, he was a vulnerable mess when it came to her. He jotted off a quick reply to her. *Great article. Send it to Max when you're ready. I'll drop by in a while when I'm in*

*the area. I think this case is about to take off. Love you,
sweetheart, Matt.*

Chapter 14

Matt arrived at the coffee shop before Tanner. The place was hopping. He waved at Jessie on his way to order lunch. "I'll be in later," he called out to her. She smiled, nodded at him, and gave her attention back to the woman standing at the counter.

"Hi, Chief, what will you have?" Kenny asked, then grinned at the surprised look on Matt's face. "I like to help Molly on my day off. It makes her happy, and besides, I like being with her."

"I can understand wanting to be with her. I find myself next door as often as I can get there."

"It must be all those books, eh, sir?" Kenny laughed.

"You're off the clock. You can call me Matt. Sure, I like to read," Matt grinned, "but I like the owner even better." Matt placed his order.

"I hear you. Find a table, and I'll bring your order out when it's ready."

Matt found a table near the front of the shop where it was a little more private. He sat with his back to the wall. It was a good place to see everyone walking in the door. A few minutes later, a man walked in with a leather satchel stashed under his arm. He screamed teacher to Matt with his striped polo shirt in the school colors, khaki pants, and sneakers. "Mr. Tanner?" Matt asked as he stood.

"That's me." He shook Matt's hand.

His tousled brown hair, black glasses, and warm smile made him approachable. Gordon had a nice way about him, and Matt instantly liked him. "I've already ordered. We'll begin when you're ready."

"Do you mind watching this?" He placed the satchel on the table. "It's too heavy to hold and carry anything else."

"I'll keep my eye on it," He placed his hand on the thick, heavy bag, wondering what was in it.

"Thanks for meeting me on such short notice." Gordon sat across from him after placing his order. Tanner reached for the bag. "What I found concerned me. Truthfully, I was ready to quit my job over this."

Matt watched him pull out a huge three-ring binder. "It must not be good if you were willing to quit a job you recently moved here for."

"Let's say I was shocked by what I found." He placed his arm across the binder. "I was clearing off a table, putting things back in the cabinets where they belong. My hand knocked a can of paintbrushes to the floor, scattering them. Two rolled under one of the cabinets. I had to move the darn thing along with several rolls of paper trying to get to them. When I shifted the cabinet, a crudely made door in the back of cabinet sprang open, and I found this." He pointed to the thick notebook. "At first I thought maybe it was some pictures of some of the kids' work stored in it. When I opened the book, I was stunned, and knew I had to get the police involved."

"Good call." Matt waited, Gordon's hands still covered the book.

"It seemed strange to have a book filled with pictures like you're about to see stuffed in a hidden compartment in a storage cabinet. The hiding place was hard to get at, which makes me believe someone wants it that way. If this is what I think it is, these pictures are valuable to someone. I had to get down on my hands and knees and move my hand along the back of the cabinet to find the makeshift secret door cut into the wood. I figure that's how the book was taken in and out without having to move the clunky cabinet. Whoever it belongs to, did such a great job hiding it, only they would know where to look." Gordon pushed the binder toward Matt.

Matt opened it and frowned. "Damn! Do you have any idea who this belongs too?"

"Not a clue. Being new at the school, I've only just begun to meet some of my colleagues. But…" his voice trailed off.

"What?" Matt asked. He clenched his hand into a fist at his side.

"All of the teachers in the art department have keys to the art storeroom and so does the janitor. This isn't good, is it?"

"No, sir it isn't. It's illegal. All these girls were underage." Matt turned through a few pages of the book before closing it. The photos were of young girls, all from the high school, taken in various provocative poses, and wearing little clothing.

"That's what I thought. Do you think it's some kind of child pornography ring? There seems to be a normal picture of each girl and then one that is far from a normal school picture." He reached back in his satchel and pulled out a spiral notebook. "I don't want to forget to give you this. I think it goes with it. The two were together. Whoever wrote these notes has saved your department a lot of work by numbering each of the photos and putting the names of the girls in this notebook next to their number."

Matt looked through the names. *Damn.* "One of the girls in this book was a murder victim several years ago. We recently reopened the investigation. You have found what could be a major piece of evidence. Are the art teachers the only one with access to the room?"

"If only it were that easy. The room gets a lot of use during the day, and it may be hard to narrow down who goes in and out of it. The storeroom is left open in the day. Teachers send their students to the room for supplies, and other teachers go there themselves for art supplies and graph paper for their classrooms and bulletin boards." Gordon thanked Kenny when he placed his lunch in front of him.

"Is there a camera in the storeroom?" Matt took a bite of his sandwich.

"I have no idea, but I doubt it. Most schools have them in hallways near the entrances and some in the classrooms now that it's a different world. This is just a storeroom."

"I see what you mean. We might be able to rig one. I want to make a copy of this, see if we can pull a print off it, and have you put it back. Maybe we can set a trap."

"I'm sure my prints are on it. I never thought about prints before I picked it up." Gordon frowned.

"Of course not, you had no idea what you stumbled on. Mine is on it too. Stop by the station after work. We'll fingerprint you so we can eliminate yours." The two men talked through lunch. Matt placed the binder and notebook in a large takeout bag he got from Kenny.

"I have to get back to the school. Do you have any ideas about all of this?" Gordon asked.

"Someone is pedaling porn and getting young girls at the school involved. I will need to find some of these girls to get answers, or parents, in the case of the younger ones. It looks like it's been going on for a while."

"I thought the same thing. There are lots of photos in that book. It had to be over a span of years or someone would have caught on."

"You're right. I wonder how it flew under the radar this long." Matt knew the minute she walked into the coffee shop. He turned and motioned to her. "Hi, sweetheart." He motioned her over to the table. "I want you to meet Gordon Tanner. His wife was in your shop a few days ago."

"I remember talking with her. It's nice to meet you." She stood beside Matt's chair. "How is your wife?"

"She's well, thanks to you," Gordon greeted her with a cheerful grin. "She met Molly and is getting to know the town. I appreciate you talking with her."

"My pleasure. I'm happy to hear she's getting out in the community. I know she'll love it here." She heard the bell ring above her door. "I need to get back to work. I'll see you later." Her hand brushed gently across his shoulder.

"I'll stop in before I go back to the station." Matt saw her nod before she disappeared through the open doors. "For now, we need to keep this to ourselves and my team. No one at the school needs to know. I will approach the principal, Mr. Rhodes, as soon as I know what we're dealing with. It's safe to say someone at the school is involved. We don't want to panic them until our trap is set."

"Sounds good. I'd rather stay out of the picture entirely, being new to the area." Gordon stood to leave, picking up his empty satchel. "I'll stop by the station after work."

"I appreciate it. Stay in touch. Let me know if you see anything suspicious on campus." Matt shook his hand. "It could be something as simple as someone approaching students and hanging around the school." Matt paused. "If you get the feeling a person shouldn't be near the school, call me at this number." Matt handed him his business card.

"I'll watch, and alert you if I see anything." Gordon left.

"How was your lunch, sir?" Kenny asked.

"Matt," he said and smiled. "It's always good." He bought two chocolate brownies. "These are my downfall."

"That's all Molly's doing. She's a great cook." Kenny grinned. "If I'm not careful I'll be wearing all her cooking."

"As long as you're at the academy, you'll be working too hard to gain anything."

"I know that to be fact. The classes are hard enough, but all the running is kicking my butt." Kenny rubbed his backside. "Everything is sore."

Matt laughed. "I remember those days. You'll make it. Somehow we all managed to survive. Hey, Kenny, can I have a couple of pairs of those plastic gloves you wear for food prep?"

"Sure, take all you need." Kenny handed him the box. "See you tomorrow, Chief."

"Thanks." He waved at Molly. "You have a great little business here." He paused at the open doors to watch Jessie. She was a natural with people. When she laughed with a customer, he couldn't help but smile. It was a miracle to him that she loved him.

Chapter 15

He sat down to wait. Matt leaned his head back against the chair and indulged in one of his favorite pastimes. He loved how her hair bounced on her shoulders and the gentle sway of her hips as she went about her work. She went from one customer to another in her friendly, embracing way. Picking up a book, she showed it to the woman standing beside her. He smiled when she did. Her face was animated, lighting up her eyes. Flipping the cover over, she pointed to something. The young woman started to laugh. Stretching to his left, he couldn't see what the name of the book was. He could only hear the musical lilt of Jessie's voice. Perfect was how she looked standing there in her element.

"Hi," she sat on the arm of his chair. "I wasn't sure if I'd get to you before you had to leave." She peeked inside the bag he handed her. "Oh, I do love her brownies. Thank you."

"I do too. Dylan knows where I am, and how to get a hold of me if he needs to. We need to talk."

"Sounds serious. I have a few minutes, and hopefully we won't have any interruptions, but I make no promises."

"We'll work around them." He handed her a pair of gloves. "When you're ready you'll need to put these on."

"I'll be right back." She jumped up and went to get something behind the counter. Her trusty, small notebook was clutched in her hand when she sat in the chair beside him.

Flipping through the first pages, he saw her stop on a page with lots of writing. "Are you ready?" He asked her.

"Yes." She smiled at him and slipped the awkward gloves on. "Why do I need these?"

"You'll know in a minute." He leaned back in the soft leather chair. "You have the stage." He loved the myriad of emotions that played out on her face as she read her notes.

"Do you remember what I told you I saw during the storm last night?"

"How can I forget?" He grinned at her. "Dragons and swords and who knows what else." A mischievous glint lit his eyes.

"I was going to tell you how I think it fits into this case, but if you're going to make fun of me, I might have to rethink what I tell you." She tapped her gloved finger to her temple.

"I'll behave." He slipped on the second pair of gloves. "Continue, and when you're through I have something to tell you."

"I told you what I learned from Lizzy's journals. She was being promised a modeling career by someone. I have done these stories before and what starts as a modeling photo shoot turns into porn before these girls know what hit them. The guys involved flatter, make promises, and hook them into something way over their heads. I think Lizzy was trying to get out before she was killed."

"What makes you believe that?" The bag rustled when he reached for it.

"There was a battle going on inside her. Like the one, I saw in the night sky. Good versus evil, light over darkness or however you want to describe it. She had made a decision. I'm sure of it. But she was murdered because of it. She knew too much and was a risk for the people involved. Money trumps the life of a young girl. Sick, if you ask me."

"On that topic, we both agree." He pulled the binder and notebook out of the bag. "You needed the gloves to handle these. This proves part of your theory. Take a quick look, then I want to get it out of sight before a customer comes in." He handed the book to her.

Jessie opened and turned through a few pages before closing the binder and handing it back to him. Her eyes told the story. She was mad. "I didn't want to be right." She frowned. "This makes me fighting mad. These girls didn't deserve this."

"No, they didn't." Matt reached in the bag again. It proved many of the issues Jessie had with men. "We're going to find who did this and put them away for many years." He handed her the smaller notebook. "At least we have the names of the girls thanks to our perp's organizational mind. Lizzy's name is in here."

"Does that mean what I think it does?" She glanced at him. "Her photo is in the binder, isn't it?"

"Yes, it probably is. I didn't look." He smoothed the gloves that barely fit his hands. How could anyone work with these things on? "I'll let Marcy go through the book, and we'll start to contact the girls' parents.

They were all underage at the time. Some of the newer photos are girls still in the school. We might get some of the women out of school to talk. I hope you'll be up to doing some of the interviews with them."

"I would be happy to." She flipped through the notebook to the back.

"What are you looking for?"

"Grace's name isn't listed. I wonder what that means? Why was she murdered?" She shut the notebook and glanced at him "Do you know what I think?"

"No, fill me in." He loved how enthusiastic she became once she was engaged in a case.

"Maybe Grace was trying to help Lizzy get out of the situation she found herself in." Jessie frowned. "That would be one reason to kill her. Men can be such jerks sometimes. I get angry thinking of all the girls who were told a pack of lies only to be abused by the ones giving the promises."

"I get your anger. I can't imagine how it is for you and other women." The leather on the chair made a creaking sound with his movement. It was loud to his ears in the quiet of the store.

"No, you can't possibly know. But then again you're different, and you've always treated me with respect. "Some men, though, are a real pain." She scrunched her face. "They frustrate me, and it makes it hard to trust anyone."

"Truthfully, in high school, I would have been one of the boys thrilled to look at the pictures with no thought to the girls' feelings. Now, I think about how angry I'd be if that were my daughter. I'd go ballistic." He frowned. "I can still remember the day my mother found a girly magazine in my room and my father gave me the talk."

"What talk was that?" She grinned at him. "Being a girl, if I asked a question that made my father remotely nervous, he left the room. 'Ask your mother,' was his favorite reply."

"I got *the* lecture. I'll never forget it. He told me how disrespectful I was being by looking at women as objects. I felt lower than a slithering snake wrestling with the feelings inside me. He didn't leave me there, though. He made sure I understood that what was happening to me was normal, but I should never forget girls were people with intellects, feelings, and dreams. His talk, along with a few knocks upside my head, figuratively speaking, taught me how to treat a woman with respect, starting with my mother."

"Curiosity is the name of the game when we're growing up. We all were, boys and girls. But dealing with crude men in the workplace who come on to you is another story altogether. They should know better. At least when you're older, you're more equipped to handle the pressure of it. These young girls didn't stand a chance, and that makes me angry."

She glanced at him. Her face softened.

"What?" He loved when she looked at him that way.

"Now, more than ever, I want to meet your dad. He managed to raise three sons who respect women's feelings. He's great in my book."

"I'm not saying I never slipped up, but he managed to remind me with any means he could. He's still working on Jason, my youngest brother, though."

"I remember he was a bit of a flirt."

"A bit. That's putting it mildly." Matt grinned.

"Another Liam, or living up to his older brothers' reputations, possibly." Jessie chuckled. "I hope we can find the ones who made the promises to the girls. They're as guilty as the one who murdered Elizabeth."

"We'll get them." Matt put the binder back in the bag when the bell above the door rang. He pulled off the ill-fitting gloves. "When we find them, I believe we'll find Lizzy's killer in the mix."

"I'll be right with you," Jessie called out to the visitor, and handed Matt the spiral notebook. She handed Matt her gloves.

"I'll talk to you later, sweetheart." He grabbed the bag and walked into the coffee shop. He was hesitant to leave but didn't know why. The guy in her store seemed familiar. The fact he was good looking didn't make it any easier. Maybe the name would come to him. He grabbed a coffee and decided to watch from a distance.

Hell, he knew who it was. What was he doing in town and in Jessie's store?

****

"May I help you?" Jessie asked the man.

"I hope so. Are you the Jessie Reynolds who left a voicemail on my phone?"

"If you're Chad Bennett, then yes, I am her." She smiled at him.

"One more question before you tell me what you wanted to talk to me about. Was that Matt Parker who was here when I first walked in?"

"Yes, it was. I didn't know you were coming, and I had no idea Matt would be here when you got here either. There must be the reason for it though."

"We need to put our stupid argument to rest. Still, I think I'll let him stew for a few minutes. I'm sure he recognized me too."

Jessie chuckled. "I'm sure he did. He's watching us now." She motioned to the chairs. "I wanted to talk to you about Elizabeth McKenzie. As I told you in the message, we are reopening the case."

He glanced at the coffee shop. "I would be happy to help in any way I can. I wasn't a fan of hers in our senior year. She was cheating on my friend, but he didn't want to hear it from me. She was a mess."

"In what way?"

"How much time do you have" He held her gaze. "Don't get me wrong. We were a happy threesome until our senior year. But Lizzy changed the first few weeks that fall. She did everything she could to destroy Matt's friendship with me. In the end, I guess you could say it worked."

"Why did you leave after graduation?"

"Truthfully, I was angry. Nobody saw what was right under their noses, including Matt. I had to get away from it all."

"You have to remember, Chad, he was young, and Lizzy was his girlfriend. Try to put yourself in his shoes."

"I can see that now, but in high school I couldn't, and I was angry."

"How long will you be in town? I have a lot of questions I want to ask you."

"A day maybe two at the most." Chad glanced in the coffee shop. "Do you think we should put Matt out of his misery?" His eyes lit, his mouth turned up at the corner. "From the expression on his face, I would say you're probably his girl, and right now he'd like to strangle me."

"I knew I was going to like you." Jessie patted his arm. "He's the Police Chief so he won't kill you, but he'll probably grumble." She stood, moving toward the open doors. "Matt, come in here if you have a minute. There's someone I want you to meet."

If the frown on his face was an indication of his feelings, he wasn't too happy.

Matt leaned close to her. "I know who he is. The question is what is he doing here?"

"I called him and asked him to come." She emphasized the word asked drawing it out. "I thought maybe he might remember something that could help with the case." She hoped her plan wouldn't backfire.

"We'll talk about this later," he grumbled at her.

"We," she pointed at him and then back at herself, "have nothing to talk about. But you two do. You may as well get it over with." She gave him a gentle nudge pushing him between his shoulders.

Chad stood. "Matt."

"Chad." Matt tipped his head slightly. "I'm surprised to see you."

"I felt the same way when I walked in the door and saw you sitting there. Now that we're in the same room there's no time like the present to work through what happened years ago."

"I guess you're right." Matt extended his hand. Chad grabbed it.

Jessie left them to talk and went about her work. Chad's head was bent close to Matt's. The two of them were talking. Chad was a good-looking man. With his blond hair, brown eyes, and the nice smile, he was a catch for someone. Was he married? Darn, she was slipping. She forgot to check his hand for a ring. He would be perfect for Peyton or maybe Sally. When she glanced their way again, Matt motioned her over.

"Sweetheart, we'll be back to take you to dinner. I want to take Chad over to the station to see some of the guys he'll remember." He pulled her down close and whispered in her ear. "Thanks for calling him. I owe you."

"Yes, you do, and I'll be more than happy to remind you often." She squeezed his hand. "See you later."

Chapter 16

"Jessie is stunning. You could always pick them, that's for sure. I never could figure out what they saw in you." Chad goaded him.

"I have no idea what she sees in me, but I'm glad she sees something she likes."

"I've been reading about all the crazy things happening here. Blue Cove has gone through some major changes since I left. Truthfully, I was surprised to learn you came back here after all that happened to you the last year of school. I thought you'd be happy to get the hell out of Dodge."

"I was, and I did leave for a while. I went to college, and then to the FBI National Academy in Virginia."

"What are you doing here and not at the Agency."

"I worked for a few years in the Counter Terrorism Unit. Believe me when I say I have nothing but absolute respect for the men and women at the Bureau. They're honest hard-working folks in the service of their country."

"Seems right up your alley. I think I hear a but in that answer. What brought you back?"

"The job was demanding. Dealing with domestic issues and homegrown terrorists kept us running. I don't know how the married agents did it. I fell into bed at night exhausted. I guess I'm a small-town cop at heart. I always felt compelled to come back here. I had unsettled business to take care of. Although, lately it has been stressful around here too."

"Blue Cove isn't that small anymore. The town has grown a lot."

"You're right, especially in the last few years."

"I couldn't believe when I heard Ross blew up the old gristmill."

"Wow, you remembered the man's name."

"I can read, and I do listen to the news," his voice was tinged with sarcasm. "Do you remember how often we used to hang around there as boys?"

"I remember, and it was my knowledge of the place that saved my life." Matt told him about what had happened, and how he remembered their secret entrance into the mill.

"Why did Jessie call me? Don't get me wrong. I'm glad she did. It gave me a way to save face and come back to town. I've wanted to for years."

"Jessie is my partner of sorts. It was one of her articles you might have read. She's unconventional in her methods, but she's good."

Chad gave him an odd look. "What do you mean?"

Matt spent the next several minutes explaining the strange phenomenon of Jessie's methods since her arrival. "She's a marvel. Her unique abilities are mind-blowing and surprise even her. There isn't a cop who works in this town that doesn't respect her and several at the Agency, as well. They'd like to have her at the Bureau."

"Don't tell me you believe all this psychic crap." Chad shook his head.

"Whatever her gift is, I, for one, am grateful for it. We've solved crimes that went undetected. I like to think of her as intuitive." Matt turned into the station and parked the car. "Logic often gets kicked to the curb working with her, but I'm her greatest fan."

Chad chuckled. "I noticed."

"Let her tell you why she wanted you to come to town, and if you can handle it, I'll let her tell you the reason we have reopened the case after all these years."

"I'll listen, but I won't be fooled either."

"I never thought you would." Matt opened the car door and pulled the bag out of the backseat. "Let's go. The guys will be happy to see you."

"Yeah, I doubt they even remember me." Chad followed him into the station.

Matt wasn't sure what to think about Chad's sudden return to his life. Dylan and Gary were happy to see him. He looked great, but there was something different about him. Too many years had passed, and Matt didn't know him anymore. Chad hadn't volunteered any information about what he had been doing for the past ten years. For now, he would wait and give him the benefit of the doubt.

Matt pulled the spiral notebook out of the bag and began to look at the names of the young women listed. How long had this been going on right under their noses? Someone in authority had to have known and looked the other way. With Lizzy's name in the mix, it goes back at least ten years, maybe more. Damn, every town has its own dirty little secrets, and Blue Cove was no exception. He wondered if Anderson knew what was going on and if he got kickbacks to look the other way.

"You're deep in thought." Chad knocked on the

open door, walked into the office, and sat in the chair in front of Matt's desk.

He closed the file. "I do a lot of thinking on this job."

"I can imagine." Chad moved to the edge of his chair. "Do you like your job? I don't mean just tolerate, but honest to goodness like it. Are you happy to come to work every day?"

"Yeah, I like it. It's in my blood. I take satisfaction in putting bad guys behind bars, as corny as that sounds. I even like rescuing the widow's cat out of the tree. Yes, I'd say I'm happy." Matt rested his hands on his desk. "How about you? Have the last ten years been good to you?" Matt studied his friend's face. He knew body language, and Chad was at war with himself.

"It's been a mixed bag. You know how it goes. To make a long story short, I got my college degree in business and work at a high paying job I hate. I live the life my income affords me, and I can't quit 'cause I have to pay for the lifestyle. High school was a hell of a lot easier."

"Are you married?" Matt asked.

"I was engaged once, but it didn't last. I guess you could say she wasn't the right one if there is such a thing. She cheated on me from day one." Chad leaned back in the chair.

"That could make a skeptic out of anyone. I quit believing it myself for a while, but Jessie has changed all that for me." Matt's hand gestured as he talked.

"It doesn't hurt that she's easy on the eyes."

"True, but there's more to it."

"What more is there?" Chad asked him.

"Talking about feelings is new to me, and I find it

hard to put it all into words. I was drawn to Jess the first moment we met. We fought all the time. Her strength mystified me. I thought I was in charge, but in truth, she charmed me, and I was a lost cause."

"If you're happy, who the hell cares how it happened. Dylan is getting married, he told me."

"His fiancée is Jessie's best friend."

"He filled me in on the details. After talking to the guys, I have to say you're right about one thing. All these guys respect Jessie.

"I told you." Matt drummed his fingers on the desk. "I noticed in the want ads that the town council is looking for a city manager. If you're unhappy with your job, you should check it out."

"I have an interview tomorrow. That's one of the reasons why I'm here. The pay is good, and it's right in line with what I'm doing now. We'll see."

"If it's meant to happen it will."

"Getting a tad philosophical, old man, aren't you?" Chad raised his brows.

"Jessie's rubbing off on me. She always says 'it's meant to be', and maybe it is. I don't have all the imaginative answers in this logical brain of mine."

"She's the second reason I'm here. I have a lot to say about Lizzy. I hope it won't blow our tentative reunion all to pieces."

"The time has come for honesty and getting to the truth. The McKenzies deserve to know what happened to their daughter."

"Maybe they'd be better off not knowing." Chad straightened in the chair, a frown on his face.

"What do you mean?"

"The facts that are bound to come out won't bring

them much peace. It might shatter an illusion they have of their family. We'll find out soon enough."

"As long as those facts tell the story of what happened to Elizabeth, that's what counts." Chad divulged a lot in the simple statement. They had fought over something along the same lines before he left. Chad had told him that he wasn't truthful with himself and holding on to a fantasy of who Lizzy was. Maybe he had.

"Gary is taking me back to my car. I need to get a room for the night. Where do you want to meet for dinner?" After their evening plans were made, Chad walked out the door.

Chapter 17

Jessie knew after reading Lizzy's journals that the case had links to porn, but she had no idea how many girls had been sucked into the scheme. Kendra's name was on the list. Jess picked up the phone and called her. When the younger child answered the phone, Jessie asked, "Hello, may I speak to your mother?"

The child called for her mother, but then Jessie could hear Kendra and the fight that ensued. "Give me the phone, please."

"Mine!" the younger child screamed. Whew, that little one could hold her own.

"Give it to me and go play." Kendra's muffled words still could be heard. "Hello, this is Kendra."

"Kendra, this is Jessie from the bookstore. I wanted to see if you had some time in the next week when we could get together and talk. Something has come up, and I would like to run it past you,"

"I'll see if I can get a sitter and call you back later. There's no way I can talk with this bundle of energy with me."

"What's her name? She sounded so darn cute on the phone."

"Zoe, and she keeps me hopping. When she's not talking, she's getting into everything her little hands can grab. Silence is never a good thing when she's awake." Kendra laughed. "It usually means I'm about to clean up a colossal mess. She's quite taken with Mommy's lipsticks and eyeshadows. Besides painting everything in sight with them, she likes to eat the lipstick. I have to keep them under lock and key."

"How old is she?" Jessie asked.

"She's two going on twenty. Zoe wants to do it all but sleep."

"Well, she sure sounds cute."

"We think she is." There was a sudden silence on the line. "Zoe, get down, you'll fall," Kendra shouted. "I need to go. She's climbing on top of the cabinet."

"Oh dear, take care of her. Call me when you can meet." Jessie smiled to herself. Her life was simple. She would have to meet the small whirlwind named Zoe. The bell above the door was her signal to get back to work.

She waited on several customers through the afternoon and wrote down a question to ask Chad every time she thought of another one. He didn't seem to like Elizabeth McKenzie, and she wanted to know why. Would he be free to talk with Matt present? She hoped so. He needed to hear what Chad had to say and so did she if they were going to solve the case and keep it from happening to any other girls. If it hadn't already.

She grabbed her phone out of her purse. There was one more call she needed to make while she waited for Matt to arrive. It was settled. Audrey would come early to the store so she could run with the running team in the morning. Clicking off the phone, she sorted through the stack of mail sitting on the counter, separating the bills from junk. With any luck, Lizzy would be there to greet her. Talking to Lizzy seemed like the perfect thing to do right now. Crazy ideas were nothing new to her, and a few of them had even worked. Lizzy knew better than anyone who her murderer was. Beginning her closing routine, Jessie straightened the chairs around the table and picked up the trash left behind.

"Wait a minute. I want to ask you something before you close the door." Molly waved and rushed toward her. "Have Katie and Dylan figured out a wedding date yet?"

"No, but they're getting closer to agreeing on a date. At least they've narrowed it down to one of the seasons of the year, and now all they have to figure out is which year." Jessie chuckled. "It's fun to watch the two of them. They're cute when they are at odds. Katie completely mystifies him, and she knows it. Sometimes I think she does it on purpose."

"I remember those days. It's fun and often stressful. It's a lot easier after you're married, believe me."

Jessie gave her a doubtful look. "Are you sure about that?"

"At least sometimes it is. All I'm saying is planning a wedding can be nerve-racking. Besides, we could use another wedding in town. I like a good party."

"I'm sure they'll decide on a date soon. At least according to Katie, they're closer to setting a date than they were a week ago. Dylan would like it now, and Katie wants it a year from now. I suggested eight months from now as a compromise, but that makes it a winter wedding and Katie wants an outdoor wedding when the gardens at the Inn are in full color. So that makes it either late spring or summer this year or next. I know Dylan doesn't want to wait until next year. I've been trying to convince Katie we can get everything ready this year. Fingers are crossed that I've convinced her."

"Here's hoping." Molly crossed her fingers. "Talk to you later."

"See you." Jessie shut and locked the doors. She turned the sign around to Closed on the front door. This was one of her favorite times of the day. Glancing around the store brought the same sense of satisfaction she always felt. She loved her job, this town, and all her new friends. Happy was how she would describe herself for the moment. Content at this point in her life, and yet she wanted more. She was reaching for what? The great unknown.

That was when she noticed the man standing in the cemetery. Who was he and what was he doing there? It was hard to tell his identity from where she stood. Had she ever seen him before? She needed to get a closer look at his face. He seemed to be standing near Lizzy's grave. Was he the one who placed the flowers there all the time? One thing she knew, something wasn't right. The sun was sinking low in the sky. The orange and pink colors streaked through the clouds like an artist painting them with his brush. Even with all the beauty to distract, the storm raging within him could be clearly felt. Following his progress from the graves to where he stood at the entrance, Jessie was stunned when he looked across at her store. She never noticed his appearance. How could she? Anger, tinged with sorrow and mixed with regret, flashed in rapid succession through his mind. Could he see her watching him? She ducked out of view. The man had something to do with

Elizabeth, and the battle for their lives was similar.

She was happy to see Matt's car pull into the space in front of her store. All of what she saw only added to the mystery of Elizabeth McKenzie. Who was the man, and how did he fit in her story?

Chapter 18

Jessie took a seat on the passenger side and closed the door. "Hi, how was your day?"

"No complaints." He waited for her to latch her seatbelt. "If it were up to me, we would go back to the days when a girl could practically sit on a guy's lap while he drove. Not safe, but certainly a lot more romantic."

She smiled at him. "I wouldn't know. I've been in a seatbelt as far back as I can remember. You know, click it or ticket."

"Yeah, me too. Still, I've seen pictures." He stroked his chin. "My grandparents, to be exact. Those were the days."

"Oh, I don't know about that. We live in our own great times. There are a lot fewer rules for one, and I don't have to wear a dress if I don't want to."

"All thanks to our grandparents and parents, you know the whole cultural revolution. They were active generations. No wonder they want to take it easy now."

Jessie laughed. "Did you work things out with Chad?" She turned in her seat to face him.

"Right now we're skirting the issues, but I believe all that will change tonight. I'm only guessing, but I think that was your plan all along wasn't it?" Matt glanced at her before he pulled away from the curb.

"Part of it, I guess." Her answer was demure sounding even to her.

"Come on, Jess, only part of it." He grinned at her. "You're no good at playing games, sweetheart. There's always something going on behind the scene in that brain of yours."

"Yes, of course. All pretense aside, I thought it would be good for you both to talk. I also wanted to see what he remembered about Lizzy. You two fought over whatever it was, which seems significant to the story as far as I'm concerned."

"Details escape me." Matt looked in his side mirror.

"Maybe you wanted it that way. But not him, I think. I believe Chad remembers all the details and has been bitter over how they impacted your friendship. I'm sure he can shed light on Lizzy's state of mind. If you can..." her voice trailed off.

"I know what you were going to say." He glanced back at her.

"Oh yeah." She fluttered her lashes at him. "Enlighten me."

"You're wondering if I can handle what he's going to say. Am I right?" She nodded at him. "The thing is, Jess, I've realized something important over the past few days. Lizzy doesn't have the power to hurt me anymore. She's a memory, but that's it. I'll be able to handle anything he dishes out."

"If you truly feel that way, then I think it's time to give you something." She reached in her purse and pulled out the letter Charlotte had given her.

"What is it?" he asked, glancing at her.

"It's a letter Lizzy wrote to you a few days before

she was murdered. Her mother gave it to me and told me I would know when it was time to give it to you. The letter is rightfully yours." She handed the envelope to him. "Charlotte didn't want to give it to you then. Your heart was broken enough."

"Why didn't she give it to the investigators at the time?" He frowned. "There might be something important in what she wrote. At the very least a clue to Lizzy's state of mind."

"She should've." Jessie lifted her sunglasses to see him better. "I believe, and this is only my opinion, the reason she didn't give it to them is that it doesn't put Lizzy in a favorable light. You'll understand after you read it."

He opened the letter and began to read. When he was done, he put in back in the envelope and tossed it in the back seat. "That was harsh."

"Are you all right?" She couldn't tell from his expression what he was thinking.

"We had better get on our way. I told Chad we'd meet him five minutes ago." Matt did a U-turn and headed toward Blue Cove Drive. "I'll read it again later to digest it. It doesn't sound like the Lizzy I knew, but now I doubt whether I knew her at all."

"I remember you telling me once you didn't know if I could suspect my friends because I was loyal to them. It's hard to see the people who we care for be anything but who we think they are. I guess all of us have something hidden inside us that we alone know." Jessie glanced at his handsome profile.

"True, or how else could we explain a person going from being a law-abiding citizen to a murderer." Matt glanced in the rearview mirror.

"A depressing thought." She glanced away from him.

"What's hidden in your life, Jess?"

"A little of this and that. Wouldn't you like to know?"

"Yes, I think I would. I want to know everything about you." He glanced at her.

"I'm not that interesting. Do you mind if I change the subject. For now, my lips are sealed." She playfully zipped her lips.

"Chicken." He made a playful clucking sound

"Maybe, or it's possible I'm smarter than you think." She remembered Reba's words, and she wasn't ready to think about it yet. No true confessions or deep conversations were on the agenda for tonight.

"No question about you being smart. Change the subject if you must." He clucked again.

She ignored his teasing. "Where are we going?"

"The Chowder House. Chad wanted to go there." Matt turned his signal on.

"I love that place, and I haven't seen Roger Blackman in a while." Thank heavens she had worn a dress and her low heels to work today. It was a classy place. She ran her hand over the dress, trying to smooth out any wrinkles.

"You look nice. I forgot to mention it earlier." He glanced at her. "Of course, you always do." Matt pulled into a parking space. "Wait. I want to open the door for you." He pulled his sports jacket out of the back seat and slipped his arms in it on his way to open her door.

She ran her fingers over his cheek to his chin. "You clean up nice." She teased him, remembering what she had said the first time he brought her here. It had flown out of her mouth, and her face had turned red. She could feel the familiar heat on her face.

"I've missed seeing your blush." He ran his hand over her cheek. "You look pretty in pink." He slipped his arm around her, pulling her gently to his side.

"I can't believe you remembered." She smiled at him.

"I remember lots of things you've said and done since we met. Does that surprise you?" He gazed at her. "I love how your hair smells when you've just washed it, and the taste of your lips when we kiss. Right now the scent you're wearing makes me want to skip this dinner with Chad and have you all to myself."

The look of desire in his eyes caused her stomach to flutter. "That's nice to hear after being on my feet all day."

"You can change the subject, but you won't distract me. I'm feeling romantic. I remember the first night I brought you here too."

"Are you wearing a new cologne?" She leaned close to his face, touching her lips to his cheek. "Ummm, spicy," She inhaled the scent of his aftershave. "It suits you." She pulled away, grabbing his hand with a chuckle. "Chad's waiting. We'd better get a move on it."

"Oh, Jess, love. I think paybacks are in order. I'm going to enjoy every minute of it." He opened the door for her. She waved at Roger.

"Chief and Jessie, it's always good to see you. It's been a while." Roger approached them. "Chad Bennett is waiting for you. I haven't seen him in years." He led them to the table.

"How's your wife doing?" Jessie asked Roger.

"She's well and still tolerates me, so life is good." He patted her hand. He whispered in her ear. "Our Mr. Parker is quite smitten with you, and that's very good news to me."

She nodded at him. "To me, too." She sat when he pulled out her chair.

"What was that all about?" Matt glanced at her.

"Our secret." She smiled at Roger when he handed her a menu.

"Enjoy your meal, my friends." He motioned for the waiter. "Bring them the finest bottle of my Chianti on the house. The lobster is fresh, the filet mignon is delicious, and the swordfish is cooked to perfection. *Bon appetit.*"

"Thank you, Roger. It all sounds good."

"I remember my parents bringing us here on special occasions when we were kids." Chad looked around the restaurant. "Roger's updated the place since then. He's older but still as friendly as ever. The whole town has had a facelift. I like the looks of it."

"I fell in love with Blue Cove the first time I drove through town," Jessie reflected on her first day in Blue Cove. "Everything was blooming, and Main Street looked so inviting."

"Do you regret moving here from New York? I was told you had quite a career ahead of you there."

"I haven't had time to miss the city. I moved here to be near my friend Katie and for a less hectic life. One out of two isn't bad." Jessie winked at Matt.

"I've heard you've had a few challenges since moving here." Chad placed his menu on the table.

"How could you know that?" She gave Matt an accusing look. "You haven't been here long enough to be filled in on all the particulars."

Chad grinned. "You should know by now, this is a small town, and gossip travels fast."

"In that case, I can only imagine what you've heard." She paused while the waiter took their order. She wondered how the folks in Blue Cove talked about her. It didn't matter she wasn't going anywhere.

Chapter 19

Getting the small talk out of the way, Jessie was ready to hear what Chad had to say. "Where should we start? We aren't meeting to talk about old times, or I wouldn't need to be here." She placed her napkin on her lap.

"Since I don't know you, why don't you start? I'm interested in why you called me." Chad took a sip of his water.

Jessie glanced at Matt and saw him nod. She told Chad about some of the things that had happened to her since living in Blue Cove. "The latest occurred a few days ago, and that's why we reopened this case, and why I called you." She added after seeing his skeptical expression, "You can or don't have to believe me about Lizzy's ghost, but she is the one that led me to the memorial near the woods. Finding it and seeing another body in the woods is what led us to Grace. I'm trying to reconstruct the last few months of Lizzy's life to find clues covered up with time. They've been there all along. It's a matter of igniting people's memories."

"I'm not sure what to think about the supernatural crap, but I've checked up on you. You're well liked and respected. I'm willing to tell you what I know." He glanced at Matt. "Are you going to be okay with this? I don't have to worry about you making a scene if I insult

Lizzy's memory?"

"I'll be fine. You're free to tell it as you see it." Matt adjusted the plate of salad the waiter placed in front of him. "Maybe I'll learn something." He sat back in his chair and watched his friends talk.

"Where do you want to start?" Chad asked.

"I'll leave that up to you and ask questions as they come up."

"Lizzy and I were once good friends. She was a fun girl for the most part, until our senior year. The three of us were inseparable until I saw her treating Kendra like crap and asked her about it. I saw a side of her that was scary. Either she had us all fooled, or had changed dramatically. The thing is I had seen times early on when if she didn't get her way, she could be a bitch. Pardon my language."

"What do you mean?"

"Most of the time she had my friend here," he pointed at Matt, "tied in knots. I realize boy-girl relationships in the teens are strange, to begin with. He couldn't ever tell her no. She kept him on a short leash. Because she was pretty and popular, she had quite a following among the cool kids at the time." Chad gave Matt another quick glance. "I know it's hard to believe it to look at him now, but Matt was a quiet guy until he got hooked up with Lizzy. She brought him out of his shell."

Jessie shook her head. "I find it hard to believe that this self-assured man was ever a shy guy."

"I know, but in truth, in high school most of us guys are at best nervous pimple-faced bumpkins who have no idea how to put two sentences together in the presence of the opposite sex. Too many raging hormones for our own good. The ones who could were usually obnoxious, smug, and relied on stupid pick-up lines."

Jessie laughed. "I knew a few on each side of your description. I know a few men who are still there."

"Truthfully, girls are always one step ahead of guys in the behavior and thoughts department. Sometimes I think we are only a step up from the caveman. It's women that help keep us human."

"Aren't you being a little hard on your sex?" She laughed.

"Not at all. Take high school, for example. Most of us males hung out in groups hoping to get noticed while acting like jerks. All talk, but never knowing how to treat a girl. Lizzy knew that about us, and wasn't afraid to exploit it."

"How did she do that? I'm not sure I understand what you mean."

"She had an endgame in mind. She wanted to be popular and move out of this town as soon as she could. Her dreams were bigger than what our Blue Cove had to offer. Matt served her purpose for a while. He was quiet, but he could play football and was a quarterback, no less. He fit in her plan until she was ready to move on. She was using him to advance her place until the next guy came along."

"You make her sound shameless." Jessie frowned.

"In a way she was. Toward the end of her short life, she used a lot of people to get her way, including Grace Walters."

"How did she use Grace?" Jessie glanced at Matt. He was listening.

"Grace heard how some of the girls were starting to

talk about Lizzy. She reached out in friendship to her. Lizzy had something else in mind entirely. I never knew what she was involved in. I was getting close, and that's when her older brother and a couple of his college buddies threatened me."

"How did they threaten you?" Matt jumped into the conversation.

"They beat the hell out of me. I was told in no uncertain terms to keep my nose out of where it didn't belong, or I wouldn't live long enough to talk about it. I tried to warn you, but you weren't ready to hear me out. It took a few more similar conversations between us before we finally split. After she was murdered, she could do no wrong in your mind, and I gave up."

"How close were you?" Matt squirmed inside. Why hadn't he seen this going on?

"I was following her and saw a few of the men she met with. I didn't recognize any of them. If I had to make bets about it, her brother knew something about what was going on and might have been involved. That's my take on it."

"Which brother, Bobby or Ted?" Matt clenched his hands.

"Ted." Chad's answer was emphatic.

"Are you sure?" Matt leaned back in his chair.

"No doubt about it. I knew the one who held me down while the others hit me." Chad frowned. "I was afraid to go back to school. Those were some rough days for me."

"Why didn't you tell me? I remember you were out of school for several days, and you didn't want to talk about it when I called."

"I didn't think you'd believe me after our last fight.

Besides, my black eye wasn't nice to look at, and I didn't want anyone to ask how I got it. After Lizzy's death, you were broken, and didn't want to hear anything bad about her." Chad twirled the wine in his glass. "I left town right after graduation. I didn't want to run into Ted again. My parents thought it would be better for me if I left. They sent me to stay with my uncle in Florida for the summer. I got into college and stayed."

They talked until the waiter set their meal in front of them. Their conversation turned to happier times. Matt and Chad had a lot of history between them. Jessie enjoyed listening to them banter back and forth. She had more questions now than ever.

Chapter 20

Matt pulled in the garage after taking Jessie back to her car. He retrieved the letter from the backseat and went inside. Not sure what to think about the damn letter, he threw it onto the counter. Too bad Elizabeth hadn't mailed it years ago. It would have helped him make sense of the things that were happening. As memories resurfaced, he remembered he had been disturbed by her actions at the time but had refused to acknowledge what was right in front of him. Instead, he chose to live with the guilt rather than cast any shadow on the memory of her. At least now he was capable of rational thought. He neither hated her nor loved her. Lizzy was part of his past. More than ever he wanted to solve her murder and move on to his future.

What had Ted gotten into? How could he use his sister in such a way or was it the other way around? Matt picked up his phone to call Chad and ended up leaving a message about getting together after his job interview in the morning. Chad was holding back tonight when he answered questions. He wanted gut level honesty from him, and it would be better without Jessie there to hear.

Next, he called Jeremy. "Hi, Matt. Funny you should call. I just finished talking to Jessie."

"Oh, yeah. What did she want you to do?"

"Check into a porn ring in your area using high school age girls. Believe me, there are quite a few. I found some sites that would cause you to lose sleep."

"It sounds like we're on the same wavelength."

"All the sites look innocent up front. You know the promise of a great modeling career. Digging underneath the surface is where I'm finding the real skinny on these guys. People go to prison that dabble in this junk. I have permission to track these sites working with law enforcement. I wouldn't venture there without letting them know why I'm going. Some of these idiots aren't smart about what they're doing. They walk into police traps all the time. The pictures are right out in the open. The one operating in your area has a protected site. I'm working to break the codes now." Jeremy gave Matt the website. "It looks all above board, but I would bet once I get through the firewall I'll find out that it's not."

"I know you're right," Matt told him about the binder and the notebook they had found.

"It sounds like it's been going on for a while. When you can, send me some pictures of the older girls back five to ten years ago. I want to scour through some of the porn star movie sites. A lot of these young girls are manipulated into the movies where they become trapped."

"I'll do that first thing tomorrow."

"The big question for you to answer is who in your town has access to the girls, and who is the go-between?"

"I intend to find out."

"Women have never had it easy. Thankfully, with all the women speaking out you might find some who are willing to talk. I think Jessie will be the perfect person to work with the girls. She can earn their trust and help them at the same time. She understands about abuse. If she hasn't told you already, you need to make her. She has every right to be skeptical of men."

Matt was stunned to hear what Jeremy was telling him. Some of her actions and carefulness with him suddenly made sense to him. "Thanks, Jeremy."

"You and Jessie need to talk. This case is bringing back a lot of hard memories for her. She's quiet and keeps a lot inside of herself."

"I'll talk with her. I promise."

As soon as he hung up with Jeremy, he called her. "Hi, sweetheart. How about I make you dinner tomorrow night?"

"Sounds nice. Any special reason?"

"No, I want to spend some time with you is all."

"I guess I can manage it." She chuckled. "I mean, what's not to like about hanging out with my handsome guy? No cooking is an added benefit. You can count me in."

"What did you think about the conversation tonight?" Matt sat in his lounge chair.

"I learned some things, but I believe Chad was holding back. I'm not sure why. Maybe to protect you, but most likely it was to protect my sensibilities."

"He doesn't know you like I do."

"True, but we were also in a public place, which isn't the best place to talk about a sensitive subject. It's hard to gauge another person's reaction. For example, if you hadn't remembered your surroundings at one point, I thought you might jump out of your chair when you heard Lizzy's brother was somehow involved."

"I was this close." He snapped his fingers. "I'll tell

you what bothered me more."

"What?" She asked.

"When I heard they had beat Chad up, and I never knew about it. I must have been self-absorbed at the time. Not a good friend if you ask me."

"You're no different from most teens."

"I thought I was. How come you're so smart?"

"I listened in school." She laughed. "I once heard it said, we're not half as good as we think we are, and not half as bad either."

"I haven't seen a bad side to you, yet. From every angle, you're about perfect."

"Mr. Parker, I believe you're trying a new pick-up line, or you need to wear your glasses more often. Am I or am I not the woman who stuck my tongue out at you when I first moved here? Use your sense of reason. I've given you a run for your money. If my memory serves me right, I'm the same woman who basically told you I was going to interview Gina's family whether you liked it or not. There's no mystery here. I'm out in the open with it."

"I like that about you," he told her.

"It's a good thing."

"I'll see you tomorrow night."

"What time?" she asked.

"Six works for me if that's okay with you."

"I'll see you at six."

****

Jessie disconnected the call. She wanted to talk to Chad again, without Matt. Determined, she had to find the man responsible for that binder and ruining so many young girls' lives. The powerful always tried to take away the victim's voice whether by fear or force.

Which often resulted in death. The most important thing she could do was tell their story and give a voice to those who couldn't speak for themselves. She had never regretted for a moment the time invested or even putting herself on the line for a cause, and this time was no different. Although seeing those photos came close to home, dredging up memories she would rather leave buried. For the sake of these girls, she was willing to risk it.

She turned on the TV, stretched out on the couch, and before long she dozed off. The bang of the door startled her. She struggled to sit up and to open her eyes.

He was in the room. The palpable fear raced through her. Where was he? Searching the room, her gaze landed on him in standing smugly in the corner. He leered at her with a sick, satisfied look, ready to pounce on her at any moment. He was like a panther ready to attack his trapped prey. He raced toward her, his hands grabbing at her and locking her in his grasp. Run, her mind screamed. He was bigger and faster than she was. The punch hit her jaw, causing her to see stars. His hands latched onto her hair yanking her closer, the sting of his slaps, and the smell of him nauseated her, freezing her in place. Keep fighting! She kicked, punched, and scratched him. Every time one landed, hitting its mark, a tirade of filth flowed from his mouth, and he pulled her back, slapping her again. Try, you have to try. Don't give up! She yelled. With one final swing of her foot, she kicked him. His hands went slack as he doubled over, falling to the floor. She ran, flinging open the door and running for her life into the night.

Jessie jumped up, her eyes wide open and her rapid breathing heavy. The room was empty. How many times had she relived this nightmare? Different scenes, but he was always the same. She had defeated him once, but he was due to get out of prison soon. Stronger now than before, she wouldn't let the fear paralyze her. She knew what she had to do.

Chapter 21

Matt was awake. He propped his back against the headboard with pillows. Jessie was a puzzle to him. She had been since the first day he met her. He knew they loved each other, but she held part of herself in reserve when it came to him. Each case brought a new revelation about her personality and a greater understanding of his attraction for her. His love had grown with each new aspect he'd discovered, yet he wasn't sure how he rated with her. She flirted with him, she responded to his kisses, but she seldom shared her heart's emotions. As happy as that would make some men, he wanted to know what she was feeling and thinking. Jeremy's statement earlier filled in a few blanks. Jessie would do the rest when she was ready. No wonder she was a great advocate for women. Lizzy couldn't have chosen a better person to figure this case out. Jessie wouldn't stop until she helped every girl in those photos be free from their abusers. He smiled into the dark room. He could see her in his mind as his dragon slayer. He had to abdicate his role. She had saved him often enough. Maybe she was the creature of light fighting the dragon that night. He shook his head. If he didn't watch out, he would be talking with ghosts too.

****

Her feet pounded the ground in tempo with the other runners. She set the pace, and they followed, jockeying for position beside her. Matt would have known what the boys were up to. A wily smile lit up her face. She picked up the pace and ran faster, forcing them to push harder to keep up. By the time she reached the top of the first incline, she stopped to let the huffing, sweating boys catch up and maneuver around her, giving her little more than a glance as they passed by. Jessie could hardly contain the laughter bubbling up in her. No wonder Matt's parents wanted to keep their sons busy with sports. Mr. Donovan had called Connor and Liam idiots on more than one occasion as he made them work off their energy. She was catching on.

When they got to the curve in the second incline, the boys continued on without her. "Go ahead. I'll catch up later." She saw a couple of them nod and a few others waved.

She stopped at the memorial, sat on the bench, and waited. Elizabeth McKenzie was close by even if she wasn't showing herself. "We are working on your case, Elizabeth. I don't know what you're aware of, but we found Grace's body in the woods. Her memorial service is next week. Matt Parker and I will be going. If we're lucky, one of the suspects will show up, and we'll be watching for them. You were involved in some sordid stuff that we're only beginning to put together. Why did you lead the other girls into the mess? You knew what you were doing. Was it out of spite or did someone coerce you? I'm trying to make sense of why you betrayed your friends. I believe you had a change of heart at some point, and there was a war going on inside of you." Could Lizzy hear a word she was saying? It didn't matter. She needed to say them.

Two things happened simultaneously disturbing her train of thoughts. The red-tailed hawk began squawking overhead when she jerked, glancing skyward. The rock flew by her face, narrowly missing it. The next one didn't. It struck the side of her head with a jolt. She pitched forward, sliding to the ground.

"Are you okay, Ms. Reynolds?" Jessie heard the faint voices through the fuzz in her head.

"Maybe we should help her up." One of the girls pulled on her arm.

"No. Don't touch her. Can't you see the blood on the side of her head?" a man said.

"I can't stand blood. I don't want to see it," a girl squealed.

Jessie's eyes fluttered open. "What happened?"

"I was about to ask you the same question." Bob Harmon helped her to her feet. When she began to sway, he steadied her. "I think you should sit here for a minute. You've got a nasty lump on the side of your head. You must have hit your head when you fell."

"I didn't fall. I was on the bench when something hit me." She was happy to be upright and thinking clearly again. "How did you find me?"

"I was running with the girls, and my assistant called and told me you didn't come back with the boys and to keep a lookout for you." He showed her his phone. "I always carry it in case of emergency. How we found you, is a different story altogether. We happened to see a red-tailed hawk flying in the area. When we came in to get a closer look, we found you lying on the ground."

"Coach, look at this." One of the girls brought a

rock to him that had blood on it.

"Wow, that's a good-sized rock. Hurled out of a slingshot, I think it could knock someone out. No wonder we found you on the ground. I'd say you're lucky it didn't do more damage."

She started to stand. "I need to get to work."

"I'm afraid work will have to wait. I've already called the ambulance, and now the medics will want to check you out. The smart thing to do, if you ask me, after a knock on the head."

"You're right, of course." She looked at the girls watching her. "I feel okay though, and would rather leave." Jessie leaned back on the bench.

"They should be here any minute." Harmon turned to the girls milling about. "You can finish your run back to the school. I'll start back after the ambulance gets here."

"I saw the hawk too. I remember looking up at it, and something flew past me, barely missing me. It must have been a rock. The next one didn't miss, obviously." Jessie saw them both out of the corner of her eye. One with haunted eyes flittering about, and the other behind the tree with a slingshot in his pocket. He was no ghost. She'd like to get her hands on him and give him a piece of her mind. Why had he wanted to hurt her?

After the medics cleaned the gash on the side of her head, they declared she was fine to return to work. They drove her down to her car in the parking lot. She opened her car door. "Thank you for finding me, Bob. I'll be back to run with the team."

"Not tomorrow, I think you could use a day off. If I were you, I wouldn't run alone in the area until we know who hit you with the rock. You should be okay in a group. I have to notify the police and fill out an incident report. It's school policy. I wanted you to know in case someone calls you."

"Thanks for the heads up. See you." She sat down in the car, reaching for her seatbelt. Bob shut the door and waved.

****

He hadn't meant to hit her. The rock was already sailing through the air when she turned her head. It hit her dead on. He figured he had killed her. Rubbing his hands on his pants, he frowned. The rabbits died when the rocks hit them. He figured she would die too. Watching from behind the tree, Billy could see the man watching her. He was a bad man, and Billy didn't want him to get her. Placing another rock in the sling, he was ready, but all the voices of people coming their way caused the other man to run. Billy knew the man. He had seen him before.

Pa would be mad when he found out. He hated when Pa got angry. He could hit harder than any old rock. Besides she saw him and was plenty mad too. "Darn." He kicked at the dirt. "Billy is in big trouble."

Chapter 22

Their conversation finished, Chad stood when Matt's phone buzzed. "I'll catch you later."

Matt nodded and answered line one. "What's up?"

"Chief, Coach Harmon called in a report from the high school. I thought you'd want to know since it involves Jessie. Do you want me to assign someone to check it out?"

"Thanks, Kenny. No need, I was heading out anyway. I'll stop by the school and her store. You know how to reach me if you need to."

Later when Matt entered the bookstore, she was on the phone. "Hi," he mouthed at her. Grabbing a magazine, he sat in one of the leather chairs. He couldn't wait to hear her side of the story. She shouldn't have been there alone.

After hanging up, she walked over to him. "What are you doing here? Usually you're up to your neck in paperwork at this time of the morning." She stood beside his chair, leaning her hip against the arm.

"I had a meeting with Chad earlier. He promised to stop by to see you before he leaves town later." He laced his fingers through hers. "Then I got a call from Kenny about an incident report from the school that involved you. I got Harmon's take on it, and now I want to get your side of the story. You could say I'm

159

here on official business, Miss Reynolds." He smiled at her.

"Let me check this customer out, and I'll come back to tell you my sob story."

"Did you find everything you need?" Jessie went behind the counter.

The man placed several books on the smooth surface. "Maybe a few too many. Your sale table had some good bargains I couldn't pass up. I never bought these hardbacks when they first came out, but now I can afford to buy several to add to my library at home."

His wire-rimmed glasses and full beard streaked with gray yelled professor to her.

"I'm happy we had what you wanted. If you don't see something you're looking for, I can always order it for you. If the books are on sale, you'll get the sale price too. Keep that in mind for the future." Jessie placed his books in a bag along with a store bookmark.

"I will. Reading a book in the evening is my way of relaxing after a long day. I'll be back. I love what you've done with this space. It's so inviting." He smiled at her, reaching for his bag.

"Inviting is what I was going for. Have a nice day."

"Thank you." He walked over to the coffee shop.

Jessie sat down beside Matt. "I had an interesting morning." She recounted what happened during her morning run. "While I was waiting for the medics to check me out. I saw Lizzy's ghost, but I also saw Billy, the man you told me about. He was standing behind the tree with a slingshot in his pocket."

"It's not like him to hurt anyone. At least he never has before. I'll have a talk with him. There has to be something more to the story than what I've heard so far.

If not, I'll arrest him and scare him a bit."

"Don't scare him too much." Jessie frowned. "He seems harmless. It might have been an accident."

"I wouldn't say that lump on your head is harmless. Geez, Jess, you take all the fun out of a job." He frowned when he saw how pale she looked. "Is your head okay?"

"I have a knot on the side right here." She pointed to the spot. "There's a gash where the rock broke the skin, but I'll survive. I've never had something knock me out before. It packed a punch. For me, the scariest thing was waking up on the ground not remembering how I got there."

"Maybe you should take the rest of the day off. You look a little pale."

"Why, Mr. Parker, is that a nice way of saying I look bad?"

"No way, not me. I want to make sure you're okay."

"A slight headache is all, and I checked out fine. The medic told me I might have a headache, but I didn't have a concussion, so that's good."

"It takes quite a blow to knock a person out. It's possible the force and the speed of the rock was enough to do it. I can't imagine what Billy was thinking." Matt stood and walked toward her. His hand gently pulled her hair aside to take a look at her head. "That's quite a knot."

"You're telling me."

"Which brings me to my next question. What were you doing there alone?"

"I was having a chat with a ghost. It's hard to do that with a crowd watching." She grinned. "Besides, I was with the running club and had only planned to stop there for a moment. You already know the rest of the story." She waved her hand to emphasize what she was saying.

"If Harmon and the girls hadn't found you, anything could have happened. Damn, Jess, I'm going to be gray before my time."

"You know, Mr. Parker, a touch of gray might be nice." She patted the hair at his temple. "Although I'm sure it was a fluke, Billy might have seen me as a threat. I don't know how, but I can't climb inside his head to figure it out how he thinks."

"Please don't go there alone again until I've had time to question Billy and his father." Matt gave her shoulders a squeeze.

"You said please." She glanced at him her face lighting up. "Thank you." She stood. "I won't go there alone again until you've talked to him."

"I'm learning, sweetheart." He kissed her cheek. "I'll see you tonight. I need to get back to the station."

"Bummer. I wanted to ask you how it went with Chad, but I guess we can talk later."

"We'll talk tonight." He walked out the door as a customer was walking in. Matt talked with Kenny once he got in the car. Arranging to pick up Dylan, he cleared his schedule for the afternoon. It was time to visit Billy and his dad.

****

Jessie hung up the phone. Kendra would be there in the morning after finding a babysitter for Zoe. She jotted down a couple of questions that came to mind while she talked to Kendra. Waiting for her customers to check out, she glanced several times at the door.

Where was Chad? Matt hadn't said what time he'd be there. She'd be a wreck if she didn't stop this.

"How's your day going?" Molly stood in the open door.

She went to stand beside her friend. "Interesting is the best way to describe the morning I've had."

"I'm not surprised because I see Reba crossing the street right now. She usually comes around when something is happening or about to." Molly pointed with her chin toward the door.

"You're right, Reba always is right on time. I'll wait to tell you both what happened earlier."

"Hello, girls." Reba walked in with a determined look on her face. "I don't have much time, but I knew I needed to see you before I go to a meeting at the church."

"I'll be right back. I need to take care of a customer." Molly went to take their order.

"While she's gone, I think I'm safe in saying you're beginning to understand what I told you before, aren't you? You know what is holding you back and that you must face it. Remember, my dear girl, you have someone who loves you. You'll not have to walk through this alone."

"I know. I'm beginning to understand."

"Good." Reba patted Jessie's shoulder, then smiled and acknowledged Molly coming through the open doors "You're back. Now, Jessie girl, you can tell us both about your morning."

Jessie told them about being knocked out. "I have a goose egg for my trouble, but other than a bump, all is well." Jessie leaned her shoulder against the wall.

"There's more to this story."

"Matt said the same thing."

"Billy may have had the slingshot and even hurled the rock, but it wasn't with you in mind. Watch out for the man you can't see. He's the one you need to keep your eye on." Reba reached for Jessie's hand. "Don't frown, my dear. We don't want worry lines. No amount of moisture cream will reverse deep-set wrinkles. There are no miracle cures, no matter what they say."

"Something every woman knows all too well." Jessie agreed.

"As if you need to worry, dear girl, with your beautiful young skin. It's never too early to start taking care of it, though. No frowning, dear, that's an order. I need to be on my way and you young ladies need to get back to work." She squeezed Jessie's hand. "It'll be all right. You'll see," Reba said quietly to Jessie. She turned on her heels and headed for the entrance. Waving goodbye, she closed the door on her way out.

"She's like a white tornado. It should be a crime for one woman to have all that energy bundled up in her small body." Molly stared dumbfounded at the door. "I think I would shake in my boots if I ever thought she was coming to see me. I don't know how you do it, my friend."

"She always reassures me that all will be okay, but I still am left with my head spinning. The most important thing is, Reba gets me, and she understands what's happening to me. I don't know what I would have done in the beginning if she hadn't come into my life."

"Well, in that regard, you're like two peas in a pod. I don't envy either one of you, and I don't want what you have." She glanced into the coffee shop. "It's back to work for me." Molly turned to leave.

"Molly, did you go to the Blue Cove High School?" Jessie asked.

"Yes, why?" Molly turned back around.

"I was wondering that's all. I should get to work, too." Jessie heard the bell above the door ring. She made a mental note to ask Molly if she ever saw or heard anything suspicious at the school. Jessie waved at Chad when he walked in. "I'm glad you're here. Matt said you might stop by before you left town."

"If it works for you to talk now, I'll get a sandwich next door and be back. I have another round of interviews with the town council this afternoon. I need to get them all in while I'm in town."

"Perfect. I'll be here when you get back."

"Would you like something?" Chad walked toward the coffee shop.

"No, I'm good."

Jessie grabbed her small notebook and pen then went to the table in the center of the store to wait for Chad. She scrolled through her text messages and read the one from Katie.

We're close to setting the date. I'm excited and afraid. I think I might be catching what you've got. Cold feet! Love Dylan to the moon and back, but I love being single too. No one to answer to but me. Lol.

Jessie chuckled. Katie had a way with words.

"A smile looks good on you." Chad pulled out the chair across from her.

"A text from my friend. She always makes me laugh. Katie is the reason I moved here."

"How long have you been friends?" Chad placed his lunch on the table and sat down.

"Since the first day of kindergarten when she told me we would be best friends." Jessie folded her hands in front of her on the table. "She was right. We have been best friends ever since."

"Matt and I went from grade school through high school as friends, too."

"What changed?"

"Lizzy happened." He rubbed his temple. "I can't blame it all on her. I saw too much, and I couldn't get anyone to listen. Basically, the authorities told me to go home like a good little boy. When Matt wouldn't listen to me, I got mad and left town. It was easier to run, or at least I thought it would be. It has plagued me ever since."

"I can only imagine. What'd you see?"

"I saw small things that didn't add up. Lizzy was changing before my eyes. There were all these girls at school talking about being the next great model and hanging out with Lizzy. No offense, but I'm talking about girls who would never get their faces on the cover of a magazine. Girls Lizzy would normally have nothing to do with." He took a bite of his sandwich and swig of his tea. "Another strange thing was Kendra and Lizzy had been best friends from the time they were young and a few weeks into our senior year, they were no longer speaking."

"Friends fight. Katie and I often did," Jessie rationalized.

"True, but Lizzy blew Kendra off. She wouldn't speak to Kendra at all. That's when she took up with Grace. I felt sorry for Grace."

"Why?"

"Because Lizzy was mean to her. Grace was trying

to be a friend and hung in there with Lizzy, taking her bitchiness. I wasn't that kind. I could give it out as much as she could." Chad frowned. "Let's leave it at we didn't hit it off."

"Do you remember anything that seemed out of place to you?"

"There were lots of things. I followed Lizzy on more than one occasion. I saw her meet with some guy in an old shack out in the woods not too far away from her memorial." He gulped down some more tea. "I told this to Matt earlier. A few days before her murder, I saw the same guy with her brother, a photography teacher, and another man. I think he was a teacher, but all I ever saw was his back. He was a tall man with dark hair. They also saw me. Later that same day, when I went to my car in the parking lot at school, they pulled me into a car, took me off-site, and beat me up. They dumped me back at my car. When I got back to school a few days later, I heard the photography teacher resigned, and Lizzy was dead."

"You must have thought about this many times over the years."

"I have." Chad rested his elbows on his knees.

"What scenario played out the most in your head? If you were going to give a police interview, what details would stand out to you?" Jessie jotted down a few notes as he started to talk.

"I know there was something kinky going on. There were too many girls saying the same thing. I know Lizzy's brother was involved somehow and a couple of teachers at the school. I believe the police department turned a blind eye, and that's why they were able to get away with it. Maybe they paid them off."

Chad leaned back in his chair. "They still could be in operation for all I know."

"What would your summation be if you had to make one?"

"Putting two and two together, I would say it was some kind of child pornography ring. It's sick if you ask me. These were people the girls should have been able to trust. I know there was someone behind it all and out of sight. I'm afraid Lizzy was the one who got the other girls involved. Peer pressure and the desire to fit in can mess with people and trap them."

"I think you're right." She closed her notebook. "I hope you and Matt can work through your differences. He could use a good friend back in his life."

"We're on our way. It may take time, but we'll keep working at it. I guess we have you to thank for it. Matt found a keeper when he found you. I told him those exact words this morning. There's no doubt he understands it, and you mean the world to him."

"Thank you. That's nice of you to say." She closed her notebook. "If you think of anything else, be sure to let me know. I guess I need to do some checking into Ted McKenzie. Do you know if he's still in the area?"

"I don't know. Be careful. He's dangerous, and so are his friends."

"I will. I hope you get the job and move back to Blue Cove. You belong here."

Chad stood to leave. "It was nice to meet you, Jessie. I'll be seeing you again."

She walked with him to the door and waved goodbye. This town had more than its share of secrets. She had walked into a hotbed of crime when she moved here.

A sudden chill ran down her arms along with the feeling someone was watching her.

Chapter 23

Matt and Dylan arrived at the small homestead. It had been there as far back as Matt could remember. Mr. Sullivan was cordial but frowned when he opened the door to them.

"What did my kid do now, officer?" He opened the screen door to let them in.

"We want to ask him some questions, is all. You got a nice place here," Matt told him.

"It was my pa's and his pa's before him. Someday it'll be Billy's if he can keep his wits about him. Have a seat. I'll get the darn boy." He went to the bottom of the stairs and yelled. "Billy, you get yourself down here. The police are here to talk to you." He flicked Billy's head when he walked past him. "What'd you do now, you fool boy?"

"Nothing, Pa, I swear."

"Get in there and be respectful."

"Hi, Billy." Matt stood to shake his hand. "You can sit. I have a few questions to ask you."

"I didn't mean to hurt the girl. She moved her head." He wrung his hands.

"What fool thing did you do now, boy? I swear I'll tan your hide." Jeb glared at his son.

Matt watched Billy's face blanch under his father's stare and thunderous voice. "I'm sure he has an explanation." Matt tried to defuse the situation. "Go ahead, Billy."

"The lady was sitting on the bench. She was looking at the hawk above her head. I wasn't trying to hit her. There was a bad man in the tree behind the lady. I've seen him before. He's bad."

"When did you see him?"

"Lots of times." He rubbed his nose on the back of his hand. "Tried to tell the policeman, but he told me to go home. Billy went home. I'm not dumb."

"Why don't you tell us now, Billy? We'll listen." Dylan folded his arms across his chest.

"You can't do nothing. She's dead, and she was nice." Billy clenched his fist tight.

"Who's dead?" Matt asked.

"Both the ladies. They killed my friend, and I killed the lady sitting on the bench. She fell down dead. She sat up again, but then the men took her away. I killed her."

"She's not dead. You didn't kill the lady." Matt leaned toward where Billy sat.

"I wanted to hit the man. He watched her. He was in the woods when you took my friend away."

Matt was beginning to make sense of the awkward conversation. "Who took your friend?"

"You did." Billy jumped up and paced.

"Was Grace your friend?"

He bobbed his head. "My friend. She waved at me and talked to me. Never called me stupid."

"Did you put her in the cabin?" Matt asked.

"Billy hid her. They left her in the cold. I brought her in where it was warm." He swiped at the tears rolling down his cheek. "Tell the lady I'm sorry. Billy likes her. She's nice,"

"Yes, she is. I'll tell her. Don't worry. If you see the bad man again, you tell me, Billy, and I'll believe you." Matt stood. "No more hitting the lady with rocks from your slingshot."

"No, sir." Billy looked Matt in the eye.

"Thank you, Jeb, for letting us talk to your boy. I learned a lot." Matt shook Jeb's hand.

"I don't know how you understood anything that boy said. I don't half the time. He's a grown man with the mind of a kid."

"He may be slow, sir, but he's not dumb. He knows what is going on more than we understand." Matt and Dylan walked out to the car.

"Did you understand that conversation? Why didn't you press him harder?" Dylan asked.

"He's afraid of his dad. One of these days he's going to figure out he's stronger than his dad. I wouldn't want to be Jeb when that happens." Matt glanced at Dylan. "Did you notice the more nervous he became, the less sense he made?"

"I noticed it all right. It's obvious Billy has been hit more than a few times by his dad. How old do you think he is?"

"Around our age I guess." Matt adjusted the side mirror. "I think Billy saw Grace murdered and he'll be able to pick the guy out when the time comes."

"Why'd he hurt Jessie?"

"He didn't mean to, but he saw the man again, which means he is still is in the area. I'm going to make sure Jessie stays with a group and doesn't wander off alone. Obviously, the guy is watching her."

"You think he can ID the guy?" Dylan glanced at

Matt.

"I do, and as soon as I narrow the field, I'll show him a couple of photos. Chad believes Ted McKenzie is tied to the crime somehow. I think we need to find out where he lives and have a talk with him."

"Talk about awful. That would be a parent's worst nightmare. Have your daughter murdered only to find out at some point her brother might be involved,"

"Even if he's not directly linked, he would have to be living with some major guilt." Matt started the car. "I'm afraid this case might open some major wounds in our town."

"Yeah, and the McKenzie family too." Dylan latched his seat belt when Matt started the car. "It's hard to believe this has been going on for so long and no one caught it."

"Jeremy is checking out the Internet. He said the site has a strong firewall. It appears reputable on the front end. We'll see what he finds once he gets in it and takes a look around. I sent him a few of the photos of the girls so he could check the site for their faces once he gets in." The car bounced over the dirt road.

"Damn, we live in a different world. Now that I'm getting married I think about it all the time. How do you protect your kids from this stuff?" Dylan braced himself when the car hit a deep rut in the road, pitching him upward. His seat belt pulled tight.

"Good question. It's changed, but this was going on when we were in high school. We've grown up in the computer age, and I think we're going to have to stop thinking like small town cops. Crime is everywhere, especially if there's money it." Matt pulled onto a paved road, leaving the bumps of the dirt road behind.

"Unless it's a crime of passion there's usually some money changing hands. If adult males are involved, you can practically guarantee it." Dylan looked out the side window.

"I'm happy to see the last of that road for a while." Matt glanced in his rearview mirror.

"Me too. I hit my head more than once." Dylan chuckled.

"I have a feeling that someone in the police department turned a blind eye to this when it was happening. I don't relish going to talk to all the parents of the girls involved. My first several are tomorrow. They have to be notified as soon as possible. I have a list for Kip and you to do, also. We'll have to move fast to set our trap to catch the owner of the book. I don't want him to come back and find the book gone." Matt stopped the car at the stop sign near the highway

"Gary had the copies done this morning. He told me to tell you it was finished and Gordon Tanner would be by during his break to pick it up. The book and notebook should be back in place before the end of the day. Gary rigged a small camera together, and he'll instruct Tanner where and how to place it. The camera will hold the pictures and send them back to the station on Gary's command."

"Yeah, Gary told me he would be able to monitor it from his office. Isn't technology wonderful?" Matt chuckled. "Especially, when it works like it's supposed to."

"On the off days, it can be a pain. I've had a few of those days lately. I wiped out a couple of reports and had to start them all over again." Dylan glanced at Matt.

"You have that expression. What are you thinking?"

"I'm wondering why the man is watching Jessie. Unless he saw Jessie talking to Kendra and is trying to find out what she knows."

"What makes you think that?" Dylan asked.

"Jessie told me the day she talked with Kendra at the store, Kendra suddenly was reluctant to talk. Jessie was sure she had seen someone in the coffee shop and got nervous."

"Is the guy stalking Kendra or Jessie?" Dylan asked.

"Both maybe, I don't know. Kendra is one of the girls in the book. He could be blackmailing her. Picture being a mother of a young girl, and I think you can understand why she's guarded and wants to protect herself and family from the past." Matt signaled his turn.

"Besides the embarrassment, there's got to be some fear involved. I can only imagine how this affected all those girls and must still be impacting them. It's a wonder any woman can trust a man at all." Dylan stretched out his legs.

"We have to close this ring down." Matt waited for an opening. "Wow, this road is busy today." He watched the steady stream of cars whiz by.

"Agree. Hell, I know what I would do if it were my daughter. We're going to have some irate parents on our hands. The school will have a few lawsuits, too, if it turns out there is a teacher involved somewhere."

"What about the police? If they closed their eyes to it, the city may be facing several lawsuits." Finally, enough space opened between cars. Matt turned onto the road leading back into town.

"That's why insurance is necessary." Dylan leaned his head back against the seat. "Can't say I miss bouncing in those ruts. Paved roads are nice."

"You've got that right." Matt grinned.

Chapter 24

Jessie stepped out the door into a beautiful morning. Everything always seemed better with the sun shining. A spring like day was in the forecast, and she was going to celebrate it with a run after work. Matt promised to run with her later. She smiled to herself. He was being kind after asking her not to run alone for a while. Honking the horn as she passed the Inn, she headed to town and the store. Putting the top down on her convertible sounded mighty tempting. Her fingers kept time to the beat of one of her favorite tunes.

Last night, Matt did everything possible to make her feel at ease and comfortable. He was super sweet, but it seemed as if he was walking on eggshells. The question is why. He told her about his visit to Billy's house and his conversation with Chad. The details he added made her laugh on several occasions. Their conversation was lively, dinner was great, and the only real surprise of the evening is when she learned about the man watching her. It was a bit unsettling, but nothing new. It seemed to come with the job. At least she knew that Billy wasn't trying to kill her. He was her defender in an odd painful kind of way. She rubbed the small knot on her head. It was starting to shrink, which was good.

Matt was charming, and though she had wanted to

tell him, she didn't want to spoil their evening with her sob story. Was it possible that he knew something? There was no way he could unless Jeremy said something to him. A demon from her past, the events of that day still had the power to paralyze her. Matt would have listened, been kind, but she wasn't ready to talk to him, which made no sense at all. It wasn't like it was her fault or anything. Darn, why did life have to be so complicated sometimes?

"Face it, girl, you're all grown up and have dealt with a lot scarier junk." She gave herself a pep talk. "You've seen ghosts, faced down a serial killer, and yet here you are, afraid for no good reason. You can do this, Jessie. I know you can."

Parking her car at the back of the store, gathering courage, she grabbed her phone out of her purse. Her fingers began moving across the small letters. She read the message, and before she lost her nerve, she hit send. Her text to Matt was on its way and still staring her in the face. *We need to talk before I lose my resolve.* There was no turning back now.

With that settled in her mind, Jessie walked into her store to get ready to open. Kendra would be in later, and she had several questions she wanted to ask. Taking the money from the safe, she opened the cash register and placed the cash neatly inside. The bills always started lined up in an orderly fashion but got sloppier as the day wore on. Looking around the store, Jessie noted how it sparkled. The new cleaning service had done a great job. Her father told it was a good business investment on a weekly basis to bring in an outside service. From the smell and appearance of the store, she was inclined to agree that it was money well spent.

Audrey had left the mail stacked on the counter. She saw the envelope with her name on it. No return address, but she knew the handwriting. She had received enough of them over the years. Matt would get to read this one. Stuffing the letter into her purse, she wasn't about to read it now and let her old stalker's awful words ruin her day.

"Hi, Molly." She opened the doors between the businesses.

"Isn't a gorgeous day? It makes me want to get outside." Molly walked over to where Jessie stood.

"I know what you mean. Matt promised to run with me after work. It's perfect weather for running outside, not freezing or sweltering."

"Why anyone likes to run beats me." Molly laughed.

"If you didn't make such wonderful treats, I wouldn't have to." She grinned. "I'm not telling the truth. I run because I like it. What can I say? I'm an oddity."

"Not so odd, millions of others run too." Molly turned to leave. "Can I get you anything?"

"No, I'm good." Jessie walked to the front of the store to unlock the door. The longer she stood there, the greater the sensation became that she was not alone. She took a quick peek around but didn't see anyone. The tiny hairs on her neck stood up. Seen or unseen, some presence was in her bookstore.

****

Matt read Jessie's message on his way out of City Hall after a meeting with the Mayor. Maybe his girl trusted him after all. "Hey, sweetheart. I got your message."

"I figured you might call."

"When do you want to talk?" he asked.

"How about we have pizza at my house after we run? You did promise you'd run with me.

"I did. I'll meet you there after work. I'll order the pizza for six-thirty, which gives us time to run and get back to your house to meet the delivery man."

"Thank you, I appreciate it. See you later."

"Okay, have a nice day. Oh, and Jess, remember I love you."

"You must, you're going to run with me, and I know you hate jogging. If that's not love, what is?" He could hear the laughter in her voice.

Matt chuckled. "I'll have to remember that in the future. Instead of flowers, I'll jog with you. See you."

"I wouldn't mind the flowers too. See you soon."

Matt would pick up some roses on his way to her place. Why not flowers to celebrate their run together? Jess was taking his request seriously. She agreed not to run alone until he knew who was watching her. Billy didn't like the guy, and he was a good judge of character.

When Matt walked into the station, Kenny handed him a list of phone calls he needed to make.

"Chad, this is Matt. I'm returning your call. I hear congratulations are in order."

"How'd you hear already?"

"I'd say it's a small town and all that, but I was in a meeting at town hall, and the Mayor told me. I want to be the first to welcome you back to town."

"Thanks, man, I know being here is what I need at this time in my life. I was looking for an excuse to come home, and Jessie handed it to me. Then I saw the job ad, and it seemed like a perfect time. If you were still angry, I might have decided differently, but it seems like the timing was right for both of us."

"I agree. As usual, Jessie knew."

"She's something. You've got a good one there. Jessie is a looker, but there's a lot more to her than that. Five minutes into my conversation with her I knew she's worth giving up your freedom for. Treat her well."

"I intend to. When do you start your new job?"

"The first of the month. I checked out a place today, and I'm going back to sign the papers. I liked it. I've had my condo on the market for a couple of weeks. My realtor called this morning, and I have an offer. I countered, so we'll see."

"Good luck with it. If you need help moving into your new place, let me know. I can get a few of the guys to help.

"Thanks, but the city pays for movers. I like that idea. I'll see you in a few weeks. I'm heading out of town this evening."

"Take care and let me know if I can help in any way."

Gordon Tanner was next on his call list. He wanted Matt to know the book was back in its hiding place and the camera was in operation. Now all they had to do was wait. Matt hung up, turning his chair to look at the window. The weather was perfect for a stroll in the park. Several people must have got the memo. Young kids were on the playground with their moms looking on as they played. After the cold days, and a few humid hot ones, today was perfect, and a welcome change. Winter still could have a gasp or two left in her, but people were ready to enjoy the good weather today. A knock at his door reminded him he still had work to do.

"Come in," he called out.

Dylan walked in. "Kip and I were doing the research on pornography rings in the area you asked us to do. I think you might be interested in what we found." He laid the papers on the table, and the spent the next hour poring over the pages in front of them.

"Damn, this is bigger than we thought. Thankfully, the book is back in place now before news of this starts to get out. It will spread like wildfire, once parents are notified."

Chapter 25

The odd sensation wasn't going away. Jessie stood by the open doors into Joe's again, looking for some unnamed, unseen visitor. Customers came and went all morning, but the other presence never left her store. Not one ghost, manifestation, or weird person had appeared that would account for the strange feeling making her spine prickly. Friend or foe, she didn't know, and it seemed to grow stronger as the day wore on. An eerie sense of being watched crept over her off and on. Another thing to add to a growing list of strange occurrences that have happened in her life.

Knowing all of this she still wasn't prepared for what happened when Kendra came into her store a few minutes later. It was as if hell had broken loose around them, but everything remained the same. All Jessie could think of as she went to greet Kendra was the stormy night a few days ago.

"Kendra, I'm glad you could make it. How's Zoe today?"

"As active as ever. My mom is watching her. She loves to watch her but is always ready for me to come home. Zoe can be a handful. You have to be on your toes when she's awake. It's constant movement and chatter." Kendra smiled.

"Sit back and relax for a few minutes. You could

use it." Jessie pointed to the two leather chairs. "Those chairs are nice and comfy. Would you like a coffee?" Jessie asked.

"I would love one." Kendra sat, leaning her head back against the soft leather.

"I'll be right back." Jessie went to Joe's and returned a few minutes later with two cups of coffee and some lemon bars.

Kendra took a sip of the coffee. "I love my daughter, but this quiet moment to sip my coffee without one hundred and one questions by a two-year-old is sheer heaven. So are these lemon bars."

Jessie wasn't sure she'd call what was happening around them heaven, but she'd wait and see. "You told me the last time we talked that Lizzy had changed. Everyone I talk to says the same thing, but nobody seems to know why. Do you?" Jessie saw a dark shadow cross Kendra's face. There was a battle playing out around her. She knew the moment Kendra made up her mind. The other presence was gone.

"I do. I'm ashamed to talk about it." Tears trickled down her cheeks. "I've carried the secret for too long, worried that someone would find out. I need to tell someone." She took the tissue Jessie handed her.

"You can tell me when you're ready."

"When you're in high school, it's all about having fun. I was an A student, with a dream of becoming a teacher one day. I think I would have made a good teacher." She sniffed. "Lizzy came to me in our senior year and told me about this man who thought I had the makings of a model. Being in the fashion industry had never been on my radar, but being told you have a lovely face and great bone structure can turn the head of most girls. As a matter of fact, it did." She sobbed. "It started with people I knew and trusted doing a photo shoot of me. Then I was told a professional photographer would be taking over." She grabbed another tissue from the box Jessie was holding.

"Take your time." Jessie patted her hand. "What happened?"

"This has been bottled up for so long. I'm not sure I can hold it back or that I'll make any sense at all. My parents don't even know about it. I'm not sure I can do this now. What if someone comes in?"

"I will close the store for as long as it takes. Take a deep breath." Jessie jumped up and locked the front door and the ones leading into the coffee shop.

"When I met the photographer, he was young and handsome. He was very persuasive, smooth, and dreamy, which is a lethal combination for a teenage girl. He convinced me I had to remove some of my clothes. He told me that companies wanted to see the girls that they would be hiring in various stages of dress for different commercial shoots. It started with him lifting my skirt to show more of my legs. When he told me to remove my shirt, I said I wouldn't do it. He got close to me like he was going to kiss me, but he ripped open my shirt instead. At first, I was stunned, I stood there exposed for the world to see. He said something, but I didn't hear him. At some point, I fought back. I kicked him as hard as I could right where it hurt, and ran out clutching my blouse together. Somehow I managed to go to my locker and put on my coat. Unnoticed, I went home.

"What happened next?"

"Lizzy berated me for being a chicken and told me

I was going to ruin everything. I no longer cared. I felt violated and lied to. I wanted no part of it. A lot of other girls were trapped and weren't as lucky as I was at getting away."

"I've seen the book with all the girls in it. I want to be honest with you."

"Oh, God, you've seen the pictures. Who else has?"

"The police. A new teacher at the school found the book, and there's an investigation under way. You'll have to be quiet about it for now. A trap has been set to catch the people who are a part of this."

"I'm so ashamed," she cried. "What they did was wrong. I felt helpless to stop them. They threatened me. Told me to keep my mouth shut, or they'd shut it permanently."

"Who are they?"

"I'm not sure I should tell. I need to think it through." Kendra blew her nose. "Once I got married, I didn't want it to come out at all. My husband doesn't know anything about it."

"I won't pressure you to tell me, but I hope you'll tell the police someday. These guys need to go to jail." She knew all too well the emotions Kendra was feeling.

"I felt dirty and ashamed. I should've told someone, but I couldn't do it. I just wanted to forget it ever happened. Now I live with the guilt."

"Kendra, it wasn't your fault. You were assaulted by the very people you should've been able to trust. This happens too often, and we're going to close their operation down." Jessie paused. "Is that why Lizzy died?"

"I don't know why they killed her. It still doesn't

make sense. She was the one who brought the girls to them."

"Is it possible she wanted out?"

"Anything is possible, I guess. As far as I know, Lizzy was messed up with it until she was found murdered. With all my heart, I hope she found a way out and made peace with her life. I will live with the guilt of it forever. I should have told someone, but I didn't." Kendra cried.

Jessie reached for her hand, holding it. "Look, Kendra, I know what it's like to be a victim. You heap guilt on yourself no matter what you do. The real guilty people here are the those who were supposed to be looking out for you and the other girls. You were young, and they were in a position of trust. Maybe you couldn't do anything about them then, but you can do something about them now. I'm here to help you. We can do this together. You'll find strength when you start to fight back." She was talking to herself. It was time to face and fight the fear she had carried in the back of her mind.

"Where do I start? I don't want this to ever happen to my little girl."

"Keep Zoe in the front of your mind. Do it for her. It's time to talk to the police. Why didn't you go to them before?" Jessie grabbed some tissues from the box and slipped them into Kendra's hand.

"I didn't trust anyone. I lived in fear my pictures would end up on a porn site on the Internet." Kendra wiped the tears running down her cheeks.

"I don't want to worry you, but they may already have. We have someone looking into it now."

"I'll think about what you've said. If I do decide to

tell my story, will you go with me?" Kendra gathered her tissues in her hand. "I can't do it alone."

"You don't have to. I'll be with you from beginning to end." Jessie promised her.

"I need to pick up Zoe. My mother made me promise not to be gone long and you should open your store. Thank you for listening to me." Kendra stood and hugged Jessie.

"One last question. You don't have to answer it, but I'm hopeful that you will. Did anyone ever touch you inappropriately?"

The tears began again. "Yes." She hurried toward the door. "Yes, and it still makes me angry to think I was too weak to stop him."

Jessie unlocked the front door to let Kendra out. She watched until she was safely in her car and driving away. She knew the pain. She'd seen it often enough and experienced her own. Arranging the books on the display table, Jessie felt a new sense of determination rise in her. She would help these girls no matter what.

Chapter 26

Jessie grinned at the man running beside her. The sweat ran down his neck, the sound of his shoes hit the path in tandem with hers. He was all sleek and lathered like a panther in motion, a real turn-on. What was not to love about him? Besides being handsome, he was honoring his promise. Yep, he was worth keeping.

"What are you smiling at?" He asked glancing at her.

"It's a girl thing. You wouldn't understand" She picked up her pace.

His speed matched hers. "I might. I've been known to like all things about girls." He chuckled.

"I'm sure you have." She grinned. "It's personal." She darted past him.

He caught up. "What are you trying to do, kill me?"

"Who me?" she asked playfully. "Never, I'm still discovering what I like about you." She picked up her pace again.

"Would you quit leaving me in the dust?" He strained to match her pace. "It's hard on my male ego to admit that you're a much better runner than I am. Prettier too. Although, I admit that running behind you has few perks."

"Mr. Parker, you have a way with words. I bet you

say that to all the girls." She pushed up the final hill to the cottage and beat him to the door. She laughed when he grabbed her by the waist, swinging her off the ground.

"I've got you now." He swung her around in a circle, letting her slip to the ground in the circle of his arms.

"You sure do." She gazed into his eyes, the heat visible between them.

"Well, if it isn't my long-lost neighbor. I'm sorry I didn't mean to interrupt anything." Liam laughed.

"Why don't I believe you?" Matt rolled his eyes and let go of Jessie.

"Sorry, old man, I couldn't help myself. You two looked too cozy. What can I say?"

Jessie did a few leg stretches and tilted her neck to one side and then the other. "You'll never grow up. I can't wait until you're serious about a woman, and I get to torture you. I think it should be great fun."

"You'd never do it, Jessie. It's not in you. Let's face it. You're too nice. But me, on the other hand, I live for these moments." Liam grinned at them. "Carry on. I need to get back to work." Liam turned to leave, then stopped. "You two should come by the bar some Friday or Saturday. We have live music, and folks are enjoying it. We've had some great reviews."

"We should go, Matt. It might be fun."

"We'll plan for it." Matt opened the door to the cottage holding the screen and motioned for her to go in before him. "Pizza should be here in a few minutes." Matt glanced at his watch.

"I'll be back in a few." Jessie walked past him into her room and closed the door. When she came out again, Matt was dressed and sitting in his favorite chair. "You're fast." She smiled at him.

"Nothing to it." He grinned. "You girls have more stuff to do."

"I wonder what that says about us. It takes us more to look presentable, or what?"

"I won't touch that one. When you come out looking like you do, it's worth every minute spent. I haven't been disappointed yet." Matt looked her over and whistled.

"You're sweet." Jessie walked into the kitchen. She took two plates out of the cabinet and began to set the table. After filling the glasses with ice, she placed a pitcher of tea on the table.

"Pizza is here. I'm hungry. Let's eat." He came into the kitchen carrying the box.

"Me too. Smells yummy." Jessie placed a slice on her plate along with some salad.

Matt scarfed down his first slice of pizza and reached for the second one. "Gino must have made the pie tonight. He gets the crust perfect. He still tosses it. It's great to watch him in action."

"You're right. it's especially good tonight. I've seen Gino toss the dough a couple of times. It's always fun to watch him spin it."

"Are you ready to tell me what your cryptic message was all about earlier?"

"I will when were through eating. Did Jeremy talk to you?" she asked.

"What do you mean?" His expression was wary.

"Did he tell you anything about my past?"

"Only that you would understand what these girls were going through and you'd fight for them. He said I should ask you about it, but I figured if you wanted to talk to me you would."

"I know I need to talk to someone and I trust you." She handed him the sealed letter she had stuffed in her pocket earlier. "When we're finished you can go in the living room and read this while I clean up." She placed the letter beside Matt's plate.

They talked about the store until their meal was finished. Matt went to sit in his favorite chair, and she cleaned the kitchen. Even with the water running she could her his occasional swear words as he read the letter. She turned off the water and went to the couch across from him.

"How many of these have you received?" He waved the letter in the air.

"I stopped counting a few years ago. I quit reading them about the same time." She grabbed the pillow, clutching it to her chest. She curled her legs underneath her.

"Did you give his letters to the police?" Matt frowned. "Damn, Jess, this is vile. What the hell is going on?"

"I did at first, but it didn't stop them from coming. I guess I gave up and moved on." She turned away from him.

"He obviously didn't. You know better than to do nothing. Start talking." His hand clenched at his side.

"Well, first of all, I didn't know better, I was only in high school when this began. Between my junior and senior year to be exact. I watched their little girls several times that summer. They were sweet little girls, and I liked his wife." Jessie paused. "In the beginning it was okay, but the more I babysat for them, the weirder he got. One day I came home and told my mom I wouldn't watch the girls anymore because their dad was giving me the creeps."

"What did he do?"

"Nothing major, but I was afraid to be alone in a room with him. That's when he'd brush up against me. He'd get inches from my face and stare at me. I couldn't stand the way he looked at me."

"How did he look at you?" Matt leaned forward in the chair.

"Like I was his next meal. I can't explain it. All I know I didn't want to be anywhere near the man."

"What'd your parents say?" Matt frowned.

"Not much at first. My mom said I didn't have to babysit if I was uncomfortable. Every time they called she'd made an excuse for me." Jessie twisted the fringe on the pillow.

"What happened next?"

"I saw his car drive past me when I was running home from Katie's house one evening. He slammed on his brakes, backed his car onto the sidewalk in front of me, and jumped out. He yanked me off balance, grabbing me by the arm. I fell toward his chest. All the while, he screamed at me and twisted my arm." She paused. "I thought he was going to hit me. Thankfully, the lights of another car brought him back to reality. He pushed me away, and I fell to the ground. What he said to me was the beginning of my worst nightmare. "The next time my wife calls, you'll babysit. Before he got back in the car, he told me, 'If you tell anyone about our conversation, you'll live to regret it.'"

"Did you tell anyone?" Matt asked.

"Not a first. I was busy at school and managed

never to be around when they called. I finally broke down and told Katie. Every time I went outside, he came outside and stood on his porch, glaring at me. They lived a few houses down the block on the other side of the street from us."

"You should've told your parents." Matt moved over to the couch and put his arm around her.

"I know that now, but I was young and didn't want to hurt his wife. I liked her." She leaned her head on his shoulder. "As time went on, I started getting letters with sexual content. I gave them to my father. My dad called the police, and the police went to his house to warn him."

"What happened next?" Matt's hand fisted as his side.

"His wife left with their daughters, which made me feel guilty, so I understand when Kendra told me she never told the police she was too ashamed."

"You know you had nothing to feel guilty about." He rubbed his hand up and down her back.

"In my heart I knew I didn't, but my mind kept telling me something different." She twisted a strand of hair around her finger, her voice barely audible. He started stalking me. Everywhere I went he would be nearby watching me. From football games to nights out with my friends, I always saw him out of the corner of my eye lurking somewhere in the area. My parents got a restraining order, but it didn't do any good. One day he showed up school." She took a deep breath.

"What happened, sweetheart? You can tell me." Matt held his breath.

"He followed me into the girl's bathroom where he attacked me, slamming me against the wall. My head hit so hard I saw stars." Jessie shook her head. "Strange thing is I used to think people made that up about seeing stars. I had a hard time staying upright, but luck was on my side. I managed to fight back. I got off one strong kick that hit him where it hurts and sent him cursing to the ground. I turned to run, but he was able to grab my foot. I slipped out of my shoe and made it to the principal's office before he could recover and come after me. They called the police. I had a concussion, but I was alive."

"I'm sorry, Jess. I'm sorry the system failed you." He wiped her tears from her cheek.

"During the trial, we found out two other girls hadn't been as lucky as I was." She shuddered. He's out of prison. I was notified a few weeks ago, and then I got this. At least I have confirmation that he knows the town where I live."

"No wonder you want to help these girls and battered women everywhere. Jeremy said I'd understand, and he was right. It's a wonder you'd want to be anywhere near a man." He touched her cheek tenderly. "How are we going to solve this case and keep you safe from this creep at the same time?"

"If anyone can, it's you. The thing is, I know he's coming. I had a dream about him the other night, and I have to face him again. I want to be able to go into my future without always looking over shoulder."

Matt pulled her tight against him. "What's his name? I want to see if we can track him."

"Stuart," she said in a soft voice. "Stuart Adler." She hugged the pillow tighter.

"I have a new nickname for you. Did you know that?" Matt pushed her hair out of her eyes.

She turned to look at him. "What?"

He shook his head. "Someday I will tell you what it is, but not today. Right now all I want to do is hold you."

Chapter 27

Matt flipped on the light in the kitchen on his way to his laptop and favorite chair. Jessie was in his thoughts. He was angry for her, and all the young girls at the high school who had become victims of men who should have known better. How scared and vulnerable she must have felt all those years ago. A budding beauty in high school. Stuart was obsessed with her.

Logging into Records he found Stuart Adler's rap sheet. Jessie's father had called several times, and the police had issued warnings with each call. Damn, Jess was right. He had been released from prison a couple of weeks ago. Stuart made his first parole meeting with his counselor a few days ago. After reading the letter, Matt knew it was only a matter of time before Adler would come after Jessie.

He wrote an email to the lead investigator in charge of the case, wanting to know if any of the other girls had received threatening letters. The letter Jessie had let him read was not only threatening but obscene. How many had she received over the years? At least now he understood why she held something of herself back. Why wouldn't she?

Grabbing the remote, he turned on the sports channel. Spring baseball training was in full swing. He needed to buy tickets for a Yankees' home game. They could take in a game, catch a Broadway show and have dinner, a nice weekend date. The popcorn sound on his phone notified him that he had an email. After reading the reply to his note, he was more concerned than ever.

She answered the phone after a few rings "You miss me already?"

"I missed you after you closed the door and locked it."

"What's up? Something tells me you didn't call to pass the time. You read about Stuart, and now you're worried about my safety, aren't you?"

"Maybe, which has me wondering how did a cold case turn into porn trafficking, and the possibility of dealing with a vindictive man seeking revenge."

"I have no clue," she laughed.

"We're about to find out." Matt muted the TV. "Jess, I don't want to upend your life again. Is it possible for you to sleep at the Inn at night? I would rest easier if you weren't alone. I could stay at your place if you want. Would that work better for you? I have no idea how long we have until Adler comes looking."

"Let me think about it. I hate to always need a babysitter. I'm not that girl any longer, and I think I could handle him."

"True, if he plays fair. I don't think he will. He'll be looking for a chance to take you by surprise. His letter says it all. He holds you responsible for his obsession. I know it doesn't make sense, but his anger has been building all these years in prison." Matt paused. "The other thing is you're the only one he's kept in contact with. No one else. That doesn't bode well, Jess. Let me know tomorrow what you want to do."

"I will. Goodnight, Matt, and don't worry."

"Easier said than done, sweetheart. I read the letter, remember?"

****

Jessie woke up with a start. Plumping up the pillow behind her head, she tried to focus in the dark. Adler filled her dreams again. Each nightmare was more intense than the one before. It made her wonder if her showdown with Stuart was getting closer. How was she going to handle the first moment she saw him again? Memories of him seemed to freeze her in place much less the real-life version standing in front of her. Older now, she would like to believe things would be different, but she wasn't sure she could rely on any training when it came to Stuart Adler. Pulling the covers up to her chin she rolled onto her side. He was a violent man, and she was afraid of him.

She glanced at the clock out of her one open eye. Daylight saving time might give more light in the evening, but it was darker in the mornings. Not even a trace of light showed as she peeked out the window over her bed. The sun should at least be out before she had to get up. She pushed the hair out of her face and sat on the edge of the bed. "Oh, well, you can't have everything your way. Get moving," she mumbled as she shuffled her way into her morning ritual.

Putting bread into the toaster, she opened the file on the table. The paper was running the first article on Elizabeth McKenzie today. Matt had read it and thought it would stir the waters. Charlotte had loved the article, and Jessie was feeling hopeful some of the girls would be willing to talk after reading the story. She buttered her toast and turned off the whistling teakettle. Pouring hot water into a mug, she put a tea bag in the water. Carrying her tea into the living room, she opened the curtains to watch the sunrise over the cove. "Okay, now this makes it all worthwhile." She sipped her hot tea. "Another beautiful morning," she sighed. Would she ever tire of watching the sun rise over the cove?

First the article this morning, then later today, Matt, Kip, and Dylan would begin speaking to the parents and the girls found in the book. There had to be a few of the girls who were around at the time and knew something about the murders of Elizabeth and Grace. Maybe like Kendra, they were too afraid or ashamed to talk to anyone. With any luck, the article would start the wheels turning. Jessie turned on the computer and went to the Sentinel website. The story made the front page. "Wow!" It still thrilled her to see her name in print and her words on a page. Jessie pulled her ringing phone from her purse. "Hey, Katie, what's up?"

"My mom told me this morning Stuart Adler is out of prison. Hopefully, he doesn't know where you live."

"He does. He already sent me one of his sweet letters." Jessie walked into the kitchen and put her mug in the sink.

"Doesn't that scare you? How can you be cool about it?"

"One look at me and you'd know I'm not exactly excited about it."

"Speaking of excited, I was so upset about Adler that I forgot to tell you my good news."

"You've finally set the date," Jessie shouted with joy.

"We did. I love Dylan, and I started to wonder why I was dillydallying He wanted it this year, and I said why not. We still have a few months to plan and get ready."

"We can do it." Jessie couldn't stop smiling. "Don't keep me in suspense. When is it?"

"The last Saturday in August," Katie squealed an octave higher. "I'm having a summer wedding this year. I've already booked the Marina for the reception, and of course, the wedding will be here in the garden."

"My best friend is getting married to the love of her life." Jessie's eyes teared.

"Don't you dare start crying, or we'll both be bawling like babies. I know you, Jessie, wipe your eyes. We have some celebrating to do. I'll make plans. All you'll have to do is show up when you're told and be happy."

"I'm thrilled for you and ready to celebrate. You name the place and time, and I'll be there with my hunky cop."

"Sounds good. Don't forget to honk on your way to work. It's tradition, and you know how I love tradition."

Jessie shoved her phone into her purse and walked out the door with a smile plastered on her face. In a few weeks, this place will be awash with color, a perfect place for a wedding. Katie's wedding. Jessie honked more than once as she passed the Inn.

Chapter 28

Matt walked into the station. Kenny handed him several messages on his way to his office. Dylan and Kip were standing in the hall waiting for him.

"Chief, can we talk to you a minute?" Dylan pushed away from the doorframe.

"Sure, come in. What's on your mind?" He motioned for them to sit.

"Gary called Jeremy this morning. With his help, they were able to get around the firewall on the website. It's a porn site all right, and several girls from town are on it. I think most of them without their knowledge. Today is going to be a rough day for a lot of families." Dylan's fingers gripped the arm of the chair.

"Gary is tagging the girls' photos in the book with those on the Internet site. We should probably start with girls he has already identified to be on the porn site." Kip flipped through the notes he had taken earlier.

"I'll call the agency and talk to Tom before we start our rounds this morning." Matt jotted a reminder on his desk pad. "It would be great to put these guys out of business permanently."

"I have a sister and nieces, and this makes me fighting mad." Dylan frowned.

"I'll tell you one thing, Jeremy knows his way around a computer. He's a wealth of information." Kip leaned back in his chair. "I learned a lot listening to him tell Gary what to do. Jeremy seems to think cyberspace is where a lot of crimes are committed now and will be the hotbed of the future. The internet opens a whole new frontier for law enforcement to have to battle. I'd say his job is secure for quite a while and we'll need more people like him."

"You're right. There are great job opportunities opening in this field for people coming up through the ranks with computer skills. He's one of the best." Matt went to close the door to his office and leaned his hip against the corner of his desk. "We may have a sensitive issue to contend with. Chad thinks Elizabeth's brother is involved in some way. We talked about this before, Dylan." Matt made eye contact with him. "We have to check him out thoroughly behind the scenes. If he is, we'll nail him along with the others. There is something else I may need some help with." Matt told them what he had learned about Stuart Adler. "He's out of prison, and it's only a matter of time until he comes to town."

"Does he know where she is?" Dylan leaned forward in his chair.

"Yes." Matt pulled out the letter she had received and handed it to Dylan. "Go, ahead and read it. It will give you a sense of the man's state of mind."

"Damn." Dylan shook his head. "He's one vile man."

"He's obsessed with her. The lead investigator said none of the other victims had received any letters over the years from him, only Jessie."

"He's already subdued them. She's the one that got away." Dylan handed the letter to Kip to read.

"How's she dealing with it?" Kip asked.

"I can't tell if she's putting a good spin on it or what."

"She's not the same young girl he targeted years ago. He might meet his match in her now. We've all seen her in action." Dylan's fingers drummed the arm of the chair.

"True, but if we can prevent him from getting at her, I'd rather not test the theory." Matt handed them each a photo of Stuart Adler. "This is a recent photo of how our guy looks now, and we need to watch for him. They'll let me know if he leaves town on their side."

"Cases sure as hell aren't simple anymore." Kip ran his hand through his hair. "Where do we start? You saw the research we did. What a mess, and this crime has been going on for at least ten years right under our noses." He flipped his small notebook closed. "Guys like this one ruin it for the rest of us." Kip waved the picture of Adler in the air.

"You've got that right. We'll leave in twenty minutes as soon as I'm done making these calls. Is there anything else we need to discuss?"

"I have one more thing," Dylan smiled at them. "Katie and I've set a date, and you are both in the wedding, so you'll need to save it."

"Congratulations, we've been waiting." Matt shook his friend's hand.

"As I've learned, you can't rush these things. Weddings are a big event for women. Katie wasn't about to be moved until she knew it would be the perfect time. Pencil in the last Saturday of August, this year." Dylan grinned as he emphasized this year

"At least you don't have to wait until next

summer." Matt went to sit at his desk.

Kip pounded Dylan on the shoulder. "I can't wait. Who knows? Maybe I'll meet that someone special myself. They say weddings are a good place to meet a girl." The two talked as they walked out of the office.

Matt picked up the phone. "Hey, Tom, this is Matt."

"Don't tell me you have another big case and you need my help." He chuckled

Matt updated Tom about the case they were in the middle of. "While I have you on the phone, could you look into something for me?"

"Sure, what do you need?"

"I want information on Stuart Adler." Matt read him his prisoner number and gave him details that he had learned. "I want to find out as much as I can on him." He explained why.

"Let me get this right, a cold murder case, and a porn trafficking ring in the local high school, plus a violent pervert after Jessie. Sounds like another one of your routine simple cases to me. Not!" He chuckled. "It should be a piece of cake for your team. I'll call you if I find out anything on your guy. I'll give Gary's number to the right department. They'll want to talk to him. Let's take this group down."

"I'm with you on that. This has been going on for at least ten years and maybe longer."

Matt spent the rest of the day contacting parents and, in some cases, grown women whose photos were in the book. It wasn't an easy day. He was leaving the last house for the day. Gary called to say someone was getting the book out at the school. He had him on the screen in front of him. Matt turned on lights and sirens and headed to the school with Dylan and Kip in his wake. He was too late. But they had a photo.

"Can you enhance or make it larger. Matt stared at the grainy shot.

"I'll work on it." Gary put the disc in his computer and began to play around with the quality. He sent it to the FBI to see if they could do a scan for him. They promised to put a rush on it.

"Technology is great if it works, and this seems to be working."

"I wonder if he's someone that works at the school or an outsider." Dylan pointed at the man's photo.

"Someone must have read Jessie's story in the paper this morning, and maybe he's starting to panic." Kip watched Gary's hand flying over the keys.

"Great article. She didn't mince words. I guess this was all a part of the plan, visit the girls, and the story coming on the same day." Dylan grinned. "Once you stir the pot, the rats come out of their holes."

"Her stories do stir up trouble." Matt grinned. "I'm headed to her place now."

Chapter 29

Whew, this day flew by. Jessie glanced at the clock. The book table was in order once again. How had Matt's day gone with the girls and their parents? It couldn't have been easy for any of them. Her own father had been a mess after he realized how serious the Stuart Adler situation had become. He took all the steps the police told him to do to protect her, and it still wasn't enough. The guilt dogged him for the longest time. Maybe that's why he was always strict and protective. She straightened the bookmarks in the basket. Someone had tossed them carelessly back in after picking out the one they wanted.

Jessie had often wondered what happened to Stuart's wife and little girls. They were another casualty of his choices. Once the police had told Sylvia what her husband was being charged with, she left and took the girls with her. No one in the old neighborhood knew where they had moved.

From research and articles, she had worked on over the years, it was clear most female victims knew their attacker. Family members were often involved in one way or another. Keeping those girls away from Stuart was smart.

She motioned to Molly to come to the doors. "Do you have a minute before I close?"

"Did you want something?" Molly leaned against the door frame.

"Have you talked to Katie today?"

"No, was I supposed to?" Molly turned to make sure someone wasn't waiting at the counter.

"I thought maybe Katie would call you." Jessie paused, her eyes lighting up. "They've finally set a date." She clapped her hands in excitement. "It's the last Saturday in August."

"When did you find out?" Molly asked. "I haven't heard from her yet."

"I'm sure you will. I found out before I left for work. She's over the moon with excitement. Katie never does anything in a small way."

"True. I have a feeling her wedding will be a lot of fun." Molly smiled.

"I know it'll be. I get misty-eyed thinking about it. We've been friends for so long, it's hard to believe my best friend will be a married woman soon."

"What about Matt and you?"

"What about us?" Jessie countered. "I'm being facetious." She laughed.

"I thought you were. Seriously, are you two ever going to get married?"

"You never know, anything is possible. I do love the man." She batted her eyelashes playfully.

"Everyone in town knows he loves you. We're all waiting to hear."

"I'm not talking, but I wouldn't hold my breath." She laughed. The bell above the door rang. Darn, why hadn't she locked them earlier? It was after closing time. She walked toward the front of the store. "May I help you find something?"

"No, I wanted to check your store out. I noticed it's closing time, so I'll be back tomorrow." The tall, well-dressed man walked toward the counter and left her standing behind him.

Jessie was uncomfortable, but she had no idea why. She straightened the book table trying to watch him when she could. He took a bookmark after going through the basket. She saw him reach behind the counter. "Did you find one you liked?" She walked toward him.

"I did. Now I have the store's number too." He stepped past her, waving the bookmark in front of her. "We'll meet again."

He walked out the door, and she locked it behind him. Closing the doors into Joe's, she went to the counter. Something was off about that man. She shifted the papers on the countertop and looked behind it where he had reached. That's when she saw the note.

You have no idea who you're messing with. If I were you, I wouldn't stick my nose where it doesn't belong. You're new, and you don't get how things work around here. Walk away while you still can. The people involved would think nothing of snapping that pretty neck of yours.

"Well, isn't that nice." The story had only been out for a day, and it was already upsetting folks. She started her closing routine.

She grabbed her ringing phone off the counter. "Hey, Matt."

"I'm on my way. We could go to dinner if you want."

"Sounds good. I'm done, why don't you meet me at the house, and we can take my car?"

"I'll be there in a few."

She shoved her phone into her purse, turned off the lights, and headed for her car, locking the back door behind her. How would Matt feel about another note to read? The drive home was a quiet one. It was still light. If she hurried, she could freshen up before Matt got to her place.

****

Matt pulled in beside her car. Walking the path to her cottage had become a familiar habit for him over the past year. He was about to knock, but he saw her standing in the opened door, smiling at him. He took a deep breath. This was the best moment in an otherwise tough day.

"You're a sight for these tired eyes." He held the screen door open for her.

"I imagine you've had a hard day."

"I can't blame the parents or the girls for being upset." He turned the knob to make sure he had locked it.

"Did any of the girls know the reason they had been photographed?"

"Not today. These were all the young girls still in school now. It was a nightmare. We're meeting the principal at the school at midnight. Gary is going to check the girls' locker room and shower for a hidden camera. None of these girls had posed for any photos." He took hold of her hand, and they strolled to the car.

"Why so late?" she asked.

"We don't want to tip our hand too soon. No one should be there at that time of night. We also have a photo of someone taking the book. Gary got in on video, and the FBI is running a facial recognition scan on it. We should know more in the morning." He opened the car door for her.

"The case is starting to break open." She latched her seatbelt. "Where are we going?"

"An Italian place Dylan told me we had to try." Matt shut his car door.

"Perfect." She glanced at him. "Did Dylan tell you they set a date?"

"He sure did. He was telling anyone who'd listen how happy he is."

"Katie is happy too." Jessie's eyes were misty.

"Surely it doesn't make you sad, sweetheart. Why the tears?" He handed her a tissue.

"These are tears of joy. I'm excited for my friend. The first time I met you, Dylan was there. I could see her feelings shining in her eyes. He didn't reciprocate her feelings, so she bounced around for a while, but it was always Dylan that had her heart."

"It's awesome, and we played a small part in it." Matt reached for her hand at the light. "How was your day?"

"It was interesting." She turned to look out the window.

"With an answer like that, I know I need to ask you why."

"I'll tell you later. Let's enjoy our evening together. We can pretend for a few minutes we're on a date. There're no murder victims, abuse of young women, and angry men coming after me. All the problems will still be here after dinner."

"I guess that's mean we'll talk later." He laughed, and she nodded.

Chapter 30

Dimmed lighting, candles that floated in cut crystal holders against white tablecloths, and gleaming silverware greeted them as they walked into the main dining area. Hand in hand they followed the host to a table in the corner. The chamber music was romantic and soft.

"I love you," he whispered in her ear. He held her chair for her.

She gave him a broad smile and whispered back, "The feeling is mutual."

Sitting across from her, he glanced at the menu the waiter handed him. "What sparkling wine would you suggest?"

"This sparkling rosé is an especially good one." The waiter pointed to it on the wine menu.

"Jess, does that sound good to you?" He handed the waiter the wine list.

"Yes, perfect. I like a nice sparkling wine." The waiter walked away.

"What looks good to you?" Matt glanced over the top of the menu at her.

"The Chicken Bryan sounds delicious to me."

"I want the Chicken Marsala. The mushrooms sold me." Matt placed his menu on the table and reached across the table for her hand. Matt gave the waiter their order after he filled their wine glasses.

"Dylan has great taste in restaurants. He knows how to pick them, and you can tell him I said so." She took a sip of her wine.

"You look beautiful tonight. The candlelight makes your skin glow." Matt ran his thumb over her hand. "I love special times together. They don't come often enough for me."

"Thank you. It's nice to have a few quiet moments even though I know trouble will come roaring back as soon as we leave this place." She withdrew her hand from his as soon as the waiter approached the table with their salads. Placing her napkin on her lap, she reached for her salad fork.

"You're right, but for now we'll talk about anything but the case." He smiled at her.

"Sounds like a plan to me."

****

They walked out into the starry night hand in hand. "Well, I guess it's back to reality." She glanced at him. "Thanks for a great evening. Dinner was a nice reprieve." She slid into the passenger seat after he opened the car door for her. As soon as he got in and shut his door, she handed him the note. "I thought you might what to read this."

"Another one?" He asked. "Is it as vile as the last?"

"No, it's from a different person." She told him about the man who had come into her store before closing.

"Geez, Jess, your article has only been out one day, and already the goons are coming out of hiding." He turned toward her. "This ups the ante. You can't watch for Stuart and this guy. How many others are out there we don't know of? It's settled. You're at the Inn, or I'm staying in your guest room, and you'll have someone watching your store while you're there." He winked. "I'll be on the clock so I'll behave." He started the car.

"I'm not worried about you." She turned away from him and looked out the passenger window.

"What is it then, Jess?"

"I've spent the last several years learning to be strong on my own. I feel like I've been going backward since I moved to the Cove." She toyed with the strap on her purse.

"Did you ever see ghosts in New York?" Matt glanced at her.

"You know I didn't."

"It seems to me you are dealing with different energy here altogether, sweetheart. Every new situation has handed you a learning curve, and you've had to face unique new challenges. I have too since I've been in my position as chief. Blue Cove has presented you with an excess of stuff to deal with. You're strong, and you've handled it all. We'll be there as your backup. I never ask my guys to investigate alone. They go with a partner to have their back. It's how it works." He made the turn off the highway heading back to town.

"You're right, but it isn't how I planned it." She shifted in her seat, stretching out her legs.

"Who could plan for or even imagine the things you've seen since coming to Blue Cove?"

"You're telling me. I never saw it coming, but I'm okay with it. I only want to find a way of living a normal life in the process." She gave him a half smile.

"We'll figure it out. For now, all I'm asking is that you let us help whenever we can. You've helped me often enough." Matt drove through town, headed toward the Inn.

"I'm good with it. We've managed before, and we'll manage again."

"That's my girl. I know Adler isn't on his way yet. I have someone watching him. They'll let me know as soon as he leaves town. For tonight, I'll give you space. Someone will be watching your house as soon as you're at home, starting tomorrow." Matt pulled the car next to his.

"Do you want to come in?" She unlatched her seatbelt. "You're not on the clock."

"Are you sure?" He grinned at her, taking her hand.

"I'm positive."

"I have a couple of hours before I have to be at the school."

****

Matt met Gary and his team at the school. They went over the locker room and found several small cameras strategically placed in the dressing area and showers. Principal Rhodes was shocked.

"Look at this, Chief." He opened some of the ceiling tiles, and the wires ran through them. Kip went up in the catwalk area above the drop ceiling and followed them into the classroom on the same floor. Rhodes unlocked the door and Gary began to search the area.

"Who is the teacher?" Matt asked.

"Often, several teachers use a room." The principal rubbed his balding head.

"What would be taught in this room?" Kip checked out all the computer desks.

"Computer application, computer science,

computer programming, and computer labs are a few of the classes in these three connecting rooms."

"Chief, look at this. Is this a normal setup for a computer class? This is a listening device. Someone was not only watching the girls, filming them, but they've been listening in on their conversations too."

"Damn, how long has this been going on?" Rhodes looked closely at where Gary pointed. "This equipment shouldn't be in this classroom. It doesn't belong to the school. He checked for the school's identifying mark on the property. There are no school numbers etched into the equipment which means it's not one of ours."

"I'm going to need a list of all the teachers who have access to these classrooms daily. Also, I'll need the names of the art teachers now and any who recently retired along with the photography teachers."

"No problem."

"Gary, we have to disable those cameras. Hopefully, our suspect will come to fix the problem, and we'll catch him. I can't in good conscience leave here knowing those cameras are operational."

"I agree. I'll take care of it." Gary took Kip with him to disable the equipment. A few snips later and the cameras were off.

"How do you keep a daughter safe from a sophisticated operation like this? Parents are going to flip when they hear about this." Rhodes shook his head.

"We are beginning to notify the parents and the girls already, but now it appears it may be all the girls. Someone had to know this was going on and turned their head. Maybe got a payoff." Matt frowned, disgusted.

"We might need to write a letter to the parents of

daughters and have a school-wide meeting, which you could address. It would be the easiest way to deal with it and answer their questions and concerns. We could have a victims' advocate, counselor, and whoever else we need to address the parents' concerns," Rhodes suggested leaning his hip against a computer table.

"You're right. Set the time and date, and I'll be there," Matt told him.

"If a school official or city police knew about this operation and turned their head, I can see the lawsuits piling up and rightfully so." Matt flipped the small camera over in his hand.

"It will get messy long before it gets better. The first thing we have to do is to protect the kids and then get the people responsible for the crime." Matt stood next to Principal Rhodes. "We're dealing with people peddling child porn. We'll get them and shut it down. With any luck, we'll solve two murders from ten years ago."

"Has it been going on for ten years?" Rhodes frowned, the wrinkles on his forehead standing out.

"Yes, with and without the girls' knowledge. It started as a modeling scam, but from the equipment found here, I have a feeling it turned into peddling porn by blackmailing the girls. They're all afraid to talk, even the girls that are women now. I believe they have been threatened."

"Do you have proof?" Rhodes asked.

"We're close," Matt told him.

"Well, at least these won't work for a while. They'll have plenty of repairs to do to get it operational again." He held up clipped wires, small memory boards, and various parts of cameras and mics.

"I've arranged for a special agent to watch over the school and these classrooms. He'll be watching the teachers and students in these rooms during the day. You can tell your staff he's a student teacher. For now, we'll need to keep his identity secret."

"I'll do whatever you want. The sooner we put a stop to it the better."

"I couldn't agree more!" Matt responded.

Chapter 31

She poured the steaming, hot coffee into the cream in her cup and gazed out the kitchen window at the clear bright morning sky. Only a few wispy white clouds floated through the sea of stunning blue. It looked like another beautiful day was on tap. Her sleep last night had been an interrupted and fitful one. Dreams of Grace and Lizzy and nightmares of dragons and wars left her feeling on the tired side. Had Matt found anything last night? The mere thought of a camera hidden in the girls' locker room filled her with anger.

These crimes against girls and women were the reason she had become an activist. The once helpless feeling she used to live with had given way to the determination to fight back. She did it with her pen, the causes she supported, and by making sure the men around her treated their women colleagues with respect or she would say something.

Of course, over time, she had learned to tone it down, but she still could feel her blood boil at the injustice in the way some men thought they could talk to and treat women. But there were still plenty of good guys around too, like Matt. She sighed.

"Enough thinking, already." She wiped the kitchen counter before grabbing her purse. She would know soon enough what they found. Matt would fill her in on the details. He was good about making her feel like a part of an investigation.

Locking the door, she fumbled around in her purse in search of her ringing phone. "Good morning, this is Jessie."

"We need to talk. Do you have time for coffee this morning?" The woman's shaky voice came over the phone.

"I'm sorry, do I know you? Who is this?" Jessie asked.

"My name is Carolyn Edwards. You don't know me, but I read your story about Elizabeth McKenzie. I would like to talk with you if you have the time. Lizzy and I were friends in high school."

"I'll be at my store Idle Time Books. You're free to stop by if you'd like. The store is located next to Joe's coffee shop. Customers might interrupt us, but I manage to talk to people there all the time. I'd be happy to meet with you, Carolyn."

"I'll be there this morning." Carolyn disconnected the call.

Honking the horn and waving, Jessie passed the Inn on her way out to the road. Carolyn had been nervous when she called, judging from the sound of her voice. Why? What piece of the puzzle could Carolyn Edwards provide? Matt was right. The article was already starting to shake things up.

She flipped on the lights on her way in the door. What she felt there made her want to turn around and walk back out. The hair on the back of her neck stood up. Grabbing a hammer she had in the back room, she searched the store. No one was there, but she wasn't alone. Someone, or maybe she should say something, was watching, and they weren't friendly. She shuddered. Rushing through her opening routine, she hummed a song and then began to sing the words out loud. With relief, she opened the doors into Joe's at nine. Molly was near if she needed her. Turning the sign around, she unlocked the front door.

"Thank you," she whispered as Reba pulled up in front of the store. She held the door open for Reba.

Reba stepped across the threshold. "Whoa, what is going on in here? It feels like I'm in a strange place of turmoil and not your wonderful store."

"I was beginning to think I was losing my mind I almost turned around and ran out of here after I arrived. I thought maybe someone was hiding in the store, but I didn't find anyone."

"Did you check in the attic area?"

"No, should I?" Jessie reached for the hammer she had placed on the counter.

"Not you, let's get an officer over here. If no one is up there, you'll know for sure you're dealing with another strange situation. I think you know what I mean." Reba patted her hand and called the police station.

Kip and Gary arrived a few minutes later. "What's up, Jessie?"

Reba stood in front of Kip. "Would you please check in the attic, young man? Jessie felt something was off in the store on her arrival this morning. I've felt it too as soon as I walked in. We want to make sure the premise is empty, and no one is hiding up there."

"We'll check it out for you." Kip grabbed the key from Jessie and started up the stairs.

"I don't believe anyone is hiding in the attic, but it's good to rule out the possibility." Reba stood at the base of the stairs listening to the two men talk. "Jessie, was the attic door locked?"

"Yes, I've kept it locked since they found the bugs planted there before I opened the store."

"There may be a problem then," Kip shouted down to her.

"Why?"

"What did you find, young man?" Reba asked Kip as he walked down the stairs.

"Did you know the attic door was unlocked? The lock was broken," Kip said as he stepped off the last stair.

"No, I always keep it locked. I haven't been up there in months."

"The good news is we didn't find anyone, but the bad news is someone has been watching your store and listening in again. We'll check your entrances for signs of damage. They had to get in some way."

"I don't see any damage on your exterior doors." Kip stood beside her.

"Could this be an entry point?" She noticed new marks on the doors opening into the coffee shop.

"That's what I was looking for. They look fresh too." Kip bent down to look.

"Have you ever noticed them before?" Gary dusted for prints.

"No, but I wasn't looking for them." Jessie watched over Kip's shoulder.

"I'll check entrances next door." Gary walked into Joe's and went to talk to Molly.

"I wonder who planted it this time. This is getting

ridiculous." Jessie greeted a customer coming through the doorway, "May I help you?"

The older woman's face lit up once she saw Reba. "I didn't expect to see you here."

"It's always nice to see you, Millie, dear. Let's get a cup of tea and chat if you have time. Later I can help you find some great books to read. Jessie has helped me often enough."

"Yes, it sounds like a perfect way to spend the morning. I'll be back after we've had tea." The woman smiled at Jessie.

"I'll take care of Millie so the officers can talk to you, dear. I'll be sure to sell her a few books while I'm at it." Reba spoke softly. "No frowning, dear. Your customers will wonder what's going on. Remember the wrinkles. Don't make them because you can't erase them." Reba followed Millie into the coffee shop.

Jessie went to answer her phone. "Idle Time Books, may I help you."

"I hope so, sweetheart. Gary says we have a problem at your store again."

"It looks that way."

"I'll be over in a while to check it out and fill you in on what we found."

"Do you know Carolyn Edwards?" Jessie asked him.

"She was Lizzy's friend in high school, why?"

"She called me this morning and is coming to see me. She said she wanted to talk."

"I guess we'd better buckle up. It looks the case is taking off, and it's about to get bumpy. I'll see you later."

"Okay." She put the receiver down. No doubt

about it, the air was bumpy and charged with something. More than what was visible, something unseen was going on too. Jessie hummed as she straightened the book table. Her morning was off and running.

Chapter 32

Reba was true to her word. She kept Millie entertained, brought her back to the store, and encouraged her to buy several books. Jessie admired the way Reba led her from one shelf to another, discussing several of the books. Maybe between Reba and Sadie, Jessie would be able to enjoy a few more days off. Those two could bring in business.

"I'll be back, dear. We have much to discuss. I want to know what you know about the presence that was in your store earlier."

"What makes you think I know?" Jessie walked Reba to the door.

"I wasn't born yesterday, my dear girl. You're way ahead of me when it comes to supernatural events. I'm playing catch-up."

Jessie chuckled. "No way. I'm the one running to stay up with you." She kissed Reba on the cheek. "You're always welcome to visit me any time. I was thinking earlier you would be a great asset to work here occasionally. The way you sold those books, you were smooth."

"Aren't you sweet, my dear, I wouldn't mind getting out of the house every now and again. Sadie and I would make a great team."

"I agree the two of you would raise my revenue in

a few days." She held the door open, and Reba swept past her, patting her cheek on the way out.

"Jessie, could you come here a minute?" Molly asked, motioning to her. "Can you believe they broke into my store and then got into yours?" Molly lowered her voice. "It freaks me out. I mean nothing was missing, which seems strange."

"I can't believe it's happened again." Jessie shook her head.

"You mean it's happened before."

"Yes, someday I'll have to tell you the story. You'll have to have a lot more time." Jessie eyed the line forming at the counter. Molly was about to get busy. "It was one way that I was welcomed to town. You were working in the coffee shop at the time."

"Wow, how could I have forgotten that piece of information. It was less than a year ago." Molly looked over her shoulder and saw the customers. Her new hire was waiting on them.

"You were in love, and I don't think my store was at the top of your radar at the time. Cummings owned Java Joe's then. The wires went from your store into mine in the attics."

"No wonder Gary wanted to check my attic."

"Did he find anything?" Jessie asked.

"If he did, he didn't say anything. He was only up there for a few minutes. Weird stuff has been happening to you for a while, hasn't it?"

"At first I didn't understand why all the crazy stuff was happening to me. I fought it, complained, and whined about it all, but I try not to anymore. Such is my life in Blue Cove, and I'm doing my best to live with it."

"What else can you do? It is what it is." Molly looked over her shoulder again.

"Exactly! All my complaining didn't change a thing."

"I'd better get back to work or at least look like I'm working." Molly turned around.

"We'll talk later." Jessie went behind the counter and opened the mail sitting there.

Thankfully the morning had calmed down. She sat in one of the chairs with a steaming cup of hot tea. The notes of the song she was humming earlier skipped through her mind, coming and going from time to time. She wasn't going to take this invasion of her space without a fight. As far as she was concerned, she had two safe havens, her store and her home, and they were worth fighting for.

****

Gary and Kip were in Matt's office showing him the small camera and bug they had found in Jessie's store. "I cut some wires and removed a few working parts like we did at the school."

"You see these markings." Gary pointed them out. "These are the same brand we found in the locker room."

"We have to be dealing with someone local. Or at least a front man that works here. Someone is monitoring the equipment and maintaining it."

"I agree." Kip held up the camera. "This stuff was a recent addition to Jessie's store. The lenses are all clean. Not a lot of dust has had time to accumulate. The marks on the door were fresh and visible enough to see with the naked eye. Kip took out his notepad, flipping through the pages. "A few things surprised me. The attic door's lock was broken, and there was no attempt to hide what they were doing in there. The cameras' layout seemed like a rush job to me. Jessie would've seen them if she had gone upstairs. Our suspect must be feeling the heat and isn't bothering to cover his tracks. He must've planted them in the last week. Molly hadn't noticed the marks on the door until a few days ago as she came in the back door."

"In other words, they're taking risks and getting sloppy. It seems a bit strange to me after operating under the radar for so long to risk it now. Jessie's article only came out yesterday. It makes me wonder if someone is leaking information." Matt stood, leaning his hip against the desk.

"Who knows besides us?" Kip asked.

"The people who placed the cameras, of course, Rhodes, a few members of the city council, and the man who's been watching Jess that Billy told us about. We should probably add a few teachers to the list." Matt's hand clenched at his side.

"Could there be someone left over from the time of Anderson working here at the station that might be privy to inside information?" Gary turned the small camera over in his hand. "It's amazing how small this stuff has got. There was a time they would've had to use a boxy video camera. Obviously, they've adapted to the times."

"Anything is possible. Except for getting the city manager to budget new equipment for the police, that is. Maybe I should send you and Gary to do a presentation on this and cybercrimes. They still think of Blue Cove as a sleepy little town."

"I could open their eyes with a few stats. Might be

fun." Gary chuckled.

"Let's get to work. Gary, trace the serial numbers and see if you can find where and when the suspects purchased the stuff. Maybe they'll have a name or credit card on file. Kip, contact a couple of the schools on the list and see if any of them have searched for video equipment in the girls' locker rooms or showers. You might want to encourage them to do it. Ask them if they find anything to send us a copy of the serial numbers."

"Will do." Kip stood up to leave. "What about the guy who found the book?"

"Gordon Tanner?"

"Yeah," Kip replied.

"He seemed like a nice enough man, but I haven't ruled anyone out. It doesn't make sense for him to bring attention to a crime he's involved in." Matt frowned. "But only the evidence will decide who's in and who's out."

****

She heard the bell above the door ring. "Hi, Kendra. I wasn't expecting to see you. How's your daughter."

"She's good and with Grandma for a few hours. This is my friend, Carolyn Edwards."

"It's nice to meet you, Carolyn." Jessie reached for her hand and felt it tremble in hers. She was nervous, and Jessie sought to put her at ease.

"I wanted to talk to you, and I didn't want to come alone. Kendra said she'd come with me. I hope you don't mind."

"Of course not, you're both welcome any time." Jessie smiled. "Get comfortable and hopefully we won't be interrupted, but if a bus comes, I can't promise anything."

"Before we get started, I could use a coffee." Kendra grabbed her wallet out of her purse. "Can I get either one of you anything?"

"I'd like coffee too, black." Carolyn sat in one of the leather chairs. Her finger began twirling a strand of her long, dark brown hair. "Do you want me to help?"

"No, I can handle it. How about you Jessie? Would you like a coffee or anything?"

"I'm good, thanks." Jessie added another chair in the grouping and sat beside Carolyn. "How long were you friends with Lizzy?"

"We met in middle school. She was always fun to hang around. You know the type—pretty and popular—part of the in group. Things changed in high school. Reading your article yesterday morning reminded of a few things that I've tried hard to forget. I need to tell someone." Carolyn shifted in her chair. "The police investigating Lizzy's murder at the time didn't ask most of us many questions. They didn't seem to care. I'm sure I'm wrong, but it seemed that way to me." Carolyn reached for the coffee that Kendra handed to her. "It was strange and scary for me, so my perception could have been all wrong. I'd never had a friend die before, much less murdered. All of us girls were really scared."

"I can imagine," Jessie responded. "It must have been a hard time for all of you."

"I had nightmares for weeks." Kendra sat in the empty chair placing her coffee on the table. I wish I would've had someone to talk to at the time. I'm still afraid to say anything. Can anyone hear us? I mean, do you think this place is bugged?" Kendra lowered her voice.

"I can honestly say as of this moment there are no listening devices in my store. You're free to talk." Jessie glanced at Kendra. "What made you think of a bug?"

"Strange things were happening before Lizzy was murdered. No matter who I talked to, Lizzy could tell me what I had said word for word."

"I didn't know it was happening to you too. I thought I was the only one." Carolyn frowned, reaching for Kendra's hand. "How could Lizzy have known? I told a friend while we were changing after gym there was no way I would ever let those guys take my picture. They gave me the creeps." Carolyn leaned forward in the chair. "They said they wanted models for teen swimwear. What a crock. According to Lizzy, we all had a chance. A model agency was recruiting for their catalog, and they wanted all shapes and sizes. Look at me. I'm not exactly the type. I know they were feeding me a line. The only thing I could have modeled for was a porn movie. All the models I had ever seen weren't built like this." She pointed at her bust. "I developed early. The same day after school, Lizzy and her brother were waiting for me at my car. Ted told me to keep my mouth shut if I knew what was good for me. I had ruined my chance, but I shouldn't ruin it for the other girls. Lizzy repeated my words back to me. I have no idea what kind of scam they were running, but I wanted no part of it."

"I know what they were doing. They were lying. Those guys wanted to take a picture of girls with clothes on and then without. I ran out when they tried it on me, but a lot of girls weren't so lucky. I still feel ashamed. I came close to being just another gullible young girl with her picture on some dumpy porn site." Kendra swiped at the tears on her face. "I will be happy to help take these guys out. I know they're still operating at the school. There are some new people involved in the group and some of the same old ones. I wanted to talk before but was too afraid. Since meeting you," she pointed at Jessie. "I'm not afraid anymore, and I know there are others who are willing to talk, too."

"It's time to get the police involved." Jessie pulled out her phone.

"I tried before, but they wouldn't listen." Kendra took a sip of her coffee. "Lizzy heard about it and stopped talking to me. That was the end of our friendship.

"I did too. Basically, I was told go home. He'd call me if he needed me. He never called. I kept my mouth shut." Carolyn leaned back and reached for her coffee. Her brown eyes glistened with unshed tears.

"I know a group of police who will not only listen but will fight for you like I'm going to do." She called Matt. "I'm sending Kendra and Carolyn Edwards over to talk to you. They have some information you need to hear. I'll tell them." She hung up. "He said he'd be waiting."

Chapter 33

Matt spent the next few hours talking with Kendra and Carolyn. He was starting to get a clearer picture of what had gone on at the high school. Ted and Lizzy were at the heart of most of the problems. Lizzy had the trust of the girls and Ted played on their guilt and fear. How could he have been so clueless at the time? Carolyn was right. The investigating officers didn't seem to care. What troubled him the most was, he couldn't find any police files of interviews conducted with Lizzy's friends, or any of the other girls either. While searching the old files during the past few days, he had concluded there was a massive cover-up. Who were they protecting, and why? Even old Mike in records couldn't find anything. He knew where to find the files and evidence of every case over the past twenty years.

Making a call, Matt later slipped out of the station to meet with Charlotte McKenzie. She agreed to meet with him away from the house. By the time he was through talking with her, he had filled in a few more holes in his working theory. Charlotte reminded him that Byron was a council member at the time of Lizzy's death and couldn't finish out his term. They suddenly come into money right before the murder and had been thinking of moving after Lizzy graduated but lost the desire to do anything after her murder. Bobby was away at school, and he had coped better than Ted had. Charlotte was most worried about Ted, or Teddy as she still liked to call him. Matt recalled the end of their conversation as he drove back to the station.

"We're getting close to solving this case. I'm afraid some things may come out in the next few weeks that could hurt your family. I wanted you to know. You'll be reliving some hard memories," he had told Charlotte.

Mrs. McKenzie had leaned toward him and grabbed his hand. "Matt, you were always good to my Lizzy. Ted and his sister were involved in something, but I don't know what. More than once, I overheard them in heated conversations that stopped as soon as I walked in the room. I doubt much can shock me anymore. Teddy has been slowly dying since we lost Elizabeth. He is carrying a heavy load, but he refuses to talk about it. He's rarely sober and won't go into rehab. Lizzy was lost to us before she was murdered. I guess the best I can hope is to put the person behind bars that destroyed what was left of her."

What a mess. If this case were heading where he thought it was, Charlotte would probably be shocked despite her words to him.

He pulled into his spot at the station and answered his ringing phone. "This is Parker."

"We think Adler is headed your way," the voice on the other end said. "He rented a car—a one-way rental to New York. We think he'll pass your way first."

"Thanks for letting me know." Matt hit the steering wheel. He would tell Jessie later. Matt walked into the station with new information to chew on.

"Any messages for me?" He stopped at Kenny's

desk.

"Dylan and Kip wanted to talk to you as soon as you got back." Kenny handed Matt his phone messages.

"Tell them to come into my office." Matt headed down the hall reading his messages as he walked.

****

She wondered how long it would take before the person who planted the devices would realize they weren't hearing or seeing anything. Jessie waved at Audrey as she walked in. "Thanks for getting here early."

"No problem. I have no idea why you'd be in a hurry to go running, but have at it." Audrey smiled at her.

"I am supposed to pace the running club at the school. The coach said their times have improved since I've been running with them. I won't be able to run with them for a while. I wanted to get another one in before I take a few days off." Jessie grabbed her purse and keys. She changed into her running clothes before she left for the school. The thought of changing in the girls' locker room didn't sit well with her. "I'll be back to close the store," Jessie called out.

"Okay, see you in a bit." Audrey waved.

Driving to the school, she had no idea what to expect this time. Her time with this group had proved interesting from the first day. Seeing Lizzy's ghost, the hawk after hearing Frank's story, and being beaned with a rock, what was next? After she parked, she sent Matt a text. *Hey, I wanted you to know I'm pacing the team today. I'll stay with them and not go off on my own. See you.*

Both teams began at an easy pace jogging a mile

on the track before they started running the path leading up to the first of several small inclines. Soon they would pass the area where Jessie had first heard Lizzy's ghost. Would her spirit be there today?

Running in the late afternoon was different from in the morning. It was warm, and the sweat was already forming beads on her neck trickling down her back and arms. The trees offered only shade, but little else. No rustling leaves, no breeze, only a calm, eerie stillness that made the sound of their feet hitting the ground rumble like thunder. The kids jockeyed for position. Occasional laughter made her smile. The sheer feeling of elation kept them all running day after day. Most of them loved it as she did. She would miss them, but until Adler was no longer a problem, she couldn't risk it for the kids' sake.

Some of the kids fell off the pace. She encouraged them to push harder, singing "Pick them up, come on, move those feet," like an auctioneer's rhythmic chant. Their pace automatically improved, returning to the rhythm. The stragglers soon caught up with the first group, and eventually they all made it back to the school without incident. One by one the kids bent over to catch their breaths, stretch out their tired muscles, and then head to the gym to shower.

Jessie stood at the car, waiting until the last one went inside. Putting on her sunglasses, she saw Lizzy's ghost. She was near the football field. Not far from her was Grace, surrounded by light. What was she seeing? She lifted her glasses. The dragon rose up on its haunches, but the light sent it fleeing away. She opened her car and slid inside. Why a dragon? She always thought of them as magical. This dragon was dark and menacing. It had to mean something significant, but she had no idea what.

She answered her ringing phone.

"Hi, sweetheart."

"Did you get my message?" she asked.

"I did, and thanks for letting me know. I trust all went well."

"Yep, we're finished, and I'm leaving the school now. I need to go back and close up the store."

"I'll bring dinner tonight. I heard earlier that Stuart might be on his way here."

"I figured it would be happening soon. I told Coach Harmon I couldn't run with the kids for a few days. I wouldn't want them to be put at risk."

"Good. You're one step ahead of me. I'll see you in a while and fill you in on today's activities."

Ghosts, dragons, and beings of light. What did it all mean? Nothing was as she had been taught as a child. It was far more complicated. Maybe Sadie could tell her something to give her clarity. Jessie parked her car in front of the store. She wouldn't be there long. "Audrey I'm back."

"Did you enjoy your time with the kids?"

"They're fun to run with. They keep me on my toes." She straightened the front book table as they talked.

"You had a few customers come in. Rachael Tanner stopped by to say hello and said she'd be back another day. She seems like a nice lady."

"She is. Her husband is a new teacher at the school. Thanks for watching the store."

"Do you want me to help clean before I leave? The two of us can get it done faster."

"Oh, that would be nice." Jessie took the feather duster and cleaned the counter, straightening the bookmarks.

"I don't do much in the evening. Once I'm home, I spend most of the night reading or watching TV." Audrey removed the trash from the tables and wiped the surfaces clean.

Jessie closed the doors between the stores, waving at Molly as she did. Locking the front door, she turned the sign to Closed. "I'll put the money in the safe if you'll make sure the back door is shut and locked. We can go out the front."

"I'd be happy to."

Jessie turned the dial on the safe after shutting the door.

Ready to leave, Audrey picked up her purse from the counter.

"Audrey, where's your car? I didn't see it parked out front."

"It's in the church parking lot. It was so pretty outside, I wanted to walk a little today."

"It was a gorgeous day. I don't blame you."

"There's a cold front coming in tomorrow. I suppose that means I must pull my coat out again. I was hoping I could put it away until fall. I guess we're never safe from cold weather until the end of May. Still, I was hopeful. The last few days have been delightful." She held the door for Jessie.

"I know what you mean." Jessie turned off the front lights and walked out the door, testing to make sure she had locked it. See you tomorrow."

"Go home, and no more running tonight." Audrey laughed.

"Enjoy your evening."

"I will."

Jessie watched Audrey walk until she was safely in her car. With the turn of the key, the engine purred to life, and she patted the dash. "Good girl." Jessie loved this vintage car.

Chapter 34

As soon as Jessie opened the door, Matt came in. His overnight bag slipped from his shoulder, hitting the floor with a thud. He had no free hand to grab it. "Let me help. What were you thinking?" Jessie's hand reached for the handle of the paper bag he was holding on the tips of his ring and pinky fingers before it tumbled onto the ground next to the other one.

He leaned close and kissed her on the cheek, trying to balance what he was still holding. "Hi, sweetheart. I thought I could make it in one trip."

"You're lucky you didn't lose our dinner on your way to the door." Jessie took another bag.

"Luck had nothing to do with it, doll. I had it all under control." He grinned, flexing his muscles.

"Sure, you did." Jessie smiled at him playfully squeezing his biceps. "Yes, I can see how you might think you could carry it off." She laughed, drawing out the word think. "What's for dinner?" She carried the bags placing them on the counter.

"Patterson's had a roasted chicken special. It sounded good to me. I hope you're okay with it." Matt pulled the containers out of the bag, placing them on the table that was set and ready to go.

"Sounds delicious." Jessie filled her plate with salad, a slice of chicken breast, and roasted potatoes.

"How was your day? Mine was interesting."

"I went to see Charlotte McKenzie after talking to Kendra and Carolyn. I wanted to forewarn her that the case was picking up steam. The more we're finding out, it looks like Ted and Lizzy were both at the heart of the mess at the school. She didn't seem too shocked by the prospect of her family going through some hard times with the new revelations." Matt took a bite of his chicken.

"I find it strange she wasn't more upset. I think as a mom it would be heartbreaking to consider your son had anything to do with your daughter's death, intentionally or unintentionally." She shook her head. "I would be devastated."

"From what she said, I think she's suspected something for a while. She told me Ted is drinking and hasn't been the same since his sister's death." Matt shared more about the conversation with her.

"The whole thing doesn't make sense to me. From what I've seen and heard the past few days, there is more to this story than just Ted and Lizzy's complicity."

"What do you mean?" Matt reached for the roasted potatoes.

"They were being used. What were they getting in return? Elizabeth had only one photo in the book. She looked like a model in that picture which could've been used to entice the other girls into the scheme. There were no other pictures of her in the book or on the website according to Jeremy." Jessie took a bite of her salad.

"That's odd." He stopped the glass halfway to his mouth.

"I thought it was too," she said. "Once we discover which adults are implicated in the operation, we'll probably have a clearer picture. I have a strong sense they found themselves entangled in something they couldn't extricate themselves from."

"Give me your theory." Matt took a drink of his tea.

"If they made money, others would've noticed a change in their lifestyle. I'm sure if you look back, or if Charlotte does, she'll know who spent money she doesn't remember giving them. After Grace was murdered, and I think she died first. They died maybe days or moments apart, but Lizzy was beside herself with grief. A note in her diary that she'd written claimed someone promised her that no one would get hurt. It was underlined several times and with four exclamations points at the end for emphasis." Jessie paused to take a breath. "I have no idea when she wrote that, but a war raged inside her, and she's still not at peace. There's a reason she's here, and we're going to need her help to understand what happened that day ten years ago." Jessie pushed the salad around on her plate with her fork.

"You never cease to surprise me. I take it from what you told me, you've seen the dragon again." He smiled at her. "I may as well tell you my new name for you."

"If it's crazy, I'd rather you didn't tell me."

"It's fanciful. You've called me your knight in shining armor." He reached for her hand. "I think of you as my dragon slayer."

"Why?" Her eyes widened, and brows arched. "I'm curious to know why."

"I'm only beginning to put it together in my head. Besides saving my hide a few times, you're willing to go to bat for anyone in need. You hear their cries when no one else can. Sweetheart, I mean it as a compliment in every way possible. You have a way of putting the ghosts from the past to rest while finding a way forward in every case."

"I don't know what to say. I'm surprised. You're sweet. I can't say I've ever seen me quite that way."

"You're the one that saw the night sky turn to a battleground. I've enough of an imagination to envision it the way I'd like to see it." Matt chuckled. "I'll keep the rest to myself for now. This will be our secret and my fantasy. Besides you invoke a sexy image wielding a sword."

Laughter bubbled out of her. "You have some imagination, Mr. Parker."

"Aw, sweet lady, when it comes to you, my mind travels down many roads. You're one of my favorite subjects." His hand stroked her cheek. If I were a writer, you'd be the heroine in my book, but you know about me and the writing process."

"Are you serious or teasing me? I don't know how to take you sometimes."

"I'm serious." He leaned toward her, framing her face with his hands. He brushed his lips across hers. "Tell me how your day was."

"The morning started with a strange presence in my store, which brought Gary and Kip to check for spyware. They found it, as you know. After talking with Kendra and Carolyn, I ran with the running club and saw a couple of ghosts. All in all, it made for a noteworthy day."

"It's not over yet." He stood, placing his dish in the sink. "Because Adler is on his way here, I'll be staying, or if I can't, someone else will."

"I was wondering why you'd brought an overnight bag." She walked up behind him, wrapping her arms around his waist and leaning the side of her face against his back.

"What's this?" He turned around to face her.

"I appreciate you. As often as you've had to stay here to keep me safe, it's hard to see how you can think of me as strong. But I love that you do."

"I may have more than a few fantasies with you in them, but nothing beats the real thing." He held her close. "Let's do these dishes." He rinsed, and she put them in the dishwasher.

Jessie cleaned off the table, put the food away, and wiped the counter. "Do you want to watch some TV?"

"I have some reports to work on, but I don't mind if you do. I like just having you near." He flipped off the kitchen light. "Have you heard when Sadie will be here?

"I'll write her an email and find out." She went over to her computer and turned it on.

"Sounds good. If you finish, you can watch TV. It won't bother me." On his way to the couch, Matt grabbed his briefcase. He sat, spreading all his papers out on the coffee table. He turned on his laptop, scanning the written reports, and copying them into their case files on his computer.

Chapter 35

Matt glanced at the closed bedroom door. Jessie went to bed a while ago. He had enjoyed watching her work on the computer. She had a habit of twisting her hair around her finger and smiling at something she read. He liked how she winked at him when she caught him watching her, too. Matt felt like he was back in high school. She kept him off-center with her flirting. Not much of his work got done, but it was worth it.

Stuart Adler's rap sheet was a lengthy one. He counted thirty-six instances including Jessie's and the two other girls'. His record was clean until the year before Jessie had started babysitting for the family. A speeding ticket, a few minor infractions, and then it escalated. What set him off? Something in his life must have changed. Jessie's father had filed ten complaints.

The neighbors were worried about his wife. There was a reason no one knew where she was. Sylvia was in the witness protection program with their little girls, now teens. She feared for her life and the lives of her daughters. Mrs. Adler called the police on her husband numerous times—once after he hit their older daughter with such force her head snapped back and hit the wall. The police rushed them out of the home a few weeks before they arrested Adler on assault and rape charges.

Matt's phone vibrated. "This is Matt."

"Chief, this Joe."

"Hi, how are Sarah and the baby? I've missed seeing you at the front desk."

"They're fine. The baby will be a year soon. With Kenny's first classes nearly complete. I'll be able to work several day shifts again."

"What's up?"

"I know it's late, but Maxwell called and said he needed to get in contact with you ASAP. He said it was important. Did you have your phone off? He said it kept going to voicemail."

"I have the ringtone off, but I heard it vibrate. I'll give him a call."

"Tell Jessie Sarah's sending her an invitation for Abigail's first birthday."

"I'll let her know. Talk to you later."

"Tom, I got the message you called," Matt said as soon as Tom picked up the phone.

"You're hard to get a hold of."

"I was out of the office most of the day, and now I'm babysitting Jessie. I'm not complaining about this part of my job."

"I take it Adler is on his way there."

"Yes, they called today. I was reading over his rap sheet. He went downhill quickly. He had no troubles most of his life, then in a short window of time, boom, it all changed. It always makes me wonder happened to cause it."

"Who knows? It could have been almost anything. It could have been something as simple as an obsession or a boss riding him every day," Tom replied.

"It seldom justifies their action. What's up?" Matt asked.

"I sent the name of the man we identified from the face scan. Our department was able to enhance and clean up the grainy photo. He's not a nice person, to put it mildly. I'm wondering how he was able to get anywhere near a school. How did he get an operation going? He had to pay somebody in the town to turn a blind eye to him. A simple background check would have given anyone interested in doing business with this guy a clue to his character. It's too bad Anderson isn't alive. I'd have a few questions to ask him. This guy has a record. I sent a copy to your email so you can take a look at it. His dad is one of the big guys in the porn industry. You know the type a bully with lots of folks around him to do his dirty work. He's made it big in the adult entertainment industry, but the agency has always believed he used kids. I think it's possible we'll finally get him this time. His son will be the bait."

"Does that mean you're coming to Blue Cove?"

"We'll have a team there to work with you. We've been trying to get this guy for a long time. I want to see him locked up for what he has done to young girls. We're talking about scum."

"From what I've been learning, I would say some locals are colluding with him. You never know about people beyond what you see in public view." Matt told Tom about the cameras and listening devices found in the girls' locker room, showers, and Jessie's store.

"I'll see you soon, and we'll talk more."

"Sounds good." Matt disconnected the call. He checked the locks and carried his laptop with him into the guest room. Propping himself up against the headboard with some pillows, he read the extensive record of Trevor Valentine, sometimes called the love doctor. Somebody's idea of sick joke, Matt guessed. Calvin, his son, was the man in the photo.

Ted McKenzie was the next person on his agenda to question. From every indication, Ted was living with a boatload of guilt, which was a possible reason for his alcohol problem. Matt sent Jeremy an email and asked him to find any information he could on Ted McKenzie. Could Jeremy connect Ted to Trevor Valentine? Matt was hopeful. He shut off his computer and leaned his head back against the pillow. Damn, how was he going to keep Jessie safe with everything happening at the same time?

The soft knock at the door came a few minutes after midnight. "Come in." The door slowly opened. He expelled a deep breath. The vision in front of him was lovely. The light from the hall highlighted her hesitation and her tousled curls. He loved how she looked all warm and sleepy. Even in her ill-fitted robe, she was a beautiful woman. "I hope I didn't wake you." He gulped, staking his hands behind his head.

She sat in the chair closest to the door. "I heard you talking earlier and was wondering what was going on."

"Why are you still awake?"

"I couldn't shut my mind off." She fiddled with the tie on her robe. "Adler is a part of my life that I've tried hard to forget, and now he's back. The idea he's on his way here makes me nervous."

"I can understand your concern. I have a gnawing feeling in my gut every time I think about all this stuff happening at once. I even wondered how I could keep you safe, but I'm only your backup. Jess, sweetheart. You're not the same girl of ten years ago. You've rescued kids, shot a hitman, and outsmarted a serial killer. Adler has no clue what he's in for. I feel sorry for him. I give you my permission to make his life hell."

"Thank you," she said softly. "Now, you can answer my original question. Who were you talking to? Unless of course, it's top secret, and you can't tell your partner." She smiled sweetly at him.

"Tom called to give me the name of the man in the photo." He told her what he learned so far about Calvin and his dad, Trevor Valentine. "What I find odd is that Trevor's son was in the school photo, and not one of his henchmen. No one has been able to touch this guy because of his goons. He usually has multiple layers of protection around him. Because the Valentines are involved, and because of the nature of the crimes, we're going to get some help from the FBI."

"I'm glad to hear the cavalry is coming. These guys have messed with a lot of lives, and I want to help take them down. Besides, Lizzy is counting on me. It's time for her to rest."

"You say the strangest things, but they make more sense to me all the time. I wonder what that says about me."

"It tells me you're growing and seeing the world around you with new insight. Or maybe you've been around me too long," she chuckled. "It also means fewer lectures and more conversation. I'm happy."

"I aim to please." He smiled.

"Okay, goodnight." She kissed him and was out the door before he realized her intention.

Her quick movement stunned him. He scarcely had time to get his hands out from behind his head, and no time to pull her into his arms. They were empty, and so was the room.

"You're slipping, old man." He turned over, and his mind went into overdrive. It was going to be a long lonely night.

Chapter 36

Jessie had slept well. Raring to go, she got ready for work. By the time she got out to the kitchen, Matt had made her coffee. He looked tired. "Didn't you sleep?"

"If you must know, a certain beautiful woman came into my room last night, kissed me, and before I could kiss her back, she was gone."

"Feeling a tad frustrated, are we?" She glanced away from him. Her eyes lit up. "You should keep your door locked. We can't have strange women kissing you in the middle of the night and keeping you from your beauty sleep." She bit her lip to keep from laughing.

"This particular woman is free to come into my room anytime. Since I was denied the pleasure of last night, I'll take it as the opportunity arises." He pulled her into his arms and kissed her.

She sighed, leaning her head against his chest. "You have to behave. You're on the clock." She pulled out of his arms and poured coffee into her cup, saving room for plenty of cream.

"It beats me why you drink coffee in your milk."

"It's the only way I can drink it. All the grownups drink this stuff, and I wanted to fit in at college. This is what I came up with in my quest to fit in. Coffee flavored milk. I think it's more about holding the warm cup for me, but I like the French vanilla cream too."

He grinned at her. "Works for me. Jess, if you see or hear from Stuart, let me know. I'll keep my phone with me. I have a full day, but I have someone who'll be watching the store, and they can be there quick."

"I appreciate you letting me know. I'm going to visit with Lizzy today. Before you ask the question I know is on the tip of your tongue, I'm going to the cemetery and visit her grave. I hope she shows up. I need answers to a few questions, and she has the answers."

"Well, that brings another question to mind." He held her hand in his.

"Oh yeah, what's that?"

"How will she answer those questions?" He put emphasis on the word answer. "Does she talk?"

Jessie shook her head. "It's a little hard to explain, but I'm able to communicate with them. I usually figure out what they're trying to say. Mostly I want to ask her for her help. She knows who her killer is even though we have no idea."

"I'll take your word for it."

"You'll have to or try asking her yourself." She turned away to hide her smile. "Are you ready to leave? I need to get to work." She poured the coffee into her favorite travel coffee mug and handed another one to Matt.

He filled the cup and put the lid on tight. "I'm ready, now." He grabbed his briefcase. Jessie reached for her purse at the same time, and they bumped into each other. "Sorry." He turned around, kissed her, and gave her a nudge between the shoulder blades to get her moving. He reached for her hand after he locked the door. "I'll call you later."

"Okay." She slipped into the driver's seat.

"If something comes up, you call me, got it?"

"I will. See you later." She latched her seatbelt as he closed the door. Honking, she waved at Katie as she made her way out to the road into Blue Cove.

****

Matt got to the station, he was only there long enough to pick up Dylan and send Kip and Gary to visit several more families. The pace would be brutal. It was one of those kinds of days, pushing his team to their limits. A list of concerned parents was growing, teachers were getting wind of the trouble at the school, and the principal was struggling to keep up with the demands for answers. It was all hitting the fan.

"What should we expect today?" Dylan glanced at Matt.

"That's a good question. We should prepare for anything. Charlotte told me Ted is rarely sober. I attribute it to guilt. He knows something. How he'll react to our questions, I have no idea."

"I wonder how far into the mire he's waded. Is he on the outside or is he one of the key players?" Dylan frowned. "Hell, I always thought Ted was a straight shooter, growing up."

"I did too. People aren't always what they seem," he stated. Matt turned left onto Old Homestead Road as the GPS instructed, then made a quick right into Homestead Estates.

"I guess we are about to find out how deep." Dylan gave a low whistle. "These are some big homes. I haven't been out here in a while. These bad boys must be sitting on five to ten acres."

"I like land, but I prefer an ocean view." Matt went several more streets winding through the homes. He turned on the road leading to a huge house sitting back off the main road. From the drive, there was a beautiful view of the ocean in the distance. "Whatever he does for a living, it must pay quite well."

"Nice place. I could live here."

Matt chuckled. "Not on your salary."

"You've got that right." Dylan got out of the car.

Matt rang the doorbell. "Is Mr. McKenzie at home?" Matt asked the maid who opened the door.

"Come in." She motioned for them to enter. "Do you have a card I can give him?"

Matt handed her his business card and followed her into a small parlor. "Thank you." Matt sat in one of the chairs.

"Damn, the man lives like a king." Dylan stood at the window, watching a beautiful quarter horse grazing. "He's one fine looking horse."

Matt stood to look. "I bet he's fast."

"He is." Ted shook Matt's hand. "What took you so long?"

"What do you mean?" Matt had a puzzled look on his face. He noticed Ted's trembling hands and bloodshot eyes.

"I know your reputation, Parker. It's been ten years since my sister's death, and no one asked me anything. But here you are. God, I wished you would have come years ago. This weight is killing me."

"I'm here now, and I have questions. We can start there." Matt searched his face. Ted looked like hell, at least ten years older than he should. There was no sign of the guy Matt once knew.

"Fire away. Hell, you caught me sober. I need something to bolster my confidence. Do either of you want a drink?" He poured himself a shot of whiskey and soda on the rocks.

"No, thanks." Dylan shook his head.

"None for me." Matt took the notebook out of his pocket. "What do you know about your sister's death?"

Ted moved nervously to the edge of his chair. "Too damn much. I've lived with the picture in my mind for ten long years. All of this is mine, paid in full to keep me quiet." He motioned around the room. "It couldn't shut off the screaming in my head, though. I've lived one endless nightmare, lost my wife and kids, all because I couldn't live with myself."

"Why didn't you tell the police?" Dylan asked.

"That's a joke. Are you trying to be funny?" He frowned the lines deepened on his forehead "The chief was dirty and up to his eyeballs in the middle of it. You were too young to realize they were framing you." He pointed at Matt. "Hell, we were all too young. They would've sent you to prison in a heartbeat if they could've manufactured more evidence against you. Believe me, they were trying." He set his empty glass down and poured another shot. "Damn, none of us knew what we were getting into. We were just a bunch of kids with dreams, and they were the adults who trapped us with our own dreams."

"Who are they?" Matt asked.

"All of it is written in a letter. I have the paper in my safe and another copy with my lawyer in the event I should have an untimely demise. Believe me, they'll kill me if they think I'm talking. I'll come to the station tomorrow with my lawyer. I need to make a deal before

I talk."

"I'll have to see what you give me before I can offer a deal."

"I know how it works. I would have come a few years ago, but Anderson was still the chief. I wanted to see how you did and make sure I could trust you. For a while, it seemed like Anderson was grooming you. But you took him out. The problem is, by waiting these people kept messing with peoples' lives."

"It took a while for me to see what he was." Matt frowned, remembering how close he came to losing Jessie.

"Can I ask you a question?" Ted stared at the liquid swirling in the glass as he twirled the cut-crystal tumbler in his hand.

"Sure, go ahead."

"Why now after all this time? It's been forever."

"Did you read the article in the paper?" Matt asked.

"I did. I thought it was good. It made Lizzy look good."

"The writer is the reason. As she told me, it's past time to solve Lizzy's murder." Matt shared how Jessie came across the memorial while running with the team and how they found Grace's body. He didn't mention about her seeing Lizzy's ghost.

"I'm glad you found Grace. She didn't deserve to die. She was trying to help Lizzy, and it was working. I couldn't reach my sister. I was a part of the problem, as you'll see as soon as you read my confession." Ted stared at the empty glass in his hand.

Matt stood. "Ted, I'll do all I can to work out the best deal for you. I can't promise anything, but I'll give it my best shot."

"I believe you'll try, but it doesn't matter. I can't live with it anymore." Ted's had went slack, sending the empty glass to the carpet near his feet.

"I have a bad feeling about this. I think you should come into town with us now. Let us put you in protective custody." Matt tried to convince him he needed to be in town.

"No, I'll be there tomorrow and not any sooner. I want to stay a free man as long as I can." Ted walked them to the door. "I keep her grave," his voice softened. "I want her to know someone cares and remembers her." He shook their hands as they left.

"Do you think he'll come?" Dylan opened the car door.

"He'll be there, if Trevor Valentine doesn't get a hold of him first."

"You don't mean the king of porn, do you?"

"That's the one. His son is the man caught in the photo at the school."

"Damn, we'd better watch his house."

"My sentiment exactly." Matt started the car.

"When do we start?"

"You and Joe will be on tonight and see that he's escorted safely to the station tomorrow. You'll need to go catch some shut-eye after work and take over at ten. Jessie and I can have dinner in the car and watch the house until you relieve us." Matt texted Joe and Jessie his message. "We'd better come up with a backup plan. Valentine won't take this sitting down."

Chapter 37

Jessie left the church, and before she went back to the store, she made her way to the cemetery. Walking among the graves, she found Lizzy's headstone. "I know you came to me for a reason. I'm getting a clearer picture of what happened to you, but we need your help. You're the only one who knows who murdered you." Jessie placed her hand on top of the headstone. "You were trying to break free from the tangled web, and someone murdered you for trying to leave. Lizzy, you're the only one who knows who murdered Grace too."

Jessie walked over to the bench by Gina's grave and sat. She remembered the moment she saw Gina's ghost for the first time and the profound impact it had on her life. Less than a year had passed and yet it seemed like a lifetime ago. Murders left so many unanswered questions for the families. If only these folks could talk.

Jessie looked around the cemetery. The faint rustling of the leaves sounded around her as the gentle breeze skipped from tree to tree. It was peaceful sitting there. Then she became aware of another presence. Lizzy was watching her with a soft expression on her face. "I want your story to end well. Help us," Jessie whispered. She stood, strolling slowly toward the gate, aware that Lizzy followed her every step of the way.

The mystery book club was in the middle of one of their animated discussions when she walked into her store. Little did they know a ghost closely watched the commotion. Jessie smiled. No one would believe her if she told them. Well, maybe Reba might get it and even chuckle once or twice as she shared with her the description playing over in her mind.

The bell rang, drawing her attention to the man who walked in. He was tall, with dark hair, and was wearing retro black glasses. He grabbed a book off the shelf without looking at the cover and sat in one of the leather chairs. The book he chose was a serious romance story which seemed odd, but Lizzy's reaction to him was even stranger. Swaying back and forth, she swirled around him, spinning like a mini tornado. Jessie rubbed her arms feeling the chill across the room. As the book club got louder, Lizzy moved faster in a frenzied motion. The man threw the book onto the chair as he jumped up and ran from the store.

Jessie couldn't stifle the giggle that rolled up her throat and out of her mouth. What had just happened? If she didn't know better, she would swear a reality TV show had orchestrated the whole scene.

After reading Matt's text earlier, she arranged for Molly to pack them a box supper, topped off with one of her great desserts. The woman promised she'd make one of her house specialties for them, oriental salad with grilled chicken, a croissant, and her gooey chocolate brownies for dessert. Jessie planned to pick it up at five.

The book club ladies were packing up their books and enjoying their conversations while Lizzy sat where the man had been. That is, if you could call floating above the chair sitting. A better word to describe it might be levitating. Jessie grinned.

"What has you smiling, dear girl?" Reba stood in the open doors of the coffee shop.

"I've had an enjoyable, but odd last few minutes." Jessie glanced to check if Lizzy was still hovering over the chair.

"Let me get my tea and brownies to take home, and you can tell me all about it."

The boisterous group of women finished gathering their belongings and headed for the door. As they passed Jessie, they thanked her and promised to see her again the following week. They probably would be ordering their new books soon.

"Thank you for telling me about this group." Rachael Tanner brought a book to the counter to pay for it. "They're such fun ladies. I can't wait for the next meeting. I haven't laughed this much since I moved here."

"I'm glad, Rachael. I love having them meet here." Jessie smiled at Reba returning to the store, carrying her tea. "Rachael this is my friend Reba. Rachael is new in town."

"Rachael, it's nice to meet you. I hope you're meeting new people and starting to feel this is like home."

"I am, thanks to Jessie." Rachael grabbed the bag Jessie handed to her.

"Our Jessie is a dear girl. You found a good person to help you find your place in your new sphere. I hope we will meet again."

"If you come to this store often, then I'm sure we

will. I'd best get home and start dinner. Thanks again, Jessie.

"See you soon." Jessie walked with her to the door. She came back and sat next to Reba.

"Now, I want to hear all about what had you smiling." Reba took a sip of her tea.

"I know you'll appreciate what happened a while ago." Jessie proceeded to tell her the odd scene that had played out in her store. Jessie smiled when Reba chuckled.

"There's never a boring moment when it comes to you, dear." Reba patted her hand. "Besides getting dessert for tonight's dinner, I wanted to talk to you. I'm a woman on a mission." She patted her hair. "Is Lizzy still here?"

"Yes, she's been here since I went to the cemetery to talk to her this morning."

"I've had Charlotte on my mind often the past few days. She's found her way into several of my dreams. My dear friend will face some hard days ahead, but the truth will finally come out. In my heart of hearts, I think she knows the truth in some form already."

"What makes you think she knows?" Jessie watched Lizzy move behind Reba.

"A woman knows her family. She understands when something is wrong even if she doesn't know all that's going on." Reba pulled her sweater around her. "Lizzy is close, isn't she?"

"Yes, right behind you." Jessie leaned closer to Reba "It will be hard for Charlotte. What we have learned to date implicates Ted and Lizzy both. But I believe Lizzy was trying to get out when she was murdered."

"What makes you think she was trying to change?"

Jessie told her about the vision of the dragon. "The faces change to Lizzy's and Grace each time I see them. There was a war over her life. I don't understand what it all means, but I know it's true."

"That explains the presence in the store the other morning. I knew it was more than a bug. You do understand there are still a few surprises left in this case. Their revelation will rock our community."

"We are only beginning to see the scope of what has been going on in this idyllic community." Jessie folded her hands in front of her on the table.

"It's everywhere, out of sight and out of mind. People would be surprised by what happens around us every day." Reba looked around the store and lowered her voice. "If walls could talk, we'd all be in a bit of trouble."

"What is the purpose of this life? It seems we are too busy messing it up to enjoy what's in front of us." Jessie frowned.

"It's only my opinion, but life is about growing beyond ourselves and becoming the best human we can be for others. I doubt the masses would agree with my assessment. However, it has worked well for me, and I'll stick with it. No sense of me changing this late in the game."

"I certainly wouldn't change anything about you." Jessie squeezed Reba's hand.

"You're a dear girl. You'll be facing your share of challenges in the next few days. It's important for you to know this is your time to fly. You've been testing your wings since moving here. Not sure of why it's all happening to you. When this case is over, you'll no longer wonder. I can't wait to see what your new-found strength will cause you to do. It's all so exciting. Oh, what I wouldn't give to be young again." Reba stood, gathering up her purse and bags. "I do enjoy watching all the happenings even if I can't be involved."

"You're a part of every case we've solved." She walked with Reba to the door.

"Yes, but I would sure love to give a few of these criminals the what-for if you know what I mean."

"I do." Jessie did a karate kick movement and grinned sheepishly.

"Well done, dear. Give them a few swift kicks from me."

Jessie laughed. "I will."

When the clock's hand reached five, she locked the front door. She went into Joe's to pick up the boxed dinners Molly had created. "I can't wait to taste what you made for us." Jessie handed Molly the money.

"Those ladies in your store were having a great time today."

"I love when they meet. They get into their discussion with energy."

"You can say that again." Molly bagged the meals and handed Jessie her change. "Kenny told me the station is in the middle of another big case. He didn't give me any details, but he said it's huge."

"It's major, but there've been a few big breaks the last several days. Hopefully, it's close to being solved." She reached for the bag. "Thanks, Molly. I'm sure we'll enjoy this."

Locking the doors when she pulled them shut, she busied herself with the closing routine. Who was the man who had been in the store earlier? She'd forgotten about him. Lizzy's reaction to him was strong. Darn, she should have taken a picture. It was comical when he ran out of the store freaked out. Reba was right. There was never a dull moment when it came to her life. Contentment filled her like a warm cup of tea on a cold day, or more to her liking, running outside on a beautiful day. She took a final look around the store, shut off the lights, and carried her bag out to the car.

Chapter 38

Jessie pulled into her parking space at home. Matt had arrived before her and was waiting in the car. She placed the bag in the back seat of his car. "I'll be right with you. I want to change into something more comfortable. Do you want to come in?"

"Sure do." He walked with her to the door, carrying a suitcase. "I needed another change of clothes." Matt set the case in the guest room.

"I'm ready." Jessie walked out of her room wearing a comfortable pair of jeans, a t-shirt, and a sweater. She put her badge in her pocket

"Do you have your gun?" Matt asked glancing at her.

"Yes." She opened her sweater where her holster hooked over her shoulder to show him. "I never go with you on a case without it. You'd make me put it on. I preempted the lecture and did it." She smiled and walked out the door he was holding open.

He gave her swat on her backside. "You're something. I like it when you're sassy." He grabbed her hand and walked with her to the car. "I can't wait to hear about your day. Mine was surprising."

"Interesting and somewhat amusing is how I would describe mine." She slid into the front seat.

"Sounds to me like we have plenty to talk about."

Matt closed his door. "What happened?"

She loved the sound of his laugh as she told him about Lizzy, the book club, and the man. Of course, she embellished the story the best she could. "In his rush to get out of there, he forgot his romance novel." She chuckled. "His choice in reading material made me doubt he was a real customer I think he was there to check on me and got more than he bargained for."

"What makes you think that?"

"Lizzy's reaction to him may have seemed comical at first, but she was agitated." Jessie glanced at Matt. "She knew him, I'm sure of it. What bothers me is with all the distractions in my store I forgot to take a picture of him. It would help if we had a photo."

"It would help, but you know what he looks like. You can check out the school's yearbooks and see if he's a teacher in one of the photos. After that, you can check out mug shots at the station." Matt drove toward Old Homestead Road. "If he's involved, we'll know soon enough."

"Where are we going?" She turned in her seat.

"Ted McKenzie. He's ready to tell us what he knows. He's been carrying a heavy load and hasn't known who he could trust." Matt told her about his earlier talk with Ted. "We're going to do what we can to keep him alive until Dylan can escort him to the station tomorrow. I'm sure Valentine has people watching his house and knows we were there. We'll take the first watch. Then, as soon as Tom gets into town, Dylan and Joe will relieve us. I've been uneasy about this all day." He turned into Homestead Estates.

"Why didn't you take him in?"

"I asked him to, and he refused. He offered to

come in tomorrow and bring his lawyer with him. I tried to convince him to come in today, and we would protect him. He didn't want to. I got the feeling he wanted to die. He sent a copy of his letter to his lawyer. We have nothing to hold him on. He's still free to do what he wants. After tomorrow, it may be a different story."

"What does your gut tell you about him?"

"He's eaten up with guilt. We were young and who knows how those thugs trapped him into playing their game, but they did. I don't think he killed his sister, but he's culpable. The men involved in this will kill without blinking an eye."

"Could his lawyer be one that Valentine got for him?"

"Hell, he could be."

"Maybe we should check on him now."

"I'll call for back-up." Matt called it in. "We'll wait until Dylan gets here. Kenny's calling for help."

"I bet he's the one who's been taking care of the grave and memorial. There are always fresh flowers no matter when I go." She scrolled through her phone messages.

"Yes, he told me he did."

"What else did you learn?" she asked.

Matt slowed his speed. "Anderson was dirty, and I was being framed to take the fall. It's hard for me to believe Anderson was on the wrong side for a long time. How could I not have known it all those years I trained under him?"

"It's hard to imagine a person you respect can be corrupt. Anderson came off as a father figure and not a corrupt cop."

"He sure did." Matt pulled up near the gate turning into Ted's property.

"At least I can understand why Ted didn't go to the cops, or even talk to you once you became chief. He probably was trying to figure out if you were corrupt too."

"I get it. After talking to Ted, I think there are more people in town involved." Matt stopped the car.

"Reba told me today the town would be rocked by the revelations the next few days. We're in for a little town housecleaning. It would be nice if Blue Cove could be the peaceful little town I thought I was moving to. Boy, was I ever wrong."

Matt's phone rang. "This is Matt." He put it on speaker.

"This is Tom. I'm in town. I'm on my way out to you with Dylan and Joe. You'll need help. Valentine won't take this sitting down. As soon as we get there, we need to go check the house and make sure your guy's still alive."

"Sounds good, I was waiting for back-up." Matt looked at all the places someone could hide around the area. Way too many trees for his peace of mind.

"We need to convince him to come in now. Did you bring a vest to put on him?"

"I did." Matt turned onto the long drive approaching Ted's house.

"This is our chance to take Valentine out, and we don't want to lose a major witness. Dylan told me you tried to get him to come earlier. I'll convince him. I know plenty about Valentine's operations."

"We're ready. I have Ted's house in view now."

"Valentine has his house bugged, I can guarantee

it. They've paid him to be quiet. They are watching their investment. Dylan says we're about three minutes out."

"We're here, and we'll wait until you get here to make contact." Matt glanced at Jessie.

"Have your guns ready." Tom told them.

"We will."

Matt took his gun out of the holster. "Put this on." He tossed a vest at her, one he grabbed from the backseat. "Now we wait. You heard what he said. Get your gun ready. You may have to use it."

Jessie looked at the vest. "Are you expecting trouble?"

"I wouldn't put it past Valentine to try something. Either way, we have to be prepared." He slipped his vest on.

"Someone's coming." Jessie saw the dust swirling out on the road. She slipped into her vest.

"Duck!" He pushed her head down. Three cars raced into the circular drive in front of the house. He waited until each car came to a stop. "It's all clear. They're the good guys."

Matt stepped out of the car. "Wait here until I know what they want to do."

"I'm not going anywhere." Jessie watched Matt walk over to Dylan's car. She liked the way he was always watching out for her. She opened the door when he motioned for her to come.

"Jess, grab that vest in the backseat, would you?" Matt knocked on the door.

Jessie raced up the stairs behind them. "I hope he's okay."

Ted opened the door. "Matt, I didn't expect to see

you until tomorrow."

"You need to come with us." Matt followed Ted inside.

"Am I under arrest?"

"No, we're concerned for your safety. Valentine has a reputation for knowing and wasting those he thinks are squealing. Trust me. He knows what you're planning."

"If he does, then I won't be safe anywhere, no matter what you do." Ted ran his hand through his hair.

"You'll stand a better chance with us than you will here on your own." Matt studied the man pacing in front of him. "Look, you'll have plenty to deal with over the next few weeks. Let us work to keep you safe while you deal with it." Matt handed him the vest. "Put this on. We need to get you out of here."

Matt went out first with his gun drawn, his eyes searching the trees surrounding the property. "Damn, too many places for a shooter to hide." He motioned to Ted and the rest. "Stay low."

Two FBI agents met them on the porch. Several armed agents took up positions behind the cars. The first bullet whizzed by Matt's head, hitting the picture window to the side of him.

"Shots fired. Down, get down." Matt saw the hole in the window out of the corner of his eye.

The next bullet slammed into Ted's chest, knocking him into Jessie. Thrown backward, she raised her arms trying to shield her head from hitting the porch.

Ted collapsed on top of her. "Are you okay?"

Wheezing, she gasped for air.

"Damn, that hurts." Ted grabbed his chest,

groaning.

"Believe me, I know." She wiggled to get some of his weight off her chest. "Think of the damage the bullet would have caused inside you."

"It feels like it has." He panted for air.

The massive wooden front door was the next casualty. The splintered pieces shattered, turning into sharp projectiles skimming around them.

"Dang, that was close," Dylan protected Jessie with his body.

"Keep your head down," one of the agents yelled, "all of you. Shots are coming from the trees on the right.

"Tom," Matt yelled. "Give us some cover. We're pinned down—nothing but sitting ducks up here."

"Where are they?" Tom radioed for more back-up.

"The right side of the property in the trees somewhere," Matt shouted as he watched the next bullet split the wood in the railing not far from the agent's head and embed in the siding.

"I've got help coming." Tom and Kip shot several rounds. "They're waiting at the turnoff watching the road. Maybe they can flush them out."

One of the agents rolled down the steps and inched along the ground to the cars, drawing fire away from the porch. Bullets skipped along the ground. One hit the trunk of the car.

"They're getting off a lot of rounds. These guys mean business. How's he doing?" Matt pointed at Ted.

"He's in pain, but alive. They had him. Without the vest, he'd be a dead man." Dylan pushed Jessie's hair out of her face. "Can you breathe okay? I know he's heavy, but you can't move yet." Several pops sounded, bullets riddling the front of the house.

"I won't be moving anytime soon. Now I know what Liam must have felt after I slammed him to the ground that night. Where's a ghost the moment you need one?" She gave a nervous giggle.

"Listen." Matt shot off a few rounds near the shooters.

"You mean the sirens headed our way." Dylan stretched out his cramping leg.

"Yep, with any luck, it will spook those goons and send them into their waiting arms."

"A ghost is a spook and not a siren." Jessie grinned at her pun. "I'm sorry, Ted." She twitched, and he groaned.

"Hang in there, guys," Tom called out to them. "I hear a car starting."

"It was quiet, too quiet." Matt didn't want anyone to move until they were sure.

Pop, pop, pop, more gunfire sounded and then the sound of squealing tires. "Matt, they have them. The car spun out of control on dirt and rolled. "It's not Valentine, but a couple of his thugs." Tom ran up the stairs to check on Ted. Dylan helped Tom get Ted to the car.

Matt held out his hand and pulled Jessie gently into a sitting position. "How are you, sweetheart?"

"Sore, but happy you kept him alive to tell his story."

Chapter 39

The doctor shook Matt's hand. "The patient has bruising and two small fractures in the third and fourth vertebrosternal ribs or true ribs, which means they're directly attached to the sternum." He held up the X-ray pointing to the fine lines. "I've given him something to manage the pain. It's a good thing you put him in a vest, or he'd be a dead man. They were aiming for his heart. Keeping a bullet outside of the body is better every time. I'll release him to your agents with instructions on what to look for and how to keep him comfortable. He'll need to see his regular doctor as soon as possible. His physician will monitor the healing process." He handed Matt Ted's paperwork.

"Thanks." Matt took the release forms and papers from the doctor.

"If there's a problem, bring him back."

"Will do." Matt turned to hand the papers to Jessie. "Hang on to these for me, would you? I don't want to lay them down somewhere. I need to put copies in Ted's file."

"Of course." She smiled at him.

"Sounds like Ted fared better than it looked. He's going to hurt, as you know, but he's alive. Now we have to keep him that way until Valentine is in custody, and even then, I'm not sure he'll be safe. Trevor has long arms with friends who owe him enough to do whatever he tells them to."

"How are you going to keep him safe tonight?" Jessie shifted her weight, leaning her hip against the wall.

"As soon as Dylan gets here, we'll discuss it."

"You need to do your job. I'll be fine for tonight, or I can stay at the Inn."

"Sweetheart, Adler's on his way here. No way will I leave you unprotected. Between Maxwell, his team, and my guys, we have plenty of help. My only question is, where to put Ted for the night. We want to keep him safe, but at the same time comfortable."

"Why is Tom here? I meant to ask you earlier." She rolled her neck to the side and shrugged her shoulders.

"As you know, Valentine's son was identified in the photo. He's one tough customer, but his father is even worse. The FBI has had him on their radar for a while, and they want to nail him. He's hard to pin down because his thugs do the dirty work for him. The photo of his son from the school is unbelievable. He slipped up, and now the Agency has the leverage to lure Trevor out."

"Speaking of his heavies, how are the two from the rollover?" she asked.

"Dylan is waiting to hear, now."

"If the doctor releases them, the jail could get awfully crowded tonight." She grinned at him.

"We have room for all of them. I'm not sure it's the wise choice for McKenzie."

"What about his own house? There is a team securing it and gathering evidence. Would Valentine send people back to the same place to get him?"

"It's hard to know. The issue is that Ted's house is too big, and there's a lot of property to secure if they decided to. It's a logistical nightmare.

"What does your gut tell you?"

"Honestly, the safest place is the station. We'll have to do our best to make him comfortable."

"You've got to go with your instincts. They've been right every time." Jessie waved at Dylan, headed toward them.

"Do you have news for me?" Matt asked.

"They're treating them for minor injuries. The doctor said they'd be good to go soon. I'll read them their rights and book them. I figure we're looking at attempted murder charges against those two goons."

"They'll have several. I need a cell for Ted. The station is the safest place for him. We aren't booking him yet until I hear what he and his lawyer have to say, but he needs to be there for his safety."

"I agree it's the safest place. Anderson used to have a recliner in the lounge. We put it in the storeroom. We can stick it in Ted's cell so he can sit up. It'll make it easier for him to breathe." Dylan leaned against the wall

"We'll put him in the first holding cell upstairs." Matt told Dylan. "It's the largest we've got."

"Sounds good. You won't get much info out of those two. As of now, their lips are sealed." Dylan pushed away from the wall.

"It's amazing how a bully can rule those under him. They'll probably take a fall before they talk." Matt texted the station to get ready for incoming suspects and to be on alert for trouble.

"I'll get Kenny and Joe to move the chair." Dylan turned to leave and then stopped. "Matt, you were on you're A-game today. You knew there'd be trouble and you had all the key players in place. This day could've ended bad, bad. Get some rest tonight, boss. You can hit the ground running tomorrow."

"Thanks, man. I'll bring Ted as soon as he's released."

Jessie reached for Matt's hand. "Let's sit and wait. I'm tired of standing."

"I'm sorry. I forgot you were sore. I have no idea why we're standing out here when there's a perfectly good waiting room." Matt told the nurse at the desk where they'd be. "They'll call us once he's ready to leave."

"You look tired." She reached for his hand after they sat down. "Have you noticed how everything seems to happen at the same time?"

"I've noticed." He leaned back in the chair, closing his eyes.

"I don't get it." She pursed her lips, her fingers tapped on the arm of the chair.

"What's there to get? A case unfolds when it does." He grinned, keeping his eyes closed. "It moves at a normal pace until *you* take out your pen, and then all hell breaks loose. You're good at stirring up trouble." He chuckled.

"I don't know whether to thank you or hit you."

"I'd rather you kissed me. I've had a hard day." His arm went around her, pulling closer. Matt whispered in her ear "There's no one else in the room, we're all alone." Pushing her hair off her neck, he kissed her cheek. "I'm happy we're alive, and did I mention we're alone?"

"I believe I heard you mention that fact."

He turned her head, holding her face between his hands. He bent his head gradually, gazing into her eyes, and kissed her. He leisurely tasted her lips, at first brushing his across hers. Then his kissed devoured her with a hint of promise and deep longing, leaving them both shaken. "Jess, you're an amazing woman, and I'm happy you're on my side."

"I feel the same way about you. Not the amazing woman part, of course." She leaned her head on his shoulder and sighed. The ringing wall phone interrupted the moment.

Matt answered the phone. He motioned to her. "Ted's ready. We need to get him back to the station alive, and then, we can breathe."

Chapter 40

Ted was comfortable and safe. Matt could take a breath. He glanced at his watch. Midnight. Where had the time gone? "Jess, sweetheart," he said, lightly shaking her shoulder. She was sleeping soundly and didn't respond to his touch. "Jess, honey, let's get you home." He grabbed her hand, and she jumped.

"I'm sorry." She stretched her arms, which had gone numb from cradling her head.

"No need to be sorry."

"I sat here to wait, and I must have drifted off." She pushed the hair off her face. "Is Ted okay?"

"He's fine. We have enough firepower to keep him safe tonight." He took her hand and tugged gently. "I'm ready to be out of here. You looked uncomfortable."

"I was, and now I'm stiff." She groaned as she stood. "I put Ted's release papers on your desk."

"Perfect, thanks. I had forgotten all about them. I'm glad I gave them to you. You're good with details." She started toward the door. "Wait a minute, Jess." He put the papers in the top drawer of his desk.

"There, there, you'll be okay." She patted her grumbling stomach. "I forgot we had dinner in the car."

"I did too." They walked out to the car together.

She grabbed the bag out of the backseat and latched her seatbelt. She handed him a croissant and took a bite of the one she was holding. "When you're hungry, everything tastes better. There are some great looking brownies in this box. We won't starve."

"I never thought we would. Starting with bread and dessert is strange though. It could become a bad habit. I have a sweet tooth, as you know."

"You're not a meat and potato kind of guy?" she asked.

"Sure, I am, but I can live with something sweet to finish it off." He took a big bite of the brownie.

"What's next?" She turned in the seat so she could see him.

"Tomorrow, we find out what Ted has to offer us." He turned onto Main Street.

"You mean today, don't you?"

"Don't remind me. It's going to be a short night."

"He's familiar with the whole operation. I'd bet on it. The guilt he's been carrying around would stagger most of us. I saw him coming out of the cemetery one day. Of course, at the time I didn't know it was Ted. Even from a distance, I could sense his guilt and rage. I hope he'll fess up." Jessie polished off the croissant.

"If he wants to get a deal, he'd better have some great info for us."

"He has it. I'm sure. You only have to convince him it's worth the risk to talk." She took napkins out of the bag and handed him one.

"Today didn't help. The Valentine family has worked freely in town for several years. Someone has had to turn a blind eye to their actions." Matt pulled into the space. He took Jessie's hand as she got out of the car. "We'll find out who. Those are the people that bother me the most. Valentine is a criminal. His record speaks for itself. But men like Anderson, who try to have it both ways, make me angry."

"There's not a doubt in my mind you'll find those involved in any cover-up." She smiled at him and gave him the key.

He unlocked the door, holding it open for her. "I'm going to be busy the next few days. Adler will be in town soon, and I haven't forgotten. If I can't be with you, someone else will, or you'll be with me. You must promise you won't venture out alone until we have Stuart in custody. I know he's coming for you.'

"Yes, I know you're right, but I don't want to talk about it." Her chin edged up.

"Damn, Jess, we have to talk about it. I know it brings back bad memories, but you have to be prepared to face this guy because he's coming."

"I'm fully aware of the fact. I'll be ready. I'm not the young girl he intimidated and scared before. I'm going to be prepared for him this time even if he takes me by surprise."

"No surprises. We are trying to prevent situations we have no control over."

She patted his cheek, walked into the kitchen, and poured a glass of milk. "Do you want some to go with your brownie?" She took another glass out of the cabinet. "Enough about Stuart. He's coming, but after today I need to think about something good for a minute. Brownies with gooey chocolate icing will do the trick." She took a big bite.

He chuckled, taking another napkin from the bag and wiping the chocolate off her chin. "I get the message. You don't want to talk about him at the moment."

"Thank you."

****

Jessie woke up in a cold sweat a few hours after she had gone to bed. He had invaded her dreams again. Stuart was coming, and she would have to deal with him. Being strong was important, especially now. Women shouldn't have to put up with this junk. Turning on the light, she reached for the pen and notepad on her nightstand. Matt's snores in the next room gave her comfort in a noisy kind of way. He was there if she needed him. All she had to do was call. For the moment words would be her therapy. Contentment washed over her, and she sighed. Matt was right for her.

The sun was peeking through her blinds the next time she awakened. The pen and notepad were on the pillow next to her. Matt was moving around in the next room. She jumped out of bed and went into the bathroom. Splashing cold water on her face, she ran a brush through her hair, pulling it into a ponytail. "Ugh," she shook her head at the image looking back at her.

Matt knocked on the door. "Are you awake?"

"I'll be there in a few," she called out. Looking at her feet, she realized she had on two different shoes. "Well, that's an interesting look." She kicked off the red shoe and went in search of the matching black one. Somehow red wouldn't look right with her pink shirt.

"Good morning, sweetheart." He kissed her cheek. "How is it possible you look this good in the morning?"

"I was going to ask you the same question. Did you sleep well?"

"Not bad. I thought I heard you scream in your sleep a couple of times. I don't think you slept well."

"I didn't, but I wrote the next article for Max and

281

Neil if they want it."

"We'd better plan for the onslaught after it's printed." He reached for her hand. "If we leave now, we can get our coffee at Joe's this morning. I'm hungry, and I could use one of her breakfast sandwiches."

"I'll be ready in a minute." She gathered the stuff she needed to take to the store, including her notepad. Slipping her laptop in the case, she took it along too. "I know what you're going to ask. Yes, I have a computer at work, but I want to write my story on this one. It's how I roll."

Matt grinned at her. "Damn, but you're good. If we get married, you can anticipate what I'm going to say before I say it." He stroked his chin. "There might be merit in that, although it could get a little boring for me."

"Ha, ha." She gave him a playful shove toward the door. "Don't forget to honk. It's tradition."

"Yours, not mine." He grinned at her.

"I'm declaring it ours as long as you're driving me in the morning." She smiled after he honked on his way past the Inn.

"I wonder what this day holds for us," she muttered.

Chapter 41

Glancing at the cemetery from the window, Jessie thought about the words she had spoken earlier. How she wished she had never uttered them. Her morning had started innocently enough, playful banter with her guy, coffee at Joe's, and a sweet kiss goodbye.

Matt's parting words were a warning to call him if she was concerned. What happened? Kip was the one watching her store now. He went from being in his car across the street, to parking in front of her store, to sitting in the chair watching her, all in a matter of an hour's time. What was next?

It all started with the ringing phone, and like a dummy, she answered it before the store was open. "Idle Time Books. May I help you?"

A man's low, breathy voice came over the line. Had she heard him, right? "I'm sorry I couldn't hear you." There was no doubt the second time around. She slammed the phone in his ear. Some creep who got his high off making obscene phone calls, and she had asked him to repeat it. Jessie giggled to herself. He must have thought he had a live one. Kip had laughed aloud after she told him how she had asked the man to repeat his obscene comment. The day digressed from there.

As soon as she opened the doors into the coffee shop, a stocky man of medium height came charging into her store. She couldn't remember the question he asked or if she had even heard him. The next thing she remembered was picking herself up off the ground after he had shoved her and fled through the front door. Then what? He began screaming obscenities at her. Had everyone lost their collective minds today?

Molly texted Matt. Matt called Kip. Now here he sat with a silly grin on his face watching her for the rest of the day.

"Jessie, how is it that every criminal within a hundred miles of this town seems to have a run-in with you? I mean doesn't that seem a bit weird? We're talking two nut jobs on the same day." Kip laughed. "What are the odds?"

"I'm not sure I want to answer your question. The odds seem to be increasing with each day that I live here. Although today was strange even for me, and it's not over yet." From where she stood, she could see Lizzy was in the cemetery, and so was a man. Who was he? Jessie took the letter from the stack of mail and stuffed it in her purse.

****

Valentine's goons weren't talking. Matt needed something to move them. They were more afraid of their boss than the threat of prison. He threw their files on his desk. The phone on his desk buzzed. "Kenny, what's up?"

"McKenzie's lawyer is here."

"Thanks. I'll be out." Matt walked to the front desk and introduced himself. The man was meticulously dressed, everything about him said high-priced attorney. Ted would need a good one before it was all said and done. Matt hoped he was as good as he looked.

"I'm Arlen Rosner, Ted McKenzie's attorney." He shook Matt's hand. "I'd like to see my client."

"Of course, I'll take you to him." Matt motioned and started down the hall.

"He told me that he hadn't been charged at this time. Is that correct?" Rosner asked.

"The only reason he came in early was for his protection. We were almost too late."

"He informed me about what happened. It was a sobering experience for my client." I'll talk to him first then we'll meet with you afterward." They walked down the hall to the holding cell.

"If this isn't private enough, there's a conference room across the hall you're free to use." Matt pointed at the door.

"Thanks. I think I'll take you up on the room. We have some details to work out."

"I'll be in my office as soon as you're ready." Matt left Rosner to speak with McKenzie.

Matt read over the formal indictment against the two men. At the top of the list were attempted murder charges against Valentine's flunkies. Their arraignment was scheduled for three today. Getting them to and from the court alive would be a task he wasn't relishing. No attorney had shown up for the men yet, which didn't bode well for them. Valentine didn't like slip-ups. Trevor would send someone to clean up the mess.

Dylan knocked on his door. "Hey, boss, Ted is ready. Do want to meet in the conference room?"

"Yes, and you need to be in there with us."

"Okay, I'll grab my notebook and be right there."

Matt picked up his small recorder and walked to

the conference room. "Dylan said your client is ready to talk."

"He is. We want to work out a deal. At this time, he's going to tell you what he knows. He's willing to sign a confession after he knows the terms."

"I'll get the formalities out of the way first. I will be recording you to make sure we are getting your testimony accurately. Ted, will you please state your full name for the record."

"My name is Theodore McKenzie."

"Do you have counsel?" Matt asked.

"I do."

"And is your counsel present?"

"He is." Ted responded.

"Mr. Rosner, at any time you can direct your client not to answer a question."

"I understand." The attorney handed a few papers to Ted.

"Let's start, shall we? Ted since you have not been charged with anything at this point, you can begin."

"This is the statement I drafted with my attorney. I will answer any questions you have regarding it." He pushed the copy to Matt. "Mr. Rosner is a new attorney. My last one was from within the Valentine organization. I didn't want him to be privy to what I'm about to say."

"I'll read this as we go. Why don't you begin by telling me why you wanted to meet? Matt took out his small notepad and pen. Dylan slipped into the chair beside him.

"I've been carrying this around with me for a long time. I loved my sister. Her death destroyed me. I quit living, and only survived after they found her."

"Do you have a family?" Dylan asked.

"I was married, and I have two kids, but my drinking destroyed anything we had as a family. I couldn't face life without a drink and my wife couldn't live with me in my drunken state." His hand trembled. Taking a deep breath, he began again. "It had all seemed innocent in the beginning." Ted proceeded to tell how he and Lizzy had been the window dressing for an operation known by several influential people in town. In the beginning, he had no idea it was trapping girls at the high school into porn with or without their knowledge. It didn't take long to figure it out.

"How did you figure it out?" Matt made eye contact with Ted.

"I heard rumors, and Lizzy told me more. She told me that she wanted out of the whole mess. Some big brother I turned out to be. I told her they were all lies. I should have protected her, and instead, I fed her to the wolves. Drinking became my way to not deal with it."

Matt circled a sentence on one of the pages. "What do you mean here?" He pointed to the paragraph.

"You'll understand as you read further. He's at the heart of it for us in some ways. We trusted him, believing he would never get us involved in something that could hurt us. I underestimated the money involved and how it can change people. I hate him."

"Who else is involved?" Matt scribbled a note underlining it twice. He thought he already knew the answer.

"Besides Valentine and his group, there is a retired photography teacher, the vice principal at the school, someone still working here who's been leaking information, and one of the retired members of city council. I already told you about Anderson."

Matt pushed what he had written on the paper toward Ted to read. "Is he one?"

Ted bowed his head. "I hate the SOB."

"We'll come back to this later. Are these the codes for Valentine's operation on the web?" Matt looked at the numbers and words on the document in his hand. "If my tech guy uses them, can he get in?"

"Yes, as of yesterday. Valentine's tech guy may be scurrying to make changes."

"Dylan, take these passwords and codes to Gary. Tell him to get Jeremy working on it too. "Do you know who murdered your sister?"

"I'm fairly positive it's this guy." Ted pointed to a name on his written statement.

"What makes you think it was him?" Matt asked.

"She fancied herself in love with the jerk. He was a smooth talker. I had introduced him to her. A real lady's man, if you know what I mean. After she confided in him that she wanted out, the police found her dead." He swiped at the tears on his cheek. "People tried to talk us out of the madness. Your friend Chad was one of them. He got beat up for his trouble, and Grace ended up dead."

"You've given us lots information to digest. I want to read through your statement thoroughly and then talk to the judge. Sit tight. Would you like lunch ordered in for you and your attorney? I don't think it's safe for you to go around town. I'll send Kenny back, and you can tell him what you want." Matt left them in the room and sent Kenny to the conference room.

"Gary, what do you have for me?" Matt walked into the tech room.

"I got in, but was hit with a new firewall. Jeremy said he could get around it and started working on it right away. I'm waiting for his call." Gary's fingers flew across the keyboard.

"Call me after you get something." He walked down the hall to his office. Sitting in his chair, Matt began reading the statement line by line, making notes to tell the judge. Damn, it made someone in the department dirty. Who was here ten years ago that is still around? He would begin there. When he presented all the information to Judge Sanders, he needed all his ducks to be in a row. He began to lay out the evidence and tie it together.

Tom walked into his office. "We'll be here to help you take people into custody tomorrow. It sounds like you'll have quite a few."

"I'm not sure the jail will be able to hold them all." Matt scribbled a name on the paper. He pushed it toward Tom.

Tom read the name on the paper. "Valentine isn't going to be happy, that's for damn sure."

As soon as we check the DNA, if it's a match, we'll charge him with murder. It will take an army to bring him in safely. It'll make the firefight yesterday look like a picnic in the park in comparison."

"I hope he tries. We've been trying to get this guy for a long time."

"He's all yours." Matt whacked Tom on the back.

Chapter 42

He couldn't wait to see her. It had been a busy day with a promise of several more to come. She was at the window watching for his car and waved as he pulled into the open space in front of the store. Locking the door behind her, she smiled, slid into the passenger seat, and closed the door.

"How was your day, my little dragon slayer?" Matt asked, waiting for her to latch her seatbelt.

She pursed her lips shaking her head at him. "No dragon sightings, today."

"Not even one. That's too bad." The fantasy of Jess wielding a sword flew into his mind. His brow furrowed. "You never answered how your day was."

"Not nearly as bad as yours must have been from the expression on your face." She gave him a concerned look. It only took a minute before she had him laughing at her story, until she told him about the man who pushed her to the ground.

"What's wrong with everyone nowadays? Have they all lost their minds? I'd liked to get my hands on him." Matt frowned. "It wasn't Adler was it?"

"No, I would know him no matter how much he has changed. You'll have to trust me on that subject."

"I can't believe you asked the man to repeat his message," Matt chuckled.

"What can I say? Obviously once wasn't enough for me."

"After confirming a lot of Ted's testimony, we're beginning the process of arrest warrants. We'll soon be rounding up several members of our community. To say it's going to be a tough time in Blue Cove is an understatement."

"Ted gave you a lot, I take it." Turning in her seat, she glanced at him.

"Yes, some of it we knew already, and a lot of it was new information. We need confirmation and a bit more evidence to substantiate a few key pieces."

"Sounds like you're going to be busy." She gave his shoulder a gentle squeeze.

"We will. Thankfully, we have extra help with Tom and his team in town."

"Are you going to take down the porn site and its operator?" She crossed her fingers.

"You can count on it." He pulled away from the curb.

"All the girls will be happy to hear the news. Their photos are out there on the Internet. Removing the site is the first step. Arrests and convictions are the next deterrents." Jessie frowned. "The sad thing is someone will come along and take their place."

"I'm afraid it's the way our world seems to work right now." Matt glanced at her. "We're headed to a new place for dinner tonight. The next several days might be hectic for both of us. If I can't be with you, remember, you'll be with me. I expect Adler to be here any time if he's not in town already."

"There's a pleasant thought." She reached for her purse, digging around in it, looking for her lip gloss.

"You know I'm right. What's your plan?"

"I've been thinking about it, but let's not talk about it now. You need a break, and after my day I do too." She patted his hand. "We'll talk about it after dinner."

"Jess, what aren't you telling me?"

"I'll tell you after we eat and not a minute sooner." She turned to look out the side window.

"All right but this conversation isn't over. We'll pick up where we left off right after dinner. You've got that?" He pulled into the restaurant parking lot.

"Yes." She waited for him to open her door. "This looks like a nice place." She took his extended hand.

He leaned close to her. "I don't know what you're up to, sweetheart, but I'm not too busy to be concerned about you. All these things seem to come at once, but we can handle it. This is what we do. Don't worry your pretty head about me having too much on my plate. We are a team. This is what we do."

"I understand, but I do worry you have too much to deal with, and you don't need something from my past added to the equation."

"If I'm correct, this case started with a ghost from my past. Literally." Matt emphasized the word *my*.

"Your ghost was followed by an obsessed man from mine. We are quite the pair." She laughed.

He held the door open for her. "Before this night is out, you'll tell me."

"Is that right? Are you sure?"

"I'm confident. We're partners, and you'd never keep important information from me." He placed his hand in the center of her back. "I know I'm right."

"Probably," she whispered, "but you're wondering, aren't you?" She moved ahead of him, following the host to their table.

After giving the waiter their order, Matt leaned back in his chair. "Jess, hand it over."

"What are you talking about?" Her eyes were large with surprise.

"You got another letter, didn't you?" He extended his hand palm up toward her. "Let's have it."

"How did you know?" She pulled the letter out of her purse and handed it to him.

"Call it an educated guess." He folded the letter and stuck it in the inside pocket of his jacket. "We won't talk about this at the moment, but after dinner, sweetheart, all bets are off."

"Are you going to lecture me?"

"Probably," he whispered, leaning close to her, "But now who's wondering?" He patted her hand and sat back in his chair.

"Touché." She smiled. "You're good at deduction, Mr. Parker. It must be a police thing."

"Thank you, ma'am." He gave her a gesture of tipping his hat.

****

The smell of the sizzling fajitas the waiter placed on the table in front of them was an invitation to stop talking and start eating. "I didn't realize how hungry I was until this moment." Matt dipped a chip in the salsa.

Jessie tasted a bite of the sizzling chicken she had placed on her plate. "Oh, this is yummy." Her tongue darted out to lick her lips. "The spices are spot on, and it's cooked to perfection. I can't wait to taste it all together with all the goodies. Good choice." She spooned up the green peppers and onions, adding them to her plate.

"Watching you enjoy your food builds my anticipation." Matt rolled everything into the small tortilla and finished it off in a couple of bites.

"Did you taste anything? Wow, that was fast."

Matt chuckled. "That was only the appetizer. I'll taste the next one."

A while later after sharing a scoop of fried ice cream, they walked out of the restaurant full and content. Matt had brought her up to speed on the case details that he was free to share. Some of the questions she had asked got him thinking of more possibilities. Damn, they worked well together.

"What's next?" Jessie asked him as he got in the car.

"We take down a porn king, his thugs, and solve a couple of murders. Along the way, we'll deal with a nuisance from your past, and hopefully, help some young ladies face a brighter future and finally find our way forward into ours."

"It sounds quite industrious, but if anyone can do it, you can."

"No, sweetheart, we can. I'm nothing without you."

****

He smiled. His girl was trying to evade him. Sitting in the chair, he pulled the envelope out of his pocket and read it. His fingers curled into a fist. How did she put up with this foul junk for the past ten years? Adler was coming, and he would try to kill her. "Jess, would you come here for a minute?" He stood and waited for her to come out of her room.

"Did you want something?" She peeked out her door.

He took her hand and led her over to the couch. "I want you to read this word for word."

"Why? I've read enough of them over the years. I'm sure he's said it all before." She placed the letter face down on her lap.

"Because he's coming for you and he's giving away details about his thinking and what he wants to do. He's your enemy, and you need to know how his mind works so he can't surprise you." He stroked the side of her cheek. "You've been afraid of this guy for so long that now it's time to put this myth to bed. You've faced down a notorious serial killer and Irwin's mind games. Sweetheart, you're not the girl he attacked in that bathroom years ago. He doesn't know it, but he's met his match."

"I know that in theory, but I feel paralyzed at the thought of seeing him again." She turned the letter over and began to read aloud.

He knew the moment she went from fear to being angry. It wasn't a premonition. She stood, crumpled the letter, and threw it across the room. Jessie never cursed, but Matt thought he heard a couple of expletives mumbled under her breath. Adler's words had the desired effect on her that Matt was hoping for. "Are you okay?"

"What do you think?" She paced back and forth until he pulled her down on the couch beside him.

"You're making me dizzy watching you." He winked at her.

"Close your eyes. It helps me think."

"And have you come to any conclusions?"

"I'm mad, in case you didn't notice."

"I noticed." His hand rubbed her back. "What

295

else?"

"I'm going to have to deal with this creep, aren't I?" She turned her head and glanced at him.

"I would amend your statement to *we* are going to have to deal with him." He wrapped his arms around her holding her tight. She snuggled against his chest. "Thank you."

Chapter 43

Matt dropped Jessie off at the store, into the capable hands of Joe who was waiting for her at the front door. "Sarah made me promise to say hello. I told her I'd be watching you today. She might stop by later if she gets a chance and a babysitter. Our little one will be one soon, and she could whip these books off the shelf in a blink of the eye." Joe took the key from her hand and unlocked the door. "It's probably better if you don't stand out in the open."

"Is Abigail walking yet?"

"She's trying. It's fun to watch her take a few steps and then fall on her diaper-padded bottom. She laughs, and so do we."

"Happy to see you're finally working days. Nights had to be hard on your family." She went behind the counter and put her purse in its spot. "Before I open, why don't you go to the coffee shop and get a cup of coffee. I'll lock the doors, and you can knock as soon as you're ready to come back."

"I will, but I want to check your store and attic." Joe followed her into the back room. He checked the back door and then climbed the stairs to the attic. "All clear. I'll be back in a few minutes. Can I get you something?"

"I'm good for now." She walked to the doors and

unlocked them. "Be sure to knock when you're ready to come back in."

"Make sure the front door is locked until it's time to open," Joe said.

"I'll check it now." Jessie double-checked the door then got busy preparing the store to open. Carrying a stack of books from the backroom to the display table took all her concentration because their odd sizes made the pile of books awkward to cart. The stack began to give way with a few books tumbling different ways onto the table right before she set the books down. She sorted and arranged them in their proper order just in the nick of time. Stepping back to survey her handiwork, Jessie paused when there was a sudden knock at the window. Startled, she lifted her head, making eye contact with the sneering contorted face of Stuart Adler.

Frozen in place, she didn't move until Joe's banging on the door got her moving. She turned her back on the cursing man in the window and went to open the doors to the coffee shop.

Joe rushed in. "Are you all right?" Collins looked at her pale face.

"Do you know why Matt has you watching the store?"

"Yes, and it's not the store I'm watching. It's you. Parker said you've had threatening letters from some guy fresh out of prison who blames you for his unhappy stay. Or the short version, the guy is obsessed with you."

"Yeah, well that guy is in town and was standing in front of my store a few minutes ago. I don't think he's here to thank me."

"See if you can see him walking down the street." They stepped out the front door. Adler was nowhere in sight. Collins locked the door and sent off a text to Matt. "He needs to know the man is in town."

"Of course, but I hate to add one more thing to his long list of junk going on." She glanced at the clock. "I could use a cup of coffee." She rubbed her arms, feeling the goosebumps.

"I figured you might as soon as you saw mine. I bought you one. Here you go, just the way you like it. Decaf with cream, right?" He handed her the cup.

"Wow, how did you remember?"

"For some reason, it stuck with me. Maybe because Matt used to say he didn't know why you even bothered to put coffee in your milk."

"I should have known. He still teases me about it. Thanks for the coffee."

Joe's phone chimed. "Matt wants to know if you're okay."

"Tell him I'm fine. I'm not as rattled as I thought I'd be, but I still don't want to tangle with Adler if I can avoid it."

"You're safe, and I'm not going anywhere. The two of us can handle Stuart if he decides to come back. I doubt that he will. Stuart's a bully and bullies don't like witnesses. We have to make sure he never gets you alone."

"Sounds like a plan. It's time to open." Jessie opened the doors to the coffee shop and another day at Idle Time Books was on its way.

Joe was always where she could see him. It was comforting. He checked out every man who came into the store. Sitting in the leather chair, he made eye contact with her over the top of his book. She'd shake her head letting him know it wasn't Adler. Not a planned action between them, but it played out that way.

The phone rang several times during her morning. A couple of times customers called. A few times it was Adler. Actually, it was Adler more than a few times. The caller's vulgar language was the tip-off. Unplugging the phone became a big temptation, growing stronger with each call. By the time she closed the store and Matt picked her up, if she hadn't thrown the phone across the room she would have been at least fighting mad.

****

Matt's mind was revving as he walked out of the station. Three people were sitting in jail waiting for their lawyers. Dylan would call with the interview times. He patted his inside pocket where three more arrest warrants were waiting along with a search warrant. They were only at the beginning of the process. The team managed to get Valentine's thugs to arraignment yesterday without a hitch, which was a damn good thing. He was waiting for the ID of a new face that showed up on the camera at the high school. This case was beginning to break wide open.

They weren't out of the woods yet. Matt knew the next arrest warrant served would send Valentine over the edge. He pulled into the space in front of Jessie's store.

"Hi." She slid into the passenger seat after Collins opened the door for her. "Thank you, Joe, for keeping me company today. Tell Sarah hello from me."

"Will do." He closed the door.

"We need to grab a quick bite to eat. I have to go back to the station and, with Alder in town, you're going to have to go with me."

"Could we stop by the house to get my laptop? I need to have something to do while you work."

"It's the least I can do for messing up your evening." He squeezed her hand.

"You didn't. Stuart did, and truthfully I'm ready to have it out with him."

"Did you have a rough day?" he asked.

"I lost count of all the times he called the store with his obscene language. I wanted to throw the phone a few times. I would have let it ring, but there were several customers in the store." Jessie glanced at Matt.

"I'm sorry you have to put up with this crap. You've had your share."

"Sadie tells me when I whine that everyone has their share of troubles. You can always find someone worse off than you. I know she is right, but sometimes I wonder."

"You never whine."

She rolled her eyes. "Yeah, right."

"Speaking of Sadie, when will she get to town?" Matt patted her hand.

"The movers should be here next week with her belongings, followed by the family."

"Are you excited?" he asked.

"Sure, that's why I hope this whole thing with Stuart is settled. I haven't told my parents yet. My dad would be livid. I hope to tell him after the fact."

"We'll figure it out, sweetheart, but one thing I know for sure, we're in for one hell of a ride the next few days. I hope you don't get sick of being at the station."

"Not me. I'll find something to occupy my time. I want to learn more about police work anyway."

"Jess, I need to confess something to you."

"This sounds serious." She held her breath.

"I talked to your father. I wanted to see how many times he called on Adler and whether he felt the police did enough."

She exhaled. "I guess I can understand why you did. At least my dad hasn't flown here and camped out on my doorstep."

"Only because I talked him out of it."

"And how did you do that?"

"We had a meeting of the minds." He chuckled.

"I don't even want to know what that means." She unlatched her seatbelt once he pulled in next to her car.

"Simply put, I promised to take care of you myself. I might have said he was getting older and would maybe get in the way."

"You're teasing." She laughed.

"Nope."

Chapter 44

The station was hopping. Between the extra agents, suspects, and their attorneys, there wasn't a quiet room available. Added to the equation, Matt's officers were standing guard and interviewing suspects. It was one busy place. She found a corner in the lunchroom where she could set up her computer and get to work. Thankfully, it was quiet enough to work a little magic with her keyboard. Now, if only she could concentrate.

Her attention strayed to what was happening in the hall. Kip passed by the open door with a suspect in handcuffs. It was Mr. Dailey, the vice-principal. Geez, she had met Shawn and his wife for the first time a few weeks ago, Mr. Rhodes had introduced them. Matt was right. The town would be in shock.

"I hope you're not getting bored." He walked into the lunchroom.

"There's too much here of interest to get bored. I can't keep my mind on what I should be doing. I saw Kip pass by the door with Shawn Dailey in handcuffs. That's a shocker."

"Dailey is the tip of the iceberg. The big guys aren't even here yet." He folded his arms across his chest, leaning his hip against the table. "I'm sorry you may have to be here a while longer. I can't leave yet."

"I'm fine. Do your job." She glanced out into the

hall. Someone else was on their way in handcuffs, but she couldn't see who it was. Matt blocked her view. "I'll entertain myself," she said, leaning to see around him.

"I'm sure you can," he said and steadied her before she fell out of the chair. "Don't go outside, please. Adler is keeping tabs on you and must know you're in here. He didn't come all this way at the risk of going back to prison for nothing."

"I'm not going anywhere." She motioned with her hands. "Move along, Chief Parker. I need to work, and you should too."

"Jess, I get the distinct feeling you're trying to get rid of me."

"Not at all, but I find what's going on out there,"—she pointed toward the open door—"quite interesting. You make a better door than a window. If you'd move a degree or two back and to the right, I could see quite well." She smiled sweetly at him.

He traced her lips with his finger. "Oh, sweetheart, I'm wounded. You don't find me as interesting as what's happening around us. I must be losing my touch." He chuckled and tapped her chin lightly. "Enjoy the view," he called over his shoulder as he walked out of the room.

"I did, Mr. Parker, I did," she sighed, fanning her face.

****

Matt went from one suspect to the next. A few of them were singing, and some weren't talking at all. In conference room two, Dailey was talking and crying at the same time.

He listened to Dailey's sob story and then handed

him a tissue. "Come on, Shawn, quit blubbering. You got caught. Own it like a man. You walked into it as a grown man. What about the girls? You're supposed to be a person of trust there to protect them, and you made a profit by turning your back. I don't feel sorry for you. You've played the part of a fool, and you have to pay."

"My wife and kids will be disgraced. Who will take care of them?" He cried.

"You should've thought of that before you committed the crime. Look, I feel bad for your family, but I also feel bad for those girls. Their photos are floating out there on the Internet through no fault of their own. What if that was your daughter, man? Guys like you make me sick." Matt slammed his hand on the table. "You sold them out for what—a few measly bucks?"

Tom leaned close to Dailey's face. "I want names, and you'd better be straight with me, or you'll be going to prison for a long time."

"You don't get it, do you? It's hard to live anywhere on the salary I make with three kids to feed, and college is looming nearby."

"Not our problem. Stop feeling sorry for yourself and start talking. Maybe, and I make no promises, the judge will go easier on you." Matt turned on his recorder

As soon as he finished with Dailey, he went to find Jessie. She wasn't in the lunchroom, or in the front desk area. Only after a nervous search, did he find her sleeping on the chair in his office. She had to be uncomfortable. Scrunched up in an awkward position with her head resting on her hands, it appeared painful to him. Kneeling down beside her, he whispered.

"Sweetheart, wake up, it's time to go home."

She moaned, stretching out her legs. "What time is it?" She pushed her hair out of her eyes, sitting up straight.

"Late." He extended his hand to pull her out of the chair. "Sorry, I had no idea I would be so long."

"Did it go well?" She stood, and he held onto her until she was totally awake.

"We got a lot of information. More arrests are in the works for tomorrow, and the FBI has secured a search warrant for Valentine's house and business. I can't tell you how happy Tom is."

She walked out the door he held open for her. "It is exciting to see this case moving ahead. There was a lot of action at the station tonight and I'm surprised I fell asleep. I didn't get much writing done. I wanted to take in everything going on here."

Dylan stopped him by the car to ask questions. Once in the car, he turned to her. Her head was back against the headrest, and she was sound asleep. There had to be a better arrangement. This wasn't fair to her.

****

Over the next several days, Adler would wave at her from the cemetery and then disappear into the woods before they could get out the door and across the street. It was getting frustrating. She had turned her back when he waved today. Probably not a smart idea, but she was over it. The cat and mouse game was driving her nuts. She would just as soon confront him and take her chances. Of course, Matt didn't think her idea had any merit. But the idea of no more nightmares, or no more creepy letters and fear of him showing his face, sounded like heaven to her. In her heart, the time was coming soon. She knew it. Matt or one of his officers couldn't be with her every minute of the day. It was only a matter of time.

"Hi Jessie," Rachael called when she walked in the door. "I'm happy I joined the book club. I'm looking forward to the weekly meetings. Do you mind if I leave my stuff here while I go get my coffee?"

"Go right ahead. The ladies are starting to come in." She could hardly believe Rachael was the same woman who walked into her store a few weeks ago. Who was this outgoing, kindhearted woman? She smiled. Jessie liked to believe she had a small part in her transformation.

"I see we're about to be invaded." Kip smiled at her. "I'm not complaining, mind you."

"We'll see if you still feel the same way after this group is finished. I love listening to them, but they aren't quiet by any means. You can always go next door and watch me from the open door."

"Good try, but the chief would have my head. He told me to stick to you like glue and not to let you out of my sight."

"You do know that's not possible. I refuse to allow you to accompany me to the ladies' room." She laughed.

"The remedy is I'll be standing outside the door. Consider yourself stuck with me."

"It could be worse. You're a nice guy to have around. I can't wait for you to meet my cousin next week. She's too old for you, but she'll like you right off like I did."

"I'm sure I'll like her too." Kip rolled his eyes at her.

"Her younger sister would be perfect for you."

He shook his head at her. "No matchmaking, Jessie, I kind of like to pick my own girls out."

"How's that working for you?"

"At the moment not so good." Kip grinned.

Business picked up after a tour bus stopped in town. Her afternoon was hopping. While showing a customer a book on the front table, she noticed Lizzy and Grace in the cemetery. The struggle around Lizzy was real. Call it light and darkness, good versus evil. There was a reason she was feeling this every time Lizzy was near. It was there with her brother Ted. How she wished she could understand why.

"I'll take this book. You've sold me on it." The customer handed the book to Jessie and followed her to the counter.

"I know you'll enjoy it. The author's style is easy to read." Jessie put the book in a bag along with a bookmark. She gave the woman her change.

"Is it always this busy and noisy?" Kip glanced at her as she sat down in the chair across from him.

"No, but I'm grateful for days like this it's good for my bottom line." She smiled. "Matt will be here soon. I guess I had better start getting things ready to close. I wanted to sit for a minute, but if I stay here much longer, I'll be asleep." She went to straighten the counter.

Chapter 45

"Jess we're about to solve this murder." Matt opened the car door for her. "You and I need to talk. I've been too busy, and I need your input." He got in the driver's side.

"I'm happy for Lizzy and her family." Jessie latched her seatbelt "Ten years is a long time not to know."

"I'm afraid some hard days are ahead for the McKenzies, but there's nothing I can do about it. Ted will always bear the guilt. He's the one who introduced a college friend to Lizzy and the family. It went all downhill from there."

"I have a few ideas of my own about who murdered Lizzy and Grace. I've seen them in the cemetery a few days this week. Adler has been there too waving at me at some point each day." Jessie squeezed his arm. "Before you become apoplectic, your officers would try to get him, but he disappeared into the woods before they could get across the street. Then because you told them not to leave me alone, they wouldn't chase after him."

"They did the right thing, but I hate to think of him here in town, yet out of our grasp."

"In the end, I'll be the one to have to deal with him." She responded to his shaking head. "I have to."

"Not if I can help it."

"I know you'll do what you can to protect me. But you know that I'm right Stuart is coming after me maybe we need to control the situation instead of being taken by surprise."

"At any other time, I would say yes, but my officers are stretched thin right now. Besides the extra agents here I've asked for help from the county. I hope we can hold Adler off for a couple more days."

"I wish for your sake we can too, but I feel the confrontation is coming fast and furious and there's not much I can do to stop it from happening. Don't worry. I believe it's going to be okay. I'll get through it, but I must face it. Like you are facing Lizzy, I need to confront Stuart."

"Not going there." He pulled into the space in front of the path to her cottage. "I'm not going to let him get his hands on you."

"All I'm saying is..." her voice trailed off when she saw his expression.

"He's not touching you." His chin lifted, his body tensed.

Chiseled in granite is how she would describe his face. "We'll talk about this another time. You have enough stress for now." She opened the car door and got out.

"Sorry, I didn't listen to your idea. Right now, I'm looking over my shoulder. I know Valentine will not go down without a fight, tomorrow is the day. He must know what's coming. Billy is coming to town tomorrow to look at mug shots and a few of the perps to see if he can ID any of them. He knows the man who killed Grace that has been watching you. I'm sure of it."

"Are you going after someone related to Valentine?"

"Yes, but there's more. We have to keep it quiet until the arrest warrants are served. We don't want them to run. Between Dailey and Ted McKenzie, we have most of the players, but I still feel like I'm missing something important." He grabbed her hand and picked up the pace. "Let's get inside."

"What makes you think that?"

"I have nothing to implicate the man, but my gut tells me something is not right."

"You've always told me to go with my instinct, and I'm telling you to do the same thing." She flipped on the light as soon as he opened the door. "You've been right in your hunches every time, and you're right this time. I have no idea what you're thinking but remember Anderson. You knew, and because you had someone watching me, in the end, you saved my life." She walked into the kitchen. "Do you what something to drink?"

"I'll take a club soda with lemon if you have it."

"I do." She filled two glasses with ice and squeezed fresh lemon into both. She poured in the soda and garnished the glasses with lemon slices. "Here, enjoy. Put your feet up and watch the scores if you want."

****

Matt's day started early, and because he wouldn't let her be alone, hers did too. It wasn't fair, but it had to be. Jeb Sullivan brought his son into town to look at mug shots per his request. Matt had placed the suspect photos among different photos. The results were more than he had hoped for. Billy knew his own mind they couldn't trick him or influence him. He picked out the suspect with no problem.

"Billy, you did a fine job this morning. Thank you." Matt shook his hand. "Do you think you can do one more thing for me?"

"Yes, sir, you betcha." Billy's chest puffed out, and he sat up tall in the chair.

"Follow me. Your dad will wait here until we come back."

Do you mind if I leave for a while? The kid may not be bright, but he knows his way around town." Jeb stood. "He can find his own way home."

"I'll make sure he gets home." Matt walked out of the room with Billy following him.

"I want you to look at a few men for me. Pick out anyone you can remember. Can you do that?"

Billy sniffed. The room was empty. "I don't see no one."

"You will in a minute. Keep looking right at the window." Matt picked up the phone and told them to light it up.

Matt watched the expression on Billy's face as Ted and suspect number three came to stand in line. He had his answer. Billy pointed at the two men among the others, becoming agitated and inconsolable.

Matt pulled the curtains. "Billy, you did great, and I appreciate your help."

"Don't like those men. Don't like them at all. Billy wants to go home." He opened the door and ran out of the station before Matt could stop him.

****

Billy went to his next favorite place in his world. Whenever his pa brought him to town, he would make his way to the woods behind the cemetery. He could sit high in a special tree where no one could see him. Grabbing a low hanging branch, he shimmied up the tree and perched on one of the branches.

Pulling a wad of chew from his pocket, he stuck it in his cheek. The bad man couldn't find him here. The smooth, cool stone he had picked off the ground fit perfect in his slingshot. Flipping it back and forth from one hand to the other, he was ready.

Like a tense bow, he waited. "Who are you?" He watched the strange man.

****

Today was his lucky day. Deep down in his bones, he could feel it. Biding his time, he waited until he could get her alone and this was the day. No doubt about it. Either she would be dead, or he would, but this crazy obsession would be over today one way or the other. The plan was perfect. Practice makes perfect as they say. Wave and hide, drawing them out, patient and then strike like a snake. Boneyards gave him the creeps. Everything was gone because of her. It didn't matter whether this was the end for him. All he cared about was hurting her too.

Strutting to the front of the cemetery, Stuart waited until he saw her in the window. Waving like a fool, he remained in plain sight until the cop came running across the street. "Yes, she was following him. His lucky day for sure. Adler hid and waited for the cop to get close to enough to hit him. The man's legs buckled as soon as he struck his head with the board.

"Kip," she screamed. Jessie ran toward his quiet form. She stopped at the gate to call Matt. "Adler got Kip. We're in the cemetery." She hung up.

"Come on. This is your destiny. A little closer, sweet girl." He whispered. Stuart jumped out of his hiding place. "I've been waiting for you. You won't get away this time. Are you scared?" Obscene words spit like flames from his mouth. "Why aren't you running? I would if I were you."

****

"You're not me. I can't remember for the life of me why I feared you. I was a kid then, and you should've known better. You want me? You'll have to come and get me. I'm done running and being afraid of you." Foreboding darkness settled over him. Jessie knew the war was on. He advanced toward her, cursing as he came. She stood firm, refusing to flinch. He was slithering closer. He suddenly stopped. She could tell her calm shook him.

"What's wrong with you? Do you want to die, bitch?" He pulled the knife from his waistband.

"I won't be dying today, but your next actions will determine if you do." Jessie stood her ground. "I refuse to be afraid of you."

His hand caressed the blade. "I wouldn't mind carving my initials in that lovely face of yours. You've always belonged to me. Are you afraid now?"

She pulled her gun from her pocket. "No, I'm not afraid, but I think you should be." She glared at him. "If you move one step closer, I will shoot. I know how to hit you too. And just so you know, I belong only to me."

"We'll see. Aw, we're playing the game of my weapon is bigger than yours. Your problem, sweetheart, you couldn't shoot me if you wanted to. You're too nice, and I don't care. If you don't kill me on the first shot, I'll turn your gun on you."

The endearment rolling off his lips sounded disgusting to her. "First of all, I'm not your sweetheart. Second, you can bet I'll make the first shot count. I'm not afraid to use this." She waved the gun.

He lunged toward her, his knife in his hand. The rock hit him near the temple, buckling his knees. Her gun erupted, and Stuart was lying on the ground. She kicked the knife out of reach from his bloody hand. Billy had hit his mark, and so had she. She had shot the knife right out of his hand. The bullet had grazed his hand on its way to the knife he was waving around. Grabbing Kip's handcuffs, she slapped them on Adler.

She knelt beside Kip, lifting his head into her lap. He was breathing, thankfully.

"Are you okay, lady?" Billy scooted down the tree, racing toward her.

"Yes, thanks to you, Billy. You're my hero."

He kicked at the dirt with his foot. "It was nothing. I hit him real good."

"You sure did." She smiled at him.

"Jessie," Kip tried to sit up.

"Stay still. Help is on the way."

Where's Adler?" Kip rubbed his head.

"He's taking a nap after being felled by a slingshot. As much as I don't like the man, I didn't want to kill him. Billy gave him a nasty lump on his head."

Chapter 46

They all began talking at once after Matt and the other officers arrived. Adler was screaming obscenities at Jessie. She was ignoring him and soothing Kip who was trying to get up, but she kept telling him to lie down. Billy was mumbling to himself, pacing among the headstones. No one was paying any attention to him. "Quiet!" Matt shouted above the noise. Several pairs of eyes turned to look at him. "Sorry I couldn't seem to get your attention any other way." Matt leaned close to her and said. "Sweetheart, let Kip get up if he wants to."

"He was knocked out, and I thought the medics should look at him first." She lifted her chin.

"You're right, Jess." Matt tapped her chin and then helped Kip to a sitting position. "Let the medics check you out before you stand." Matt turned to the medic looking at Adler's hand and the large knot on the side of his head. "After you're finished with him check my officer, out will you?"

"We'll check him, Chief."

"Let's hear it. I'm especially interested in finding out what you're doing in the cemetery and not safe in your bookstore."

"He planned for us to catch him this time. I stayed where I was supposed to until he hit Kip, and then I couldn't stand there. I had my gun and badge."

"I figured that much on my own from the bullet wound on his hand."

"I shot the knife out of it. He's lucky I didn't shoot him dead." She glared at Adler.

"I want to hear the whole story and how Billy fits it into."

She told him how it went down. "Billy was the real hero. He hit Stuart with a stone from his slingshot."

"Billy, come here, please."

Matt extended his hand. "Thank you, for saving this special lady."

"It's okay." He wiped his hands on his wrinkled shirt and shook Matt's hand.

"I want you to come with me. I'll buy you dinner and take you home to your dad. Would you like that Billy?"

"Yes, Billy wants to eat. I like the lady. Can she come too?" Billy's hand stroked her hair. "Soft like my friend's. She's dead."

"I'm sorry about your friend," Jessie told him.

"Are you going to have dinner with us?" Matt grinned at her.

"I wouldn't miss it for anything." She stood next to him.

"They're both good to go," the medic said.

Kip stood. "I'm glad it worked out, but I told you to stay put." Kip ruffled her hair.

"You don't watch your partner go down and not do something about it. You guys are the ones who trained me." She glanced at Matt and back to Kip. "We watch each other's back."

"She's got you there." Kip chuckled.

"In more ways than one." He placed his hand on the top of Adler's head to keep it from hitting the car as he got in the backseat. "I'll be back for you later." His hand brushed hers. "Kip finish your shift. Keep an eye on her and put some ice on that lump."

"What are you going to do with him?" Jessie pointed at Adler in the car.

"Book him and send him back to prison, only after I scare him about further letter writing." He turned to leave. "Jess, you did well today."

A smile was plastered on her face for the rest of the day. He'd probably lecture her later, but she could live with it. After getting some ice for Kip's head, she told Molly all the happenings in the cemetery. "I guess I finally had enough. I didn't want the guy to drag it out another day. I shouldn't have stayed inside I guess, but I needed to confront my fear after all of these years." Now at least she could lay this part of her past to rest, hopefully.

"I would have run as fast as I could the other way." Molly laughed. "I don't care about being any heroine no way, no how."

"I'm going to get a cup of coffee. Promise me you'll stay here." Kip moved past the two women into the coffee shop.

"I will. You don't need to worry. The threat is over. Adler's in jail. I think it must be getting fairly crowded by now."

"Jessie, until all the arrests are made it's never over, and you know it. Stay put."

"Kenny told me, a lot is going on. They've worked lots of overtime. I've hardly seen him. He said it would be like that for several more days. You know what's going on don't you."

"I do, and you will too soon enough." Hearing the bell ring over the door, Jessie turned. "I guess I'd better get to work." She approached the customer. "May I help you?" Her body tensed when she saw the man's face. Where had she seen him before? What was the name that went with the face? It was there in the back of her mind. He was trouble in her heart, she knew it. The dark storm feeling enveloped the atmosphere of her store.

****

Matt couldn't believe the curt text he read from Kip. *Valentine has Jessie. He's threatening to kill her unless you let his son go.*

Moving into position, Kip found a safe spot to make a call and still see Jessie. "Matt this is Kip. I'm keeping a low profile in the coffee shop. I don't want Valentine to know that I'm here. I'll take a shot if I get the chance."

"How'd it happen?"

"I went into Joe's to get a coffee while she was talking to Molly. She went to help a customer who turned out to be Valentine. He hasn't seen me yet. I'm glad I didn't wear my uniform. I'm not sure she recognizes him or even knows who he is. Right now, he's talking to her, but I heard him say he'd kill her in front of you if you didn't let his son go."

"I've been looking over my shoulder for days. I knew Valentine wouldn't take this lying down. I'll talk to Tom and the others. We're on our way. Keep an eye on her for me and kill him if you have to."

Matt found Tom in the lunchroom. "Tom, we have an issue."

"Oh, yeah, what's that?"

"Valentine has Jessie. He's in the store with her right now. Kip called and is in position to take him out if he needs too."

"Hell, who tipped him off? We only brought his son in a few hours ago. It was a quiet operation."

"I have my theory on it. I've sent Dylan to pick him up." Matt frowned. "What's our plan?"

"We can't race over there we'll have to play this carefully. Valentine will take hostages, and he'll kill them without batting an eye."

"We need to get a sharpshooter in place. We can surround the store without him knowing we're there, from the back of the bookstore. I'll text Kip and tell him to open the back door of the coffee shop." Matt chose two of his officers to come with him.

"Damn I wanted to take this guy alive. He could answer so many questions that we have."

"With any luck, he'll still be able to answer them. It's been a strange day already anything can happen. Let's do this." Matt ran to his car.

****

"No skin off my back, I'll kill you, lady. You'd better lock your store, or I kill anyone who walks through the doors." He shoved the gun in her back. "Move it."

Jessie went to the front door and locked it. She shut the doors into the coffee shop. "If you don't mind can I ask you a question?"

"Hell, lady, I'm not in the mood to chat. I wouldn't waste my time on you if you weren't his woman. I'll trade you for my boy."

"No man owns me. I'm my own woman." She was

angry, her fist tightened at her side. "You'll have to kill me because the law won't let him make a trade with you. You know that."

"Shut up! You're giving me a headache. Stop moving and sit down." He pointed his gun at her.

Jessie sat in the chair. "I'm sitting, now what?"

"Call Parker and tell him exactly what I tell you to say."

She shook her head. "He's in meetings I'll probably have to leave a voicemail."

"Oh hell, tell him I don't care how you do it, just do it."

When he answered the phone, Jessie began her pretend voicemail. "Hi, Matt. As soon as you get this message call me back. Trevor Valentine is here with me in the store. He has a message for you, but it will be too long to leave. Talk to you later." She left the phone on. Matt would hear the conversation that way.

"You'd better hope he calls. My patience is running out." He walked up to the window and looked out.

She placed her hand on the gun in her pocket. "Are you looking for somebody?"

"If you know what's good for you, you'll zip your lips." He moved back and forth between the door and window.

"I find it strange that you've come into my business and feel you can order me around. Who do you think you are? I'm not your wife, thank God. If anything, I should order you to get out of my store." When he turned around, she had her gun aimed right at him. "Checkmate. Now, what do we do?" Jessie saw Lizzy, swaying around him and Grace was on the other side.

"I have nothing to lose. You shoot, or I'll shoot. Hell, we both can shoot at the same time. I've never shot a lady before, but it might be fun." He fired a shot. The sound reverberated off the brick walls.

Jessie saw Lizzy hit his arm before he had fired. The bullet whizzed past her and stuck in one of the bookshelves along the wall. "I don't plan on letting you shoot at me a second time. I'm happy to be alive." She fired and shot the gun out of his hand before he could shoot his again. His screams and curses brought Kip busting through the side doors and Matt through the front.

Tom read the screaming Valentine his rights and led him out to the waiting car. Jessie stood beside Matt and watched Tom wrap a towel around Trevor's bleeding hand.

"Jess, I wished I hadn't heard you taunt him into shooting you. I aged many years on my ride here. Do you have no fear?" Mt asked.

"I have a healthy sense of fear, but I also knew I wasn't alone. I believed he couldn't kill me, and I was right. His shot was off. Lizzy hit his arm. You'll find the bullet somewhere that side of the building." She pointed to the area. "I didn't want to kill him. It's not in me to hurt someone, unless of course, I have to. I was hoping to talk him to death until you got here."

"What am I going to do with you?"

"Before you lecture me, I hope you'll be happy that I'm alive and kiss me, please."

Chapter 47

The spaghetti sauce simmering in the kitchen smelled good enough to eat. Made from scratch, it tasted wonderful. She had tried it several times to make sure. The salad was in the refrigerator, the garlic bread was ready to stick in the oven, and her prize cooking project, a marble cheesecake, had turned out perfect. It had been a while since she had been this domestic. Matt seemed surprised when she told him not to bring dinner because she was cooking. Glancing at the clock on her way into the kitchen, she realized he would be here soon.

Like all their other cases, Matt was busy with court arraignments during the day and wrapping up the paperwork at night. For the last few weeks, he called her, but they had precious little time together since Valentine's arrest. It had given Jessie time to help Sadie get settled in her new apartment. The movers did most of the work, but she wasn't complaining. Catching up with Peyton and her parents had been fun. Surely one of the men in Blue Cove would find Peyton fascinating. It was Jessie's new mission to convince Peyton to move here. Tomorrow evening they would all get together at the Inn for dinner along with Matt and his family. The queasy feeling in her stomach would be with her until she was convinced his parents liked her. Her hand rubbed her stomach.

Matt promised to stop by and fill her in on the case tonight, when she had suggested dinner. Tomorrow was to be a work-free night. Right now, the stress of wondering outweighed everything else. She desperately wanted to make a good first impression tomorrow.

The bread was warming, the noodles were boiling, and she was lighting the candles.

He found her in the kitchen. "Wow, it smells good in here, and I'm hungry." He turned her around and planted a kiss on her lips. "I've missed seeing you."

"I've missed you too." She kissed him back. "Everything is ready. Let's eat while it's hot." She placed the salad and bread on the table.

"Perfect. Love the candlelight. Do you want me to pour the wine?" He opened the bottle.

"That would be nice." She filled his plate and then hers with spaghetti, meatballs, and sauce. She sat placing her napkin on her lap.

"Did you make all of this?' Matt tasted the sauce.

"I did. I don't cook often, but I'm not bad at it."

"I'd say you're more than good. This sauce is a rival to any I've tasted." He filled his salad bowl and grabbed a slice of the garlic bread.

"It's not out of a jar either." She smiled proudly. "There's fresh parmesan cheese in the small bowl if you want it." She spooned a small amount over her sauce.

"Are you ready to take on my brothers and parents tomorrow night?" He took a bite of his salad.

"I'm working up to it." She pushed her food around on her plate.

"What's this? My girl who taunted Trevor

Valentine into shooting at her is afraid of my parents? Honey, they're going to love you as much as I do." He grinned at her. "Well, maybe not as much as I do or definitely not in the same way, but you'll win them over easily. What's not to love about you?"

"I can think of a few things."

"Jess, they'll love you. Trust me. They already know how happy you make me. Mom drives me nuts about grandkids. It'll be fine."

As soon as they finished dinner, and cleaned up she pulled the cheesecake from the fridge and cut two slices. "We can go in the other room and eat this. I want to hear all about the case."

"I knew you would." He sat in his favorite chair placing the dessert plate on the table beside him. "Before we start, that was the best meal I've had in a long time. You constantly surprise me with your talents."

"Thank you. Now let's get to the good part." She smiled at him, taking a bite of the cheesecake. Oh, wow, was it ever tasty. She closed her eyes.

"If the look on your face is any indication, I'm in for a real treat." He took a bite and then scarfed it down.

"Where do you want to start?" She tucked her legs under her on the couch.

"It all started with Lizzy and her family. Lizzy fell head over heels in love with Calvin Valentine. He came home with Ted from college during spring break in our junior year. He was handsome and a smooth talker. Why she didn't break up with me then I'll never know."

"Maybe he didn't reciprocate her feelings. She was kind of young for a college guy."

"It's possible. At the beginning of our senior year, he came more often. At one point, he started dating her secretly. Her mom kept her on a tight leash and would have never approved, especially after her grades started to fall off." Matt leaned forward in the chair. "At some point, Byron McKenzie, who was on the city council and a good friend of Anderson's, met with and talked to Valentine. After an enticing bribe, he couldn't refuse. Byron was on board and looked the other way. Their father brought Ted and Lizzy into this whole mess. He had assurances from Valentine and Anderson that Lizzy would never be photographed nude or on any porn site."

"Lizzy had scribbled a note on a small piece of paper. I didn't understand it at the time." She grabbed the small piece of paper from the back of the journal. "It simply says how much she hated her dad. Poor Charlotte, her world must be crumbling right now."

Matt glanced at the slip of paper. "Charlotte reminded me the day we talked that Byron suddenly came into a lot of money and they planned on moving from town. I think she knew the truth in her heart."

"No wonder Ted feels so guilty. He introduced the snake to his family." Jessie shook her head and sighed.

"Ted holds his father responsible and hates him too. It's hard for me to see Byron this way. He was always a great man or at least I thought he was. Byron got his children involved in this mess. What kind of father would do that?" he asked angrily. "He thought he could control all the players because of Anderson, but it got away from him early on. Valentine bankrolled Byron and Ted to keep their mouths shut." Matt ran his hand through his hair. "Ted could no longer live with the guilt."

"Who else was involved?"

"Shawn Dailey, you know, along with a few of the teachers at the school. Valentine had the equipment installed in the school and in your bookstore. Calvin was the one watching you after he heard you knew Grace was murdered." Matt frowned. "It gets worse. Byron was responsible for her death. He didn't actually murder her but called for the hit. He also was the one who left the money for the Walters. Guilt money, like you, said. As soon as Lizzy told her father she would never lie to or recruit another girl for his sordid purposes, one of Valentine's sons killed Grace to scare Lizzy."

"Was it Calvin?" Jessie took another bite of her cheesecake.

Matt shook his head. "No, it was his twin brother Cole."

"How could Byron call for a hit on a young girl? He had a daughter." Jessie frowned. "I'll never understand people."

"His excuse was he did it to protect Lizzy. What he didn't realize was Grace had been a true friend to Lizzy. Lizzy saw Grace murdered. She was waiting for Calvin. She had something she needed to tell him. She tried to stop the murder, but Calvin's brother Cole killed her to shut her up. She had already seen too much. No one knew at the time Lizzy was pregnant with Calvin's baby. Under Anderson's orders, the files were doctored in our records department. They wrote the letter about Grace running away and forged the signature."

"Wow, Byron's actions caused his daughter's and

grandchild's deaths. I can see why Lizzy wasn't resting peacefully. I also understand the crazy stuff I saw that night. She must have been overwhelmed and felt there was no way out for her." Jessie wiped the tears from her eyes. "Who was leaking information?"

"Old Mike in the records department. He had my office bugged. One of the agents found it. That one took me by surprise, I admit."

"What will happen to all of them?" she asked.

"Valentine and his sons will go to prison. The FBI has lots of evidence against them. It was a good day for the agents. The way Valentine operates, we probably haven't heard the end of him. The search of his home and property delivered a wealth of evidence, enough to put them away for life. Byron, well he's a mess, and he will spend the rest of his life in prison too. The others will get many years. Mike will die there. Ted will get less time for cooperating."

"What about Stuart?" She moved to the edge of the couch.

"You'll have to testify against him."

"I figured I would. What will happen to him?"

"He wanted to die. His purpose was to hurt you and have a cop shoot him. His obsession cost him everything. The charges against him are stalking and attempted murder. Hopefully, his prison time will lead him to the help he needs and peace in his life."

"What a crazy case." She shook her head.

"You've got that right." He moved over to the couch and pulled her to his side. "Have I told you how proud I am of you?"

"Only a few hundred times over the past few weeks."

"Not in person." He nuzzled her neck. "You make me smile and gray at the same time." He stroked her cheek." He turned her face toward him. "I love you." He kissed her long and slow. And then he deepened it.

She pulled back to look at him. "I feel the same way about you."

He reached for the remote. "There's a good scary movie on. That means I can hold you close until it's over." He turned on the TV.

Chapter 48

Matt knocked on the cottage door. His parents were ready, and he couldn't wait for them to meet the lovely woman who had stolen his heart.

"Come in, Matt. I'll be right out," Jessie called out.

He was too excited to sit. Instead, he leaned his hip against the couch and waited. A low growl escaped his lips as she walked out of her room. She was wearing the dress she wore in Palm Springs. It was the perfect color for her eyes, which seemed to light from within. Her hair tempted him to run his fingers through the long, lush waves resting on her shoulders.

"You're beautiful. I love that dress on you." He gazed into her eyes. "I definitely need to keep you away from Jason. He won't be able to take it. Are you ready to tackle my family?"

"Yes, I believe I am." She leaned into his arms.

"I know they'll love you. Sadie has already won them over." He opened the door. "Shall we?"

Jessie went out, and he followed, locking the door behind him. "It's a beautiful night. I feel free without the threat of Stuart hanging over my head. Do you know how good it felt to stand up to him?"

"I can imagine." He wanted her to talk she was animated tonight.

She stopped on the path and turned to face him.

"It's spring. What's not to like about this time of year, and being here with you?" She grabbed his hand and started walking. "We'd better hurry. They're waiting."

Matt introduced her to his parents, and as he had assured her, they loved her.

Jason was a total pest and wouldn't leave her alone. Dinner was fine as usual, and everyone seemed to get along. Evan kept watching Peyton sheepishly when he didn't think anyone was looking.

Matt noted her hair was as dark as Jessie's was light. They were a contrast in looks and personalities. Peyton's eyes were hazel, and a few freckles dusted the bridge of her nose while Jessie's blue eyes stirred his senses, and her dimples made his heart race every time she smiled. Jessie was outgoing and as sweet as they come. Peyton was quiet and observant. She seemed to be interested in Evan, too, if her stolen glances were an indicator.

Every time Matt glanced at Jessie, she was watching him with a smile on her face. "What has you smiling?" He moved closer to her.

"It's my little secret," she said coyly. "Isn't it a perfect night? I couldn't ask for more, my family and yours together in the same room and getting along perfectly. Have you noticed Evan has finally gotten the nerve to talk to Peyton?" She slipped her hand in his.

"I've noticed," he whispered blowing in her ear. "Time will tell."

"Jason has made a pest of himself, but I'll pardon him because he's still young." She glanced from Matt to Jason who was watching her with his come-hither look. At least that's the way he had described it. Personally, it did nothing for her.

"My folks love you, and my dad wonders what I ever did to deserve you. Frankly, I've been wondering that myself and thanking my lucky stars." He watched her face, and the light turned on. He knew her secret.

"Matt, I've wanted to ask you something. I think now would be a perfect time."

He placed his hand over her mouth. "Not yet, sweetheart." He pulled her toward the door. "Hey everyone, Jessie's had a long week, and I'm taking her home. We'll see you tomorrow."

She had only enough time to say goodbye to a few family members, and he was pulling her out the door.

"What is the matter with you? I'm not tired at all."

"I know." His pace was quick. She tripped, and he picked her up carrying her to the cottage. Once inside he put her down and led her to the couch.

"Are you through? Can I ask my question now?"

He shook his head placing his fingers across her lips "I know what you're going ask and there's no way you're going to ruin my plans."

Her eyes widened, and she grinned. "You can't possibly know. How can you?"

"I could see it in your eyes. I think you're rubbing off on me. I'm right, aren't I?"

Her brows rose. "I'd still like to know how you figured it out."

"My little feminist. I'm learning how your mind works." He took her hand in his. "Jess, I refuse to tell our kids someday if they ask me how I proposed to you that I didn't, and that you asked me in a room full of people watching us."

He got down on his knees in front of her. "What I'll tell our children is I fell in love with you the first time we met. You walked into my office with fire in your eyes, and you were stunning. It was a good thing I was sitting because quite simply you took my breath away and set my pulse racing. I'll add I wanted to be your knight in shining armor, the one who stormed the castle tower to save you from the evil dragon of our day."

"Dragon? Really." She rolled her eyes and laughed.

He placed his hand over her mouth. "Yes, dragon. This is my proposal, not yours. Then I will tell them how you were my dragon slayer, how you rescued me from a bleak and desolate life. Sweetheart, you helped me lay the ghosts of my past aside and find my way forward to love again."

He took out the small box and opened it. Against a blue satin backdrop nestled a beautiful white gold solitaire diamond engagement ring. "Jess, will you marry me?"

"I have a few conditions." She saw his lips turn up at the corners.

"Go ahead." He grinned at her.

"I want to be free to work as I am now, as your partner with no restrictions. I keep my bookstore, you'll run with me at times, and most importantly, you'll try hard not to lecture me."

"Only if you try not to provoke someone into shooting at you. In that case, I'll lecture you every time. I won't be able to stop myself." He grinned.

"Fair enough." Jessie jumped up, and Matt stood as she stepped into his open arms. "In that case, my answer is yes, yes, a hundred times yes. I'll marry you." She pulled his head down and kissed him.

Tears of joy filled her eyes when she asked, "Will

you let me have a say in our story?" Jessie gazed into Matt's eyes.

He smiled and nodded at her.

"Then what I will add to our story is how my charming prince's proposal was wonderfully romantic. He asked at just the right moment, and in the most perfect of all places, at my cottage by the sea."

A word from the author…

I am a multi-published Amazon best-selling author who writes romantic suspense with a touch of the paranormal. I enjoy writing fiction. The character development, their stories, and the twists and turns in the plot intrigue me. Once I let the characters loose, I can't wait to see where they take me. I'm hooked from the first words on the paper, and I have to keep writing to see how the story ends. Layer by layer, I build it until I come to the happy conclusion.

I live in Colorado with my husband and family. I am a member of the RMFWPAL (Rocky Mountain Fiction Writers Published Authors League) and have enjoyed becoming involved in my community as one of the many authors living in Colorado. I invite you to read one of my Blue Cove Mysteries and see for yourself why Blue Cove is a special and unusual place.

Visit me at:

http://www.ionamorrison.com